The Conservative

Published in 2013 by Arktos Media Ltd.

Published in the United Kingdom.

ISBN 978-1-907166-30-3

BIC classification:
Conservatism and right-of-centre democratic ideologies (JPFM)
Social & political philosophy (HPS)

Proofreaders: Tobias Ridderstråle and John B. Morgan
Cover Design: Andreas Nilsson
Layout: Daniel Friberg

ARKTOS MEDIA LTD
www.arktos.com

The Conservative

H.P. Lovecraft

ARKTOS
London, 2013

Table of Contents

Foreword by Alex Kurtagic. 7

The Conservative, Vol. I, No. I. 21

The Conservative, Vol. I, No. II 33

The Conservative, Vol. I, No. III 49

The Conservative, Vol. I, No. IV 70

The Conservative, Vol. II, No. I 79

The Conservative, Vol. II, No. II 86

The Conservative, Vol. II, No. III. 92

The Conservative, Vol. II, No. IV. 118

The Conservative, Vol. III, No. I 127

The Conservative, Vol. IV, No. 1 136

The Conservative Vol. V, No. I. 155

The Conservative, Twelfth Number 182

The Conservative, Thirteenth Number 190

Foreword by Alex Kurtagic

LOVECRAFT

Howard Phillips Lovecraft was born in Providence, Rhode Island, on 20 August 1890. His was a prosperous, upper middle class family. His father, Winfield Scott Lovecraft, was a travelling salesman, and his mother, Sarah Susan Lovecraft (*née* Phillips), was already in her thirties when her only child was born. Following a psychotic episode while in a hotel room in Chicago, Winfield was taken to Butler Hospital, in Providence, where he was admitted and would remain until his death five years later. The most likely cause was syphilis. Lovecraft was told his father was paralysed and comatose during this period and it is unlikely he ever saw him.

Lovecraft would thereafter be raised by his mother, her two sisters, and their father, a prominent industrialist, all of whom resided in the family home. A child prodigy, able to recite poetry at the age of two, read at three, and write at six or seven, he was also a sickly child, many of whose illnesses were psychological; he only sporadically attended school until eight years of age, although this was before the era of mandatory education. Instead, he was supplied with classics by his grandfather and encouraged to read. This included the *Illiad*, the *Odyssey*, and *Arabian Nights*. His grandfather also stimulated an interest in the 'weird tale' by telling him his own improvised stories in a Gothic key. At the same time, Lovecraft also became enamoured of chemistry and astronomy, and from 1899 produced hectographed publications of limited circulation, beginning with *The Scientific Gazette*.

His life changed in 1904 after the death of his grandfather, whose estate was subsequently mismanaged, leaving the family in diminished circumstances. Lovecraft and his mother were forced to leave their ample Victorian home and move into cramped accommodation. This proved traumatic for Lovecraft, who had a strong attachment to his birthplace, and who, apparently, briefly contemplated suicide. However, there was much thrill in learning for him and he was hungry for answers, so the idea was abandoned.

Lovecraft was again under psychological stress in his late teens. He aspired to become an astronomer, but a nervous breakdown, thought to have been caused primarily by his difficulties with higher mathematics, meant he left high school without a diploma, and was subsequently unable to gain entrance into Brown University. He would later conceal his failure to graduate, constituting an acute source of shame.

For the next five years after high school, Lovecraft led a hermitic existence, during which he wrote mostly poetry—influenced by seventeenth- and eighteenth-century poets—and some fiction. He had little human contact except his mother, with whom he developed an unhealthy closeness and 'who developed a pathological love-hate relationship with her son.'[1] She would tell others that her son was averse to leaving the house due to the hideousness of his face.

His isolation ended in 1914, when he wrote (in verse) to *The Argosy*, the original pulp magazine, to protest against Fred Jackson's insipid love stories. The ensuing debate in the letters column, which went on for months and involved witty exchanges in satirical poetry, brought Lovecraft to the attention of Edward F. Daas, president of the United Amateur Press Association, which he was invited to join. An energised Lovecraft then became a productive contributor, at first of poetry and essays, and later of short fiction. Between 1915 and 1923 he would publish thirteen issues of his own paper, *The Conservative*—which truly lived up to its name—and he would later become President and Official Editor of the UAPA, also serving briefly as President of the National Amateur Press Association, a rival body. In the process he developed a wide network of correspondents, including Clark Ashton Smith and Robert E. Howard, both of whom are now the most celebrated authors associated with the pioneering pulp magazine *Weird Tales*. Indeed, Lovecraft's prolific and extensive letter writing would eventually result in an enormous volume of correspondence.

Among Lovecraft's correspondents would be his mother, who followed her late husband into Butler Hospital in 1919, having suffered a nervous breakdown after a long period of depression and financial worries. Mother and son would remain close until her death in 1921.

---

1 S. T. Joshi, 'Howard Phillips Lovecraft: The Life of a Gentleman of Providence,' available at www.hplovecraft.com/life/biograph.aspx.

Not long after, Lovecraft, who soon recovered, would travel to an amateur journalists' convention in Boston, where he would meet Sonia Greene, a Jewish-Ukrainian who managed a hat shop on New York's Fifth Avenue. They married in March 1924, and moved into her apartment in Brooklyn, New York; Greene was by then 41, and Lovecraft 33.

Initially, their prospects seemed good: Lovecraft's career as a professional writer was apparently on its way, having had several of his stories accepted by *Weird Tales*, and Sonia's business was thriving. Yet, very soon after, they faced trouble. Greene's shop went bankrupt; she became ill and was for a period unable to work; and Lovecraft, having turned down an offer to edit a companion magazine to *Weird Tales*, which would have meant an unwanted relocation to Chicago, was forced to look for employment, something he had previously never sought nor had been forced to do. In his mid-thirties, without work experience, and living among a large immigrant population, Lovecraft was, not unexpectedly, unable to find any kind of work, and therefore any financial relief.

Greene eventually found employment in Cincinnati, and then in Cleveland, following which she would be mostly on the road. Lovecraft remained in New York, and moved into a single-room apartment in Red Hook, a seedy Brooklyn neighbourhood. The apartment was soon burgled; his suits stolen, he was left with the clothes he had on. Despite having friends in New York, including Frank Belknap Long, Rheinhart Kleiner, and Samuel Loveman, Lovecraft grew unhappy, his initial enthrallment for the city having developed into a passionate hatred. The latter would be poured into a short story, 'The Horror at Red Hook', written in July 1925, and published in *Weird Tales* in January 1927. For his survival, Lovecraft was entirely dependent on his wife, who would send him a weekly allowance. This enabled him to rent a microscopic apartment in Brooklyn Heights (then a working-class neighbourhood), yet he could afford little else: in one of his letters from this period he complained of having had to live for three days on just cheese, a hunk of bread, and a can of unheated beans. In April 1926 he returned to live with his aunts in Providence. This afforded him enormous psychological relief and led immediately to his most prolific period. The aunts had always disapproved of Lovecraft's wife, whom, because she was a 'tradeswoman', they regarded as a taint on their nephew. Relocating to Cleveland was, for Lovecraft, out of the question. Conversely, the aunts vetoed Sonia's proposal to relocate and start her own business in Providence. Lovecraft, for his part, having largely been an absentee husband, seemed happy to continue his marriage by correspondence. By 1929, the couple would agree to an amicable divorce. Without Greene's knowledge, however, Lovecraft would fail to sign the final decree, so they would remain technically married until his death.

During his final decade, Lovecraft wrote not only original stories, but also undertook to revise other author's manuscripts, engaged in ghost writing, and nurtured the careers of several young writers. It is thought that Lovecraft suffered from night terrors since early in life, and that much of his later work was influenced by them. He also travelled extensively in and around New England, motivated mostly by his antiquarian interests.

Neither inspiration nor productivity, however, nor the peak in popularity of pulp magazines throughout the 1920s and 1930s, failed to stall the advancing penury, and, following the death of his aunt Lilian in 1932, he was forced to downsize yet again with his surviving relative. His stories, by then increasingly long and complex, proved difficult to sell, forcing Lovecraft to support himself by the revision, or ghost-writing, of poetry, short stories, and non-fiction. Somehow, he managed to feed himself on $2 a week.[2]

In 1936, he received the sad and perplexing news of the suicide of Robert E. Howard, his former correspondent of six years' standing. He was also diagnosed with malnutrition and terminal cancer of the small intestine.[3] The symptoms had first appeared in 1934, but he had ignored them, being too poor to afford medical care. Despite the now constant pain, he carried on writing, until, in the end, he had to be admitted into hospital, where he died five days later, on 15 March 1937.

AMATEUR JOURNALISM

The Conservative was Lovecraft's original contribution to the movement of amateur journalism. This movement originated during the 1860s, when teenagers began taking advantage of newly available, inexpensive printing presses. It became an organised institution in the 1866-1876 period.[4] 'A short-lived society of amateur journalists, including the now

2 This amounts to just under $35 a week in 2013 money, based on a simple CPI adjustment.

3 S. T. Joshi, *A Dreamer and a Visionary: H. P. Lovecraft in his Time* (Liverpool: Liverpool University Press, 2001), pp. 95, 97, 111, 221–222, 359–360.

4 H. P. Lovecraft, *Works of H. P. Lovecraft* (Boston: MobileReference, 2008). Ebook.

famous publisher, Charles Scribner, . . . existed between 1869 to 1874'.[5] Though a more lasting society, still in existence today, was founded in 1876, '[i]t was not until 1895 . . . [that] amateur journalism was established as a serious branch of educational endeavour',[6] when William H. Greenfield, a professional author, founded the UAPA, which later became the leading organisation of its kind.[7]

Amateur journalism involved much more than news and topical non-fiction: it also involved short fiction, essays, reviews, news items, poetry, and polemics.

> The extent of the movement was extraordinary, and among the famous people who had amateur journalism in their past are Horatio Alger and Thomas Edison. Edison, who in his teens had a job selling fruit, candy, and magazines to railways passengers, bought a small press and ran it on the train while he worked. Amateur journalism was primarily a youth movement.[8]

One of the pleasures of amateur journalism was the social intercourse it offered to adolescents in an age of limited communication and travel. Exchanging publications enabled the young writers and printers to make new friends from all parts of the country; this was certainly Lovecraft's experience, who may otherwise have remained a recluse. Many years later, the model would later be replicated in other areas of culture. Substituting audio cassettes for magazines, and moving from the national to the global level, for example, exchange-based distribution would be used in the 1980s in the practice of tape trading among enthusiasts of the underground Death Metal scene.

Amateur journalism was also a primarily American phenomenon, though it eventually crossed the Atlantic, after two brothers from Manchester, having visited the United States, were inspired by the amateur movement there.[9]

The motivation was never economic, but simple love of writing. The quality of the literature produced varied widely.

---

5 Ibid.

6 Ibid.

7 Ibid.

8 Christopher Hilliard, *To Exercise Our Talents: The Democratization of Writing in Britain* (Cambridge: Harvard University Press, 2009), p. 56.

9 Ibid.

> If it is generally true that most of this material [was] the work of tyros—"amateurs" in the pejorative sense—then it means only that amateur journalism . . . perform[ed] a sound if humble function as a proving-ground for writers. Some amateurs did in fact go on to publish professionally, and yet, Lovecraft was all too correct when, late in life, he summed up the general qualitative level of amateur work: "God, what crap!"[10]

One variant model for circulation involved pass-around circuits, where the publication in question would be passed around a circle of subscribers, until it got back to the original sender. In some cases, the list was interactive, particularly when the circle was one of writers, and each stage in the journey would involve the inclusion of feedback or additional content.

As *The Conservative* attests, the movement's literary zenith coincided with the involvement of Lovecraft and his friend W. Paul Cook, between 1915 and 1925. It waned as Lovecraft, by then seeking professional opportunities in New York, left the movement (though he retained links to it). Fine printing, quality materials, and small hand-presses and mimeographs brought a redevelopment of interest in the 1930s, but thereafter amateur journalism went into a terminal decline. There are still, nevertheless, individuals involved with it.

The similarity between amateurdom and the internet-based phenomenon of citizen journalism and blogging can be easily seen. Indeed, Lovecraft was once referred to as 'an internet figure before there was an internet'.[11]

THE CONSERVATIVE

Lovecraft already had a long history of amateur writing and publishing before he became involved with organised amateurdom. In 1915, *The Conservative* was simply the latest in a series of journals which Lovecraft began producing when he was very young. Most of his early juvenilia was of a scientific nature, and included the *Rhode Island Journal of Astronomy*, his most significant publication, with 69 surviving issues, which ran weekly, off and on, between 1903 and 1906, and then monthly until 1907, with two late issues in 1909; *Astronomy* and the *Monthly Almanack*,

10 Joshi (2001), p. 78.

11 Jonathan Bowden, 'H. P. Lovecraft: Aryan Mystic', *Pulp Fascism* (San Francisco: Counter-Currents Publishing, 2013).

which ran until 1904; *Planet*, of which there was a single issue in 1903; and the *Scientific Gazette*, which was begun in 1899, running initially as a daily, and then as a weekly. Lovecraft had also published numerous chemical and astronomical pieces, as well as a collection of poetry in two volumes, *Poemata Minora*.

> A good many of [the scientific] periodicals were reproduced using a process called the hectograph (or hektograph). This was a sheet of gelatin in a pan rendered hard by glycerine. A master page is prepared wither in written form by the use of special hectograph inks or in typed form using hectographic typewriter ribbon; artwork of all sorts could also be drawn upon it. The surface of the pan would then be moistened and the master page pressed down upon it; this page would then be removed and the sheets of paper would be pressed upon the gelatin surface, which had now picked up whatever writing or art had been on the master. The surface would be good for up to 50 copies, at which time the impression would begin to fade. Different colours could also be used.[12]

While, by 1915, Lovecraft was on the editorial board of several other amateur journals, *The Conservative* was the only one for which he was the sole editor. The journal ran for thirteen issues. During the first two years, it ran as a quarterly; thereafter, until 1919, it ran as a yearly. There were then no further issues until 1923, when two late numbers appeared. The full run breaks down as follows:

- Vol. 1, No. 1: April 1915
- Vol. 1. No. 2: July 1915
- Vol. 1. No. 3: October 1915
- Vol. 1. No. 4: January 1916
- Vol. 2. No. 1: April 1916
- Vol. 2. No. 2: July 1916
- Vol. 2. No. 3: October 1916
- Vol. 2. No. 4: January 1917
- Vol. 3. No. 1: July 1917
- Vol. 4. No. 1: July 1918
- Vol. 5. No. 1: July 1919
- No. 12: March 1923
- No. 13: July 1923

12 S. T. Joshi, *I Am Providence: The Life and Times of H. P. Lovecraft*, vol. 1 (New York: Hippocampus Press, 2013), pp. 84-85.

> The issues range from 4 to 28 pages. The first three issues were written almost entirely by Lovecraft, but thereafter his contributions decline considerably except for occasional poems and—beginning with the October 1916 issue—a regular editorial column entitled "In the Editor's Study."[13]

The first issue was printed locally, with a run of 210 copies; the next three issues, and probably the next three after those, were printed by The Lincoln Press, owned by 'Albert A. Sandusky, an amateur in Cambridge, Massachusetts'.[14] A local printer would have printed the next two issues, before Lovecraft possibly took advantage of W. Paul Cook's cheap printing rates for the 1918 and 1919 issues.[15] The last two issues of *The Conservative* were printed by Charles A. A. Parker.[16]

The Conservative has been mostly out of print since 1923. It was reprinted in 1977 in a low-budget booklet edition (stapled sheets of paper) by Necronomicon Press, a small press publishing house based in Rhode Island and owned by Marc A. Michaud. In 1990, Lovecraft's 28 essay contributions were collected into a booklet, edited by S. T. Joshi, and also published by Necronomicon Press. The present is, therefore, the first professional edition in nearly a quarter of a century; the first complete edition in 36 years; and the first ever that is both complete and professional.

THEMES

Lovecraft's thought was fundamentally aristocratic, and it is, therefore, an elitist, hierarchical worldview that unifies the recurrent themes in *The Conservative.*

The effect is to pull the journal in apparently contradictory directions. On the one hand, there is a very obvious rejection of the trappings of egalitarian modernity, and a corresponding nostalgia for the standards of the pre-modern era—a mixture of rigid classicism; an adherence to archaic norms of gentlemanly propriety and decorum; archaic diction, syntax, and idioms in prose and poetry; scorn for the disintegrative effects of radicalism in literary modernism; and contempt

13 Ibid, p. 177.

14 Ibid, p. 178.

15 Ibid, p. 179.

16 Ibid.

for egalitarian social movements, such as syndicalism, socialism, and Bolshevism. On the other hand, there is an equally vehement rejection of religion, superstition, romanticism, and Victorian sentimentality, which Lovecraft dismissed as products of ignorance and simplicity; Lovecraft's worldview was informed by his scientific interests and was, accordingly, characterised by extreme rationalism, 'cynical materialism', and 'cosmic indifferentism'. As will be seen during the ensuring exploration of the journal's most salient themes, however, the apparent contradictions resolve into a coherent and consistent philosophy.

Lovecraft's archaic literary style is *The Conservative*'s most immediately apparent feature, particularly in the early issues, where he dominates the content. This was not an affectation; indeed, Lovecraft condemned the Victorians for, among other things, their artificiality and affectedness: Lovecraft grew up on a diet of Augustan literature,[17] and considered the prose of the late seventeenth and early eighteenth century the most stylistically superior ever produced in the English language; moreover, in his early years Lovecraft was socially isolated, essentially a bookworm committed to a life of the mind; and finally, Lovecraft was temperamentally conservative, and grew up in a social class of rigidly conservative values. Early eighteenth-century prose and poetry, therefore, came to be treated by him as the norm—and modern literary styles as degradations of the former lofty standards.

It is unsurprising, then, that one of Lovecraft's missions was the improvement of literary standards in amateur journalism. In this he led by example and by criticism, focusing on amateur publications, prosody, and literary modernism. All the rage at the time, extreme literary radicalism—in which he included Imagism, free verse, and T. S. Eliot's 'The Waste Land'—he castigated for involving 'a grotesque display of egotism and affectation'.

At the same time, Lovecraft saw it imperative in the twentieth century to slough off the burden of the Victorians, stating:

> It is time, THE CONSERVATIVE believes, definitely to challenge the sterile and exhausted Victorian ideal which blighted Anglo-Saxon culture for three quarters of a century and produced a milky poetry of shopworn sentimentalities and puffy platitudes; a dull-grey prose fiction of misplaced didacticism and insipid artificiality; an appallingly hideous

17 Produced during the reigns of Queen Anne, King George I, and George II, ending in 1744-5 with the deaths of Alexander Pope and Jonathan Swift.

> system of formal manners, costume, and decoration; and worst of all, an artistically blasphemous architecture whose uninspired nondescriptness transcends tolerance, comprehension, and profanity alike.[18]

Lovecraft had very clear views on Anglo-Saxondom. His Anglophilia was so pronounced, in fact, that, combined with his extreme conservatism, it led him to reject the American Revolution, and to provide space in his journal for mild historical revisionism, underscoring his own lamentation of the sundering of the race. Early in life Lovecraft professed allegiance to the British King, and in *The Conservative*, writing while the Great War raged on in Europe, he fulminated against hyphenated Americans, pacifists, and isolationists, whom he accused of using 'Americanism' and 'America First' as treasonous devices to conceal and simultaneously advance an Anglophobic agenda designed to keep America apart from the 'Mistress of the Seas'—the British Empire. In his expressed scorn for Anglophobic sentiment in the United States, and in his denunciation of its biased history textbooks, it is clear that he viewed the United States as an extension of England. While he admitted the latter had not been blameless, he considered the revolution and subsequent independence as the product of the pig-headed political attitudes and mercantile interests of a seditious and unrepresentative minority.

On the Irish question, which he saw as related, Lovecraft followed a similar line: England was, again, not blameless, but the Hibernians were seeking to sow division, both in America and in Europe, when their place was within England's Empire, in subordination to the latter's greater glory.

As a militarist, Lovecraft was delighted when the United States government finally opted to join the war on the British side, and promptly sought to enlist, first in the Rhode Island National Guard (before Wilson signed the draft bill)[19] and then in the regular army, though it appears that his mother soon contrived to thwart the first attempt, while on the second he was rejected even for clerical work.[20] Desire for action in the trenches was not, all the same, born out of hatred for Germany. Lovecraft considered the Germans racially identical to the Anglo-Saxons, which to him explained their full assimilation in America. Moreover, he regarded

18 See p. 209.

19 Joshi (2013), p. 222. 20 Ibid, pp. 300-301.

20 Ibid, pp. 300-301.

the Teuton as a superior race. For this reason, he condemned the war as fratricidal and destructive of civilisation:

> That the maintenance of civilisation today rests with that magnificent Teutonic stock which is represented alike by the two hotly contending rivals, England and Germany... is as undeniably true as it is vigorously disputed. The Teuton is the summit of evolution. That we may consider intelligently his place in history we must cast aside the popular nomenclature which would confuse the names "Teuton" and "German," and view him not nationally but racially. Tracing the career of the Teuton through medieval and modern history, we can find no possible excuse for denying his actual biological supremacy. In widely separated localities and under widely diverse conditions, his innate racial qualities have raised him to preeminence. There is no branch of modern civilisation that is not of his making.[21]

For Lovecraft, the United States was purely a credit to Anglo-Saxon genius. He emphatically dismissed the notion of its being a multicultural nation, and expected immigrants to fully assimilate into the established Anglo-Saxon matrix. But even then, there were limits to acceptable levels, and Lovecraft disapproved of the number of immigrants already evident in the 1910s. After marrying in 1924, Lovecraft would spend two years in New York, where he would be maddened by the racial heterogeneity of its population and the low quality of the immigrants. He was not alone in feeling this way, for at this time Madison Grant, also based in New York, and his colleagues were pushing for restrictive legislation, which eventually resulted in the Immigration Act of 1917 (requiring immigrants to undergo a literacy test); the Emergency Quota Act of 1921, which introduced the quota system; and finally the Immigration Act of 1924, which extended those quotas and the bias towards Northern European immigration. Lovecraft does not mention this legislation, thus indicating, perhaps, his satisfaction.

Lovecraft's views on race, conventional in his time, were explicitly expressed in his controversy with Charles Isaacson, a Jewish amateur writer, who 'praised pacifism, Socialism, and the poetry of Walt Whitman', while 'denounce[ing] militarism, conscription, racial prejudice, and the movie *The Birth of a Nation*, whose "backers," he said,

21 See pp. 23-24.

"should be flogged"'.[22] Whitman had incurred Lovecraft's disapproval for popularising free verse and making allusions to intercourse in his poetry, which, in Lovecraft's view, made him a 'degraded' poet, who 'Delights the rake, and warms the souls of swine'.[23] In turn, Blacks were considered by Lovecraft 'fundamentally the biological inferior of all White and even Mongolian races'; always in favour of a strict colour line and steadfast in his belief in the superiority of the Northern European stock, he thought that "the Northern people must occasionally be reminded of the danger which they incur in admitting [the negro] too freely to the privileges of society and government'.[24] Isaacson, while praised for his talent, is deemed by Lovecraft to be partially unfit for 'considerations of tastes and trends in Aryan thought and writings',[25] on account of 'the very spirituality that gives elevation to the Semitic mind'.[26] To Lovecraft, the latter accounted for Isaacson's being 'a radical of the extremest sort'.[27]

Lovecraft's racialism followed logically from his hierarchical view of life, so he quite naturally opposed egalitarian social movements. He disdained the idea of an author's union, mocking its underlying economic ethos with satirical speculations and treating it as symptomatic of the degenerate condition of modern literature, which is what, in his estimation, made popular authors so semblable to manual workers. Syndicalism he viewed as a sort of extortion racket, and his criticism of Marxian arguments concerning the alleged 'appropriation' of surplus value by the capitalist class, though in *The Conservative* it appears only implicitly, would later be echoed by Francis Parker Yockey:[28] the workers would be lost without the brains of those who created employment for them; were they to seize control of the factories, they would be left with nothing to run, for obviously, to have factories, there must first be capital and inventions. Accordingly, Bolshevists he deemed the 'sanguinary' proponents of a 'futile revolution which would ruin all civilization, themselves included, without helping anyone':

22 L. Sprague de Camp, *Lovecraft: A Life* (London: Hachette, 2011). Ebook.

23 See p. 44.

24 See p. 45.

25 See p. 44.

26 Ibid.

27 Ibid.

28 Francis Parker Yockey, *Imperium: The Philosophy of History and Politics* (Abergele: The Palingenesis Project, 2013), p. 119.

> ... how little will the blind anarchists gain ... ! With the intelligent element removed, the rabble will use up the resources of civilisation without being able to produce more; cities and public works will fall into decay, and a new barbarism arise, out of which will spring in time the natural chieftains who will constitute the "masters" of another era of capitalism.[29]

Though not discussed in *The Conservative*, Lovecraft initially saw capitalism in Darwinian terms, and naïvely assumed that it would bring just rewards to the best—by which he understood the culture-bearing stratum of a society. Later in life, well after he ceased publishing amateur journals, and in much diminished economic circumstances, Lovecraft came to realise his error, noting that capitalism rewarded the '*shrewdly acquisitive* rather than the *intrinsically superior and creative*'.[30] His biographer, S. T. Joshi, argues that readers should be grateful for the fact that Lovecraft saw literary activity as an elegant amusement, the province of an elite—a superior type—who wrote not for money, but for their own aesthetic and intellectual indulgence, and who bore the burden of educating those beneath them, for this has assured the consistent quality and lasting value of his prose.

Clearly, then, Lovecraft's aristocracy was not one of hereditary privilege, as was the case in Europe, but of intrinsic human quality, which set the tone for the rest of society. This conception has much in common with Anthony Ludovici's, and even Robert Filmer's paternalism,[31] minus the latter's ideas of divine right and Adamic lineage. However, Lovecraft's ideal was that set by the ancients of Greece and Rome:

> The literary genius of Greece and Rome, developed under peculiarly favourable circumstances, may fairly be said to have completed the art and science of expression. Unhurried and profound, the classical author achieved a standard of simplicity, moderation, and elegance of taste, which all succeeding time has been powerless to excel or even to equal. Indeed, those modern periods have been most cultivated, in which the models of antiquity have been most faithfully followed.[32]

---

29 See p. 177.

30 H. P. Lovecraft, *Selected Letters V (1934-1937)*, ed. August Derleth, Donald Wandrei, and James Turner (Sauk City, WI: Arkham House, 1976), p. 326.

31 Robert Filmer, *Patriarcha; or, the Natural Power of Kings* (London: Richard Chiswell, 1680).

32 H. P. Lovecraft, 'The Case for Classicism', in *Uncollected Prose and Poetry*, vol. 1, ed. S. T. Joshi and Marc A. Michaud (West Warwick, RI: Necronomicon Press, 1978), p. 13.

Setting the tone clearly included support for Prohibition. Lovecraft was a rigorous teetotaller, and viewed drinkers as a degenerate rabble, their taste for drinking worthy only of a civilised man's towering scorn and incomprehension. Here and elsewhere, he skewers drinkers for their moral inferiority.

Lovecraft also ridiculed the League of Nations and the idea that war could be prevented and unity achieved in diversity. He saw humanity as inherently rapacious, hateful, greedy, and pugnacious, divided by incompatible cultures. A web of alliances between divergent nations he thought more likely to *increase* conflict, than to bring about 'fantastic and impossible' ideals of peace and universal brotherhood. Lovecraft had no time for fatuous humanism.

Lovecraft, of course, would have called this *realism*. Yet, as a writer of weird fiction, and as a devotee of science, he was aware of the disillusioning power of knowledge, and of the fact that art relies partly on mystery and mystification. For a man like Lovecraft, meaning came from art and rootedness in tradition. Hence, he proposed that, in an age when science had made prosaic much that was previously an enigma, wrapped in speculation and superstition, future art would necessitate artificial limitations to consciousness. This is a tacit indictment of the liberal project, of course, for it belied the perception that it has rendered modern life meaningless, banal, and nearly worthless. Certainly, Lovecraft took pains to escape the modern world via antiquarianism and aesthetics. *The Conservative*, however, does not contain much on aesthetic theory or Lovecraft's thoughts on the Weird Tale—his most significant work, the great bulk of his fiction, would come later, after his New York period. All we do get are glimpses here, along with the impression that Lovecraft was a man against time.

For all his eccentricity, Lovecraft's philosophy was neither systematic nor original, yet it was internally consistent and well grounded; it also found its most detailed articulation not in his essays nor even in his fiction, but in his voluminous personal correspondence, which are works of literature in their own right. *The Conservative* provides, nevertheless, a useful overview in concentrated form, along with Lovecraft's—nowadays controversial—positions on a number of topical issues of his time. *The Conservative* remains, perhaps, one journal that truly lives up to its name.

The Conservative, Vol. I, No. I

Providence, R. I., April, 1915

The Conservative desires to apologize for any errors in proofreading which may be found in this issue. Circumstances necessitated a change of printer at the last moment, and an already great delay rendered haste a prime essential.

Edited by H. P. Lovecraft

THE SIMPLE SPELLER'S TALE

(Translated into English)

When first among the amateurs I fell,
I blush'd in shame because I could not spell.
Though skill'd in numbers, and at ease in prose,
My letters I could never well dispose.
Thoughts came abundant; language was the same;
Yet none the less I scarce could spell my name!
The kindly printer (with an eye for trade)
A clumsy care for all my work display'd:
Indiff'rent as I was, I us'd his art
Till critics cry'd, "My printer should be shot"!
Thus boldly censur'd, I began to seek
A means to thwart the rude reviewers' clique:
My fever'd eye in rage I cast around,
When all at once the wish'd-for plan I found.
It happen'd on a summer's holiday,
That past a mad-house gate I took my way.

Within the bedlam was a sage confin'd,
Who had from too much study lost his mind.
Now strolling out, in watchful keeper's care,
With childish sounds the madman fill'd the air.
Still dreaming of his letter'd days of yore,
His ravings on remember'd subjects bore:
Dim came the thoughts of what he us'd to teach,
And he began to curse our English speech.
"Aha"! quoth he, "the men that made our tongue "Were arrant rogues, and I shall have them hung.
"For long establish'd custom what care we?
"Come, let us tear down etymology.
"Let spelling fly, and naught but sound remain;
"The world is mad, and I alone am sane!"
Thus rav'd the sage; inventing, as he walk'd,
A hundred ways to spell our words as talk'd.
He simplify'd until his fancy bred
A system quite as simple as his head.
In scholarship disastrous change he wrought,
And alter'd, as he went, for want of thought.
But I, attentive, heard with joyful ear
The wild distortions, and perversions queer.
Why could not I defend my ill-spell'd page
In progress' name, and with reformer's rage?
With hope renew'd, I hasten'd home to write,
And passing wondrous was my work that night;
For classic purity I sought no more,
But strove to make worse blunders than before.
O fickle fortune! In a week my name
From scholars' praise attain'd immortal fame,
Whilst other scribes with vague orthography
Seiz'd on the clever ruse, and copy'd me.
Today in ev'ry *"Skateville Amateur"*
Amorphous letters pass as language pure,
And when some pompous pedant dares to raise
A voice remonstrant 'gainst our foolish ways,
We never fail the apt retort to give,
But damn him as a blind CONSERVATIVE.

Yet why on us your angry hand or wrath use?
We do but ape Professor B—M—!

—H. P. L.

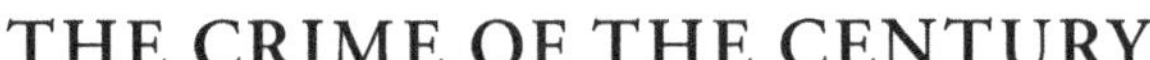

THE CRIME OF THE CENTURY

By H. P. Lovecraft

The present European war, occuring as it does in an age of hysterical sentimentality and unsound political doctrines, has called forth from the sympathizers of each set of belligerents an unexampled torrent of indiscriminate denunciation.

The effeminate idealist, half awaked from his roseate vision of universal brotherhood, shrieks at the mutual slaughter of his fellow-men, or singles out individual acts of cruelty or treachery as the objects of his well-meaning rage; while the erratic socialist, saturated with false notions of equality and democracy, raves unendingly against cruel systems of government which sacrifice a peaceful peasantry to the greed and ambition of their warlike masters.

But though the sober philosopher perceives in war a phenomenon eminently natural and absolutely inevitable; though he realizes that the masses of mankind must remain subject to the will of a dominant aristocracy so long as the present structure of the human brain endures; he can none the less find in the colossal conflict an ample cause for the deepest regret and the gravest apprehension. High above such national crimes as the Servian plots against Austria or the German disregard of Belgian neutrality, high above such sad matters as the destruction of innocent lives and property, looms the supremest of all crimes, an offense not only against conventional morality but against Nature itself; the violation of race.

In the unnatural racial alignment of the various warring powers we behold a defiance of anthropological principles that cannot but bode ill for the future of the world.

That the maintenance of civilization rests today with that magnificent Teutonic stock which is represented alike by the two hotly contending rivals, England and Germany, as well as by Austria, Scandinavia, Switzerland, Holland and Belgium, is as undeniably true as it is vigorously disputed. The Teuton is the summit of evolution. That we may consider intelligently his place in history we must cast aside the popular nomenclature which would confuse the names "Teuton" and "German," and view him not nationally but racially, identifying his fundamental stock with the tall, pale, blue-eyed, yellow-haired, long-headed "Xanthochroi" as described by Huxley, amongst whom the class of languages we call "Teutonic" arose, and who today constitute the majority of the Teutonic-speaking population of our globe.

Though some ethnologists have declared that the Teuton is the only true Aryan, and that the languages and institutions of the other nominally Aryan races were derived alone from his superior speech and customs; it is nevertheless not necessary for us to accept this daring theory in order to appreciate his vast superiority to the rest of mankind.

Tracing the career of the Teuton through mediaeval and modern history, we can find no possible excuse for denying his actual biological supremacy. In widely separated localities and under widely diverse conditions, his innate racial qualities have raised him to preeminence. There is no branch of modern civilization that is not of his making. As the power of the Roman Empire declined, the Teuton sent down into Italy, Gaul, and Spain the re-vivifying elements which saved those countries from complete destruction. Though now largely lost in the mixed population, the Teutons are the true founders of all the so-called Latin states. Political and social vitality had fled from the old inhabitants; the Teuton only was creative and constructive. After the native elements absorbed the Teutonic invaders, the Latin civilizations declined tremendously, so that the France, Italy, and Spain of today bear every mark of national degeneracy.

In the lands whose population is mainly Teutonic, we behold a striking proof of the qualities of the race. England and Germany are the supreme empires of the world, whilst the virile virtues of the Belgians have lately been demonstrated in a manner which will live forever in song and story. Switzerland and Holland are veritable synonyms for Liberty. The Scandinavians are immortalized by the exploits of the Vikings and Normans, whose conquests over man and Nature extended from the sun-baked shores of Sicily to the glacial wastes of Greenland, even attaining our own distant Vineland across the sea. United States history is one long panegyric of the Teuton, and will continue to be such if degenerate immigration can be checked in time to preserve the primitive character of the population.

The Teutonic mind is masterful, temperate, and just. No other race has shown an equal capability for self-government. It is a significant fact that not one square inch of Teutonic territory is governed save by its own inhabitants.

The division of such a splendid stock against itself, each representative faction allying itself with alien inferiors, is a crime so monstrous that the world may well stand aghast. Germany, it is true, has some appreciation of the civilizing mission of the Teuton, but has allowed her jealousy of England to conquer her intellectual zeal, and to disrupt the race in an infamous and unnecessary war.

Englishmen and Germans are blood brothers, descended from the same stern Woden-worshipping ancestors, blessed with the same rugged virtues, and fired with the same noble ambitions. In a world of diverse and hostile races the joint mission of these virile men is one of union and co-operation with their fellow-Teutons in defense of civilization against the onslaughts of all others. There is work to be done by the Teuton. As a unit he must in times to come crush successively the rising power of Slav and Mongolian, preserving for Europe and America the glorious culture that he has evolved.

Wherefore we have reason to weep less at the existence or causes of this stupendous fray, than at its unnatural and fratricidal character; at the self-decimation of the one mighty branch of humanity on which the future welfare of the world depends.

EDITORIAL

The Conservative, in thrusting upon an unsuspecting amateur public this first issue of what purports to be a paper, may well adopt that tone of trembling humility which suits the inexperienced beginner.

As another ambitious novice wrote not long ago in rugged verse:

Mid amateurs and novices, through oft they are winning,
Be it ever so humble, there must be a beginning.
A slap from the critic swiftly brings us to our feet;
Shakes up our senses, and shakes out our conceit.

Like the poet, THE CONSERVATIVE expects criticism. He does not, however, expressly solicit it; since he is well aware that critics, like other birds of prey, require but little solicitation before tearing to pieces their latest victim. That his numerous defects and weaknesses will furnish the reviewers' fraternity with a just and ample opportunity for the display of their brilliant superiority, THE CONSERVATIVE is not quite conceited enough to deny; yet he would give warning that he has made a close study of Pope's Dunciad and Paul J. Campbell's "Wet Hen," so that he is not altogether defenseless. Reference to "verbosity," "long words," "stilted, old-fashioned style," "dogmatic opinions" and the like will be entirely unnecessary. THE CONSERVATIVE has heard all this before, and is hopelessly beyond reform. Besides, he may never perpetrate another number of this modest magazine.

THE QUESTION OF THE DAY

The debate over the propriety of outside matters in the amateur papers, begun in the National association, has quickly spread to the United, where Mr. George Schilling challenges the distinguished exponents of the negative with an able article on the minimum wage. THE CONSERVATIVE, mindful of the nature and aims of amateur journalism, cannot but be opposed to the present attacks on the liberty of the press.

The agitators who would restrict the work of amateurs to subjects immediately connected with the associations base their opinions on ridiculously exalted standards of amateur writing. Endowed with an almost too great refinement of taste, they cannot endure the general article of ordinary merit, but demand that every author become a specialist in his chosen field before he shall so much as dare to express his views in public. While it is easy to imagine the supercilious displeasure with which our faultless critics must examine the average amateur's half-formed views on outside affairs, it is difficult to understand why these impeccable censors should take it upon themselves to stifle the dawning spirit of research in the beginner by suppressing his crude, nascent efforts. The uninspired and unintelligent presentation of a topic may often elicit reams of really valuable discussion, in the meantime forcing the original author to acquire a truer grasp of his subject. It is in this atmosphere of lettered freedom that the educational side of amateur journalism is best developed.

The position of those who favor the exclusive discussion of amateur journalism is peculiarly indefensible. Amateur journalism is like a great machine for the production and publication of literary matter. While it is of course necessary to keep the mechanism in running order, our greatest interest naturally centres on the product. It is only the child who becomes infatuated with the machine for its own sake; who spends all his time in watching the wheels go 'round.

THE MORRIS FACTION

Several months after The Conservative joined the U. A. P. A. he received a copy of a strange but excellent paper claiming to be the only real and original "United Amateur," together with a blank recommending him for membership in "The United Amateur Press Association." Having thought himself already a fully initiated United man, he naturally became rather curious as to the number of times one is supposed to join the same association. Nor has The Conservative been alone in this perplexing experience, which indeed seems quite the rule with United recruits. In time the new member learns of the factional division which has created this confusing situation, and in nearly every case regrets the separate existence of the small branch which though sadly struggling for its very life, yet refuses to return to the fold.

Whilst the veteran amateur may regard as grave and irreconcilable the differences that cause the Morris faction to stand aloof, the more recent element, already numerous and powerful, cannot help considering them far too insignificant to warrant continued separation. Can no means be devised to effect a reunion? A half-forgotten contest over an office ought not to keep such capable amateurs as Mr. Morris, Mr. Haggerty, Miss Merritt, or Mr. Cook from rejoining the larger, rejuvenated United, and co-operating with its members in the interests of a better amateur journalism.

FOR PRESIDENT—LEO FRITTER

In the United Official Quarterly for February occurs a sentence which may be construed as the launching of a presidential "boom" for Mr. Leo Fritter of Columbus, Ohio. The Conservative, in the best interests of the United Amateur Press Association, desires to be first in seconding such a just and eminently sensible motion. Leo Fritter is of true presidential timber, possessing every qualification which should exist in an executive. He is an attorney of trained legal mind, he is a man of highest culture and real literary taste, he is sincerely devoted to the cause of amateur journalism, he is a despiser of petty politics and factional jealousies, he has a keen feeling of fraternity and good-will, he stands as a champion of the United against the schemers who seek to destroy its identity, and he is not affiliated with any other amateur press association.

The Conservative feels that a rising organization like the United should have a strong man at its head, and he can think of none stronger or better than Leo Fritter. Mr. Fritter is not an "old-timer" in amateur journalism, which should count much in his favor, since he cannot have absorbed the ancient prejudices which make it so difficult for a veteran amateur to conduct an absolutely impartial administration. No person living is better fitted to aid in a reunion with the disaffected amateurs of the Morris Faction. Wherefore The Conservative again cries, and with redoubled enthusiasm: For President—Leo Fritter!

INTRODUCING MR. CHESTER PIERCE MUNROE

Visitors at the Slater Avenue Primary and Grammar School in Providence, examining the desks and walls of the building, or the fence and the long bench in the boys' yard, may today discern among the multitude of names unlawfully carved by generations of youthful irrepressibles, frequent repetitions of the initials "C. P. M. & H. P. L.", which the vicissitudes of sixteen years have failed completely to efface. The two friends whose initials are thus early associated have not been separated in spirit during the ensuing years, so that "H. P. L.", now become The Conservative, herewith takes pleasure in welcoming to the

United as his first recruit Mr. Chester Pierce Munroe, the "C. P. M." of boyhood days.

But while The Conservative has remained in the city of his birth, secluding himself amidst the musty volumes of his library, his friend has been in and of the busy world outside, acquiring a knowledge of men and things instead of mere bookish lore. Wherefore it is no dry replica of himself that The Conservative is ushering into the charmed circle of amateur journalism. Chester P. Munroe was always of literary tastes. Even in the old Slater Avenue days he used to write short stories in moments snatched from the study of his regular lessons, and in later years he became the author of more than one unpublished novel. His geographical description of Switzerland, composed a few years ago, inspired The Conservative to scribble off some complimentary verses which may one day appear in the amateur press.

Recently, Mr. Munroe has become a disciple of the Muses, and his credential to the United, a delightful little poem called "Thoughts," will soon, it is to be hoped, greet us from the pages of The Blarney Stone. The new member is now a thorough North Carolinian, having established himself at the Grove Park Inn, Ashville. It is therefore possible that he will be in attendance at the coming convention.

In the future politics of the United, Mr. Munroe may play a lively and considerable part, for he comes of a decidedly political stock. His talented father, the Hon. Addison Pierce Munroe, has repeatedly been elected by overwhelming majorities to the Senate of Rhode Island; his uncle, Mr. Oliver Munroe, is Mayor of Melrose, Massachusetts; while his charming younger brother, Harold, is a Deputy Sheriff of Providence County. The Conservative is certain that the rest of the amateurs will join with him in making this promising recruit feel at home in the ranks of the United Amateur Press Association.

Ira A. Cole's article on "The Gods of Our Fathers" in the November United Official Quarterly is a refreshing departure from the dull, wholly Semitic tone of ordinary theological thought. Like Wordsworth and Schiller, Mr. Cole feels the call of our own ancestral Aryan deities, and revels in the beautiful legends which form so important a part of our racial heritage.

Rheinhart Kleiner, in the concluding paragraph of "The Piper," refers very wittily to the prevalence of slang in amateur journalism. His epigram on this subject deserves versified form. Here is The Conservative's crude and hasty attempt to set it in metre:

> Slang is the life of speech, the critics say,
> And stript of slang, our tongue would pass away.
> If this be so, how well the amateur
> Takes care that English ever shall endure!

Leo Fritter's essay on "The Spiritual Significance of the Stars" in the January "Woodbee" illustrates in a most impressive manner the ennobling effect of astronomical study on the highly organized mind. The boundless heavens have become for Mr. Fritter an enlarged exposition of human life, and a faultless pattern for earthly conduct.

In the first issue of "Invictus" Mr. Paul J. Campbell has set a standard for the strictly individual paper which few other amateurs will ever attain. One cannot become too enthusiastic in speaking of this inspired brochure. As a philosophical essayist Mr. Campbell probably has no superior in the United, and his three brilliant homilies, "The Impost of the Future," "The Sublime Ideal," and "Whom God Hath Put Asunder," are notable additions to amateur literature.

THE CONSERVATIVE is often inclined to wonder just what methods are used by the United's prominent poets in composing their verses. This curiosity is aroused by the frequency with which gaps and redundant syllables are found in the lines of some of the very noblest bards. Miss Owen, in her Blue Pencil epithalamium, uses the word "Jewel" where a monosyllable should be, whilst Mr. Kleiner's "Love, Come Again" in the July Olympian contains a line whose harmony is seriously marred by an extra syllable. "A Dog for Comfort" by Miss von der Heide in the January Woodbee is supposed to be cast in decasyllabic quatrains, yet the second line of the fourth stanza is woefully defective. The moderns are prone to laugh at the strict regularity of eighteenth-century verse, yet the form of their own compositions would be immeasurably the better for a closer adherence to some of the old-fashioned rules.

Since the subject of plagiarism in its varying degrees has been brought to our notice so forcibly by the controversy between Messrs. Edward H. Cole and W. Paul Cook, The Conservative would like to know why the last sentence of his article in the July "New Member" was removed, and placed without credit at the back of the magazine as a motto.

It is to be regretted that Edward H. Cole confines his extraordinary talents so exclusively to the treatment of amateur journalistic affairs. Mr. Cole possesses a mind of unusual keenness and a prose style which cannot be approached in quality by that of any other amateur, yet his work is almost provokingly unvaried. It is really the duty of so thorough a scholar to exhibit his powers in matters of wider interest.

Mr. Ernest A. Dench of Brooklyn, a member of the United, and until his advent to America a British amateur of note, is one of the fortunate few who have published books to their credit. His treatise on "Playwriting for the Cinema" is a terse and readable exposition of the motion picture industry which stamps its author as a youth of more than ordinary ability.

The talented Chairman of the Department of Private Criticism writes The Conservative, who has been favored with the Chairmanship of the other Critical Bureau, that the reviews in The United Amateur show extreme strictness in dealing with the metrical irregularities of the amateur poets. To this charge The Conservative would like to reply, that he is really criticising the whole modern trend in verse-writing, rather than the individuals who exemplify its faults. In the present violent reaction against old-fashioned precision of metre, the art of versification is in danger of expiring. Form, harmony, even prosody itself, alike seem to be ignored by the majority today, so that some counter-reaction seems essential for the preservation of verse as we have hitherto known it. To blame the innocent amateur who merely falls into the errors of his time, the errors which are condoned and practiced by the best writers of the age, is obviously unjust; yet glaring violations of the established principles of prosody cannot be passed by unnoticed.

Wherefore, though The Conservative may appear to be something of a martinet in his conduct of the Department of Public Criticism, he desires to make it very plain that he is opposed not to his fellow-amateurs, but to that insidious breaking down of rhyme and metre which is one of the most regrettable features of contemporary literature.

"Outward Bound" comes to The Conservative as a welcome link with Old England, the land of his fathers. Editor Stokes is to be congratulated on having so talented a contributor as J. H. Fowler, whose fantastic poem on "The Haunted Forest" shows a marvellous and almost Poe-like comprehension of the dark and sinister.

THE CONSERVATIVE

Edited by H. P. Lovecraft in the interests Of The
United Amateur Press Association of America

Office of publication, 598 Angell Street, Providence, R. I., U. S. A.

Sent gratis to all amateur journalists who may desire it.

The Conservative, Vol. I, No. II

Providence, R. I., July, 1915

Edited by H. P. Lovecraft

A DREAM OF THE GOLDEN AGE

By Ira A. Cole

"Ver erat aeternum, placidique tepentibus auris
Mulcebant zephyri natos sine semine flores".
— OVID

One day, whilst wand'ring idly by a stream,
My truant thoughts forsook me for a dream.
And as I loiter'd 'neath the pleasing shade
Of those green aisles, by wondrous Nature made,
A spirit presence took me by the hand,
And in enchantment led me through a land
Whose stately beauty told of bygone days,
When Nature's children, at their simple plays,
In careless freedom wander'd o'er the lea,
Nor knew convention's curse like you and me.
And while we wander'd down that pleasant shore,
My spirit guide told wondrous tales of yore,
And strove by magic, and in mystic ways,
To show the splendour of those other days:
The days when all the world was bright and fair,
And gods and satyres breath'd the bracing air,
When nymphs and naiades of snowy hue,
In primal beauty slept 'neath skies of blue;

Nor sought a dull decorum to display,
But drest in Nature's garments, went their way.
When heroes, god-like and of mighty mien,
Sped in unfetter'd freedom 'cross the sheen
Of noble rivers, whose gay waters flow'd Untrammel'd
where first Nature mark'd the road.
Nor sought they other worlds than theirs to know;
Content as kings where now but paupers grow.
Well pleas'd were they with Earth and all her store,
Nor thought, nor car'd, nor wanted they for more.
With simple, grave, unfearing, childlike trust,
They bow'd at Beauty's shrine, nor knew the lust
Of cank'ring Gold, nor car'd they to defile
Their lives with those false creeds and doctrines vile,
On which Pollution's litter glut their souls:
They drank Life's wine from pantheistic bowls.
And not in dingy temples built by man,
But 'neath the dome that Heav'n's high arches span,
They saw their God, nor fear'd to meet Him so,
In leaf, or tree, or where the grasses grow.
Theirs was the mighty God who rul'd by love
The land, the sea, the starry worlds above.
Theirs were the days when merry minstrels stroll'd O'er all
the earth, and fairy music troll'd
Across green fields where dainty sylvan maids
With beardless shepherd lads, 'neath oaken shades,
Were wont to dance the merry time away,
Whilst piping Pan breath'd forth some wondrous lay.
Theirs was Earth's mystic, shadowy childhood time,
Ere Culture came from Hell's sulphuric clime,
To teach degen'rate Man Corruption's smirk,
And turn him to a foul, dishonour'd shirk,
Whose craven soul must bow to putrid wealth,
And for his vaunted virtues crash, by stealth,
The only friend his fancies ever knew;
The God who taught, Perdition to eschew.

NOTE: THE CONSERVATIVE wishes to call particular attention to the foregoing remarkable lines, which constitute the debut of our gifted

Western Manuscript Manager as a poet. Mr. Ira Cole, though of profoundly poetical temperament, and inspired by the natural grandeur of his native West, never attempted verse until a very recent date, his "Dream of the Golden Age" being only his second metrical effort. When we consider the extreme rapidity with which he has acquired ease in heroic verse, we find reason to expect great things from his pen in the near future. His "Lines to Lord Byron" will appear in *The Forget-me-not.*

METRICAL REGULARITY

By H. P. Lovecraft

"Deteriores omnus sumus licentia." —TERENCE

Of the various forms of decadence manifest in the poetical art of the present age, none strikes more harshly on our sensibilities than the alarming decline in that harmonious regularity of metre which adorned the poetry of our immediate ancestors.

That metre itself forms an essential part of all true poetry is a principle which not even the assertions of an Aristotle or the pronouncements of a Plato can disestablish. As old a critic as Dionysius of Halicarnassus and as modern a philosopher as Hegel have each affirmed that versification in poetry is not alone a necessary attribute, but the very foundation as well; Hegel, indeed, placing metre above metaphorical imagination as the essence of all poetic creation.

Science can likewise trace the metrical instinct from the very infancy of mankind, or even beyond, to the pre-human age of the apes. Nature is in itself an unending succession of regular impulses: The steady recurrence of the seasons and of the moonlight, the coming and going of the day, the ebb and flow of the tides, the beating of the heart and pulses, the tread of the feet in walking, and countless other phenomena of like regularity, have all combined to inculcate in the human brain a rhythmic sense which is as manifest in the most uncultivated, as in the most polished of peoples. Metre, therefore, is no such false artifice as most exponents of radicalism would have us believe, but is instead a natural and inevitable embellishment to poesy, which succeeding ages should develop and refine, rather than maim or destroy.

Like other instincts, the metric sense has taken on different aspects among different races. Savages show it in its simplest form while dancing to the sound of primitive drums; barbarians display it in their religious and other chantings; civilized peoples utilize it for their formal poetry, either as measured quantity, like that of Greek and Roman verse, or as measured accentual stress, like that of our own English verse. Precision of metre is thus no mere display of meretricious ornament, but a logical evolution from eminently natural sources.

It is the contention of the ultra-modern poet, as enunciated by Mrs. J. W. Renshaw in her recent article on "The Autocracy of Art," *(The Looking Glass* for May) that the truly inspired bard must chant forth his feelings independently of form or language, permitting each changing impulse to alter the rhythm of his lay, and blindly resigning his reason to the "fine frenzy" of his mood. This contention is of course founded upon the assumption that poetry is super-intellectual; the expression of a "soul" which outranks the mind and its precepts. Now while avoiding the impeachment of this dubious theory, we must needs remark, that the laws of Nature cannot so easily be outdistanced. However much true poesy may overtop the produce of the brain, it must still be affected by natural laws, which are universal and inevitable. Wherefore it is possible for the critic to assume the attitude of the scientist, and to perceive the various clearly defined natural forms through which the emotions seek expression. Indeed, we feel even unconsciously the fitness of certain types of metre for certain types of thought, and in perusing a crude or irregular poem are often abruptly repelled by the unwarranted variations made by the bard, either through his ignorance or his perverted taste. We are naturally shocked at the clothing of a grave subject in anapaestic metre, or the treatment of a long and lofty theme in short, choppy lines. This latter defect is what repels us so much from Conington's really scholarly translation of the Aeneid.

What the radicals so wantonly disregard in their eccentric performances is unity of thought. Amidst their wildly repeated leaps from one rough metre to another, they ignore the underlying uniformity of each of their poems. Scene may change; atmosphere may vary; yet one poem cannot but carry one definite message, and to suit this ultimate and fundamental message must one metre be selected and sustained. To accommodate the minor inequalities of tone in a poem, one regular metre will amply lend itself to diversity. Our chief, but now annoyingly neglected measure, the heroic couplet, is capable of taking on infinite shades of expression by the right selection and sequence of words, and by the proper placing of the caesura or pause in each line. Dr. Blair, in his 38th lecture, explains and illustrates with admirable perspicuity the importance of the caesura's location in varying the flow of heroic verse. It is also possible to lend variety to a poem by using very judiciously occasional feet of a metre different from that of the body of the work. This is generally done without disturbing the syllabification, and it in no way impairs or obscures the dominant measure.

Most amusing of all the claims of the radical is the assertion that true poetic fervour can never be confined to regular metre; that the wild-eyed, long-haired rider of Pegasus must inflict upon a suffering public in unaltered form the vague conceptions which flit in noble chaos through his exalted soul. While it is perfectly obvious that the hour of rare inspiration must be improved without the hindrance of grammars or rhyming dictionaries, it is no less obvious that the succeeding hour of calmer contemplation may very profitably be devoted to amendment and polishing. The "language of the heart" must be clarified and made intelligible to other hearts, else its purport will forever be confined to its creator. If natural laws of metrical construction be wilfully set aside, the reader's attention will be distracted from the soul of the poem to its uncouth and ill-fitting dress. The more nearly perfect the metre, the less conspicuous its presence; hence if the poet desires supreme consideration for his matter, he should make his verses so smooth that the sense may never be interrupted.

The ill effect of metrical laxity on the younger generation of poets is enormous. These latest suitors of the Muse, not yet sufficiently trained to distinguish between their own artless crudities and the cultivated monstrosities of the educated but radical bard, come to regard with distrust the orthodox critics, and to believe that no grammatical, rhetorical, or metrical skill is necessary to their own development. The result cannot but be a race of churlish, cacophonous hybrids, whose amorphous outcries will waver uncertainly betwixt prose and verse, absorbing the vices of both and the virtues of neither.

When proper consideration shall be taken of the perfect naturalness of polished metre, a wholesome reaction against the present chaos must inevitably occur; so that the few remaining disciples of conservatism and good taste may justly entertain one last, lingering hope of hearing from modern lyres the stately heroics of Pope, the majestic blank verse of Thomson, the terse octosyllabics of Swift, the sonorous quatrains of Gray, and the lively anapaests of Sheridan and Moore.

EDITORIAL

In this, his second issue, THE CONSERVATIVE deems it both proper and necessary to attempt a definition of his journalistic policy, and a forecast of his future endeavours. Though the title of the sheet affords a general index to its basic character, it is nevertheless well to describe and qualify the exact species of conservatism here represented.

That the arts of literature and literary criticism will receive prime attention from THE CONSERVATIVE seems very probable. The increasing use among us of slovenly prose and lame metre, supported and sustained by the light reviewers of the amateur press, demands an active opponent, even though a lone one, and the profound reverence of THE CONSERVATIVE for the polished writers of a more correct age, fits him for a task to which his mediocre talent might not otherwise recommend him.

When THE CONSERVATIVE shall have laid down his task, it is his desire that he may be able to employ with justice the closing words of *The Rambler,* who said, over a century and a half ago: "Whatever shall be the final sentence of mankind, I have at least endeavoured to deserve their kindness. I have laboured to refine our language to grammatical purity, and to clear it from colloquial barbarism, licentious idioms, and irregular combinations."

Outside the domain of pure literature, THE CONSERVATIVE will ever be found an enthusiastic champion of total abstinence and prohibition; of moderate, healthy militarism as contrasted with dangerous and unpatriotic peace-preaching; of Pan-Saxonism, or the domination by the English and kindred races over the lesser divisions of mankind; and of constitutional or representative government, as opposed to the pernicious and contemptible false schemes of anarchy and socialism. Though the first named of these items may superficially appear a rather inappropriate function for a CONSERVATIVE, it must be remembered, that he who strives against the Hydra-monster Rum, strives most to *conserve* his fellow-men.

THE CONSERVATIVE AND HIS CRITICS

It was remarked by Dr. Johnson in *The Idler,* that "No genius was ever blasted by the breath of criticism; the poison which, if confined, would have burst the heart, fumes away in empty hisses, and malice is set at ease with very little danger to merit". Thus fortified in mind and soothed in temper by the precept of the great lexicographer, THE CONSERVATIVE turns to the sneers of "Bab Bell," whose anonymous remarks against his first effort at publishing appear in *The Lake Breeze* for April. Since the whole principle of anonymous censure is so ignoble, the position of "Bab Bell" robs his "submarine warfare" of its greatest force, and renders further notice unnecessary. If "Bab" has a proper sense of fairness in his composition, he will unmask before committing any more backbiting of this sort.

From such journalistic sneaking it is a relief to pass on to William B. Stoddard's frankly signed and frankly supercilious review in *The Brooklynite.* Mr. Stoddard is a man of intensely negative nature, who cannot bear the positive philosophy and definite dogmatism of THE CONSERVATIVE, and who must therefore be excused for his slighting allusions. However, he is a little premature in predicting the evolution of THE CONSERVATIVE into a careless writer of his own type.

Rheinhart Kleiner is a critic whose keenest censure may be accepted without resentment, since his honest and serious attitude raises him far above the suspicion of petty teasing and attempted cynicism. His strictures on the "art-shot" rhyme in "The Simple Speller's Tale" are just, and the fault is herewith acknowledged by THE CONSERVATIVE. Of Mr. Kleiner's general opinions concerning "allowable" rhymes, more may later be said, yet it must be emphasized that his position, however fundamentally erroneous, has much to sustain it.

It has been asserted by some biographers, that the poet Keats "died of an article". If, however, the contemporaries of THE CONSERVATIVE hope thus to kill off the object of their censure, they sadly mistake their man. As Horace hath it:

Fragili quaerens illidere dentem,
Offendet solido.

To his favourable reviewers, THE CONSERVATIVE must express his sincerest gratitude. They have received in a truly fraternal and wisely lenient fashion the first production of a beginner, and have given him that wholesome stimulation without which the present and future issues would never have appeared. That he may improve under their kindly and encouraging suggestions, and at length become really worthy of their generous commendation, is The Conservative's cherished ambition.

SOME POLITICAL PHASES

The announcement by *The Lake Breeze* that it will put forward no ticket in opposition to Mr. Fritter's, practically clears the way for the election of THE CONSERVATIVE'S candidate. This elimination of political warfare should afford much pleasure to an association whose best energies are dedicated to activities of a more scholarly nature. The United has lately been progressing upward by swift strides and long leaps, so that it is the duty of the members this month not only to place in power without unseemly contests an official board who will ensure a continuance of present activity, but to adopt all constitutional amendments which may facilitate their work.

The dominant ticket, so far as is known at the hour of going to press, is in part as follows:

- President, Leo Fritter.
- Vice Pres., Mrs. J. W. Renshaw.
- Official Editor, George Schilling.
- Treasurer, Paul J. Campbell.
- Historian, Ira A. Cole.
- Laureate Recorder, Clara Stalker. Dora M. Hepner.
- Directors, Herbert B. Darrow. Mrs. F. Shepphird.

For these capable candidates, all of whom are distinguished by their services to the association, the votes of the amateurs are respectfully solicited. By helping to elect them, each member will assist in that enlargement and elevation of the United which is so ardently desired by all.

We are unusually fortunate this year in having as a Presidential nominee Mr. Leo Fritter, a man animated by the highest ideals, and endowed with the ability to realise them. Here is no petty politician on the one hand, and no mere dreamer on the other; but an active, sensible individual prepared to put into practice the logical principles which he has learnt from a close and discriminating observation of events and trends in amateur circles. The CONSERVATIVE has no hesitancy in repeating his cry of last issue: FOR PRESIDENT, LEO FRITTER!

The amendments proposed this year are of radical nature, yet so well calculated to further the best interests of the United, that most of them must needs win the favour of a CONSERVATIVE. They are integral parts of the great progressive movement inaugurated by the Southern and Middle Western members.

Amendment I, creating a laureateship for publishers, is least of all connected with this upward literary trend, yet has much to recommend it. Printing is an art in itself, and one which in its best phases requires far more cultivation and taste than the average person imagines. The typographical achievements of Edward Cole afford almost as much real pleasure to his fellow-amateurs as do his forcefully phrased compositions, and such art as this deserves some form of recognition. THE CONSERVATIVE cannot bring himself to disapprove the amendment as proposed by that energetic young publisher, Mr. Dowdell.

Amendment II would destroy the "cut price of admission" so bitterly ridiculed by partisans of the National, yet as Mr. Daas has pointed out, it might have a tendency to exclude the high-school pupils who are so much desired as recruits. It is doubtful if the increased volume and increased dignity would repay the United for the decreased number of promising young novices.

Amendment III should be adopted by unanimous vote. The restriction of membership to the North American continent is the summit of folly. Why should we not spread throughout the whole Anglo-Saxon world, fostering amateur journalism wherever our language is spoken and written? Besides, many Americans and Englishmen residing in foreign countries might be gained, if the United were open to them.

Most vital of all the proposed amendments to the United's immediate progress is the fourth, which provides for a monthly official organ, to be printed uniformly by a regularly established Official Publisher. The adoption of this idea would liberate the Official Editor from his most pressing cares, leaving him free to perform his purely editorial and literary duties in peace. It would likewise eliminate the irregularities in volumes of The United Amateur, which arise from the employment of different printers. Mr. E. E. Ericson of Wisconsin, celebrated for his excellence throughout amateur circles, would undoubtedly become Official Publisher, so that nothing need be said concerning the typographical quality of the proposed new monthly organ. Let every member of the United support this extremely desirable amendment.

Amendment V is a solution of the Ex-President problem which should have been thought of long ago. The present situation, with half our former executives either indifferent or hostile to the United, yet nominally active, is intolerable. Let the chief officials retire to honorary membership, as Mr. Daas proposes, when they have ceased to participate in the various activities of the association.

Concerning the Convention seat for 1916, THE CONSERVATIVE cannot see what city but Cleveland, active in clubs and publishing, has any valid claim to the honour. Ohio is the logical state, being practically the centre of the amateur world, and Cleveland is the logical city, since Columbus has so lately held a convention. The arguments for Newark are negligible. The Blue Pencil Club of Brooklyn, which would predominate there, is primarily a National body, whilst the Newark boys are all semi-professionals with mercantile rather than literary aspirations.

INTRODUCING MR. JOHN RUSSELL

During the winter of 1913-14 THE CONSERVATIVE was engaged in an extremely heated controversy concerning the merits of a certain author whose work appeared in one of the popular magazines of the day. The letters of the disputants, both in prose and in verse, were printed in the magazine, and among them appeared both the formal heroics of THE CONSERVATIVE, and the neat octosyllabics of one John Russell, Esq., of Tampa, Florida. Mr. Russell and THE CONSERVATIVE, who were arrayed against each other in the metric fray, were each separately invited by Mr. Edward Daas to join the United, but while THE CONSERVATIVE responded eagerly and almost immediately, his opponent deferred action. Meanwhile a peace had been sealed betwixt the contending bards, and a correspondence established, in which THE CONSERVATIVE continued to urge what Don Eduardo had first mentioned; the result now appearing in Mr. Russell's advent to the association.

John Russell, whose present address is General Delivery, West Tampa, is a true-born Scotsman, being a native of Penicuik, near Edinburgh. The patriotism of his family is attested by the presence of his two nephews at the front in Belgium, one with the Gordon Highlanders and the other with a Canadian regiment. Mr. Russell's poetry has appeared in the public press of Scotland, Canada, and the United States, and possesses a tersely epigrammatical and at times brilliantly satirical style all its own. Though proficient in classic English, it is in the quaint speech of Caledonia that Mr. Russell chiefly excels. Of this delightful dialect he is a perfect master, and his well-constructed lines are redolent of the atmosphere of North Britain. Upon joining the United, one of Mr. Russell's first acts was to dedicate a poem to the Blue-Stocking Club of Rocky Mount, whose study of Robert Burns at once aroused his interest. This poem, based on the motto of the club, appears in these pages, and affords a striking example of the new member's ability in verse.

We are indeed fortunate in having among us so able a specimen of the race which produced an Arbuthnot, a Ramsay, a Thomson, a Smollett, a Hume, a Blair, a Lord Kames, an Adam Smith, a Campbell, a Scott, a Carlyle and a Stevenson.

IN A MAJOR KEY

It was lately the good fortune of The Conservative to receive from The Blue Pencil Club a pamphlet entitled "In a Minor Key", whose phenomenal excellence furnishes emphatic evidence that the old National still retains some members who would have done it credit even in its palmiest days. But great as may be the literary merit of the publication, its astonishing radicalism of thought cannot but arouse an overwhelming chorus of opposition from the saner elements in amateur journalism.

Charles D. Isaacson, the animating essence of the publication, is a character of remarkable quality. Descended from the race that produced a Mendelssohn, he is himself a musician of no ordinary talent, whilst as a man of literature he is worthy of comparison with his co-religionists Moses Mendez and Isaac D'Israeli. But the very spirituality which gives elevation to the Semitic mind, partially unfits it for the consideration of tastes and trends in Aryan thought and writings, hence it is not surprising that he is a radical of the extremest sort.

From an ordinary man, the acclamation of degraded Walt Whitman as the "Greatest American Thinker" would come as an insult to the American mind, yet with Mr. Isaacson one may but respectfully dissent. Penetrating and forgetting the unspeakable grossness and wildness of the erratic bard, our author seizes on the one spark of truth within, and magnifies it till it becomes for him the whole Whitman. THE CONSERVATIVE, in speaking for the sounder faction of American taste, is impelled to give here his own lines on Whitman, written several years ago as part of an essay on the modern poets:

Behold great *Whitman,* whose licentious line
Delights the rake, and warms the souls of swine.
Whose fever'd fancy shuns the measur'd pace,
And copies Ovid's filth without his grace.
In his rough brain a genius might have grown,
Had he not sought to play the brute alone;
But void of shame, he let his wit run wild,
And liv'd and wrote as Adam's bestial child.
Averse to culture, strange to humankind,
He never knew the pleasures of the mind.
Scorning the pure, the delicate, the clean,
His joys were sordid, and his morals mean.
Through his gross thoughts a native vigour ran,
From which he deem'd himself the perfect man:
But want of decency his rank decreas'd,
And sunk him to the level of the beast.
Would that his Muse had dy'd before her birth,
Nor spread such foul corruption o'er the earth.

Mr. Isaacson's views on racial prejudice, as outlined in his *"Minor Key",* are too subjective to be impartial. He has perhaps resented the more or less open aversion to the children of Israel which has ever pervaded Christendom, yet a man of his perspicuity should be able to distinguish this illiberal feeling, a religious and social animosity of one white race toward another white and equally intellectual race, from the natural and scientifically just sentiment which keeps the African black from contaminating the Caucasian population of the United States. The negro is fundamentally the biological inferior of all White and even Mongolian races, and the Northern people must occasionally be reminded of the danger which they incur in admitting him too freely to the privileges of society and government.

Mr. Isaacson's protest is directed specifically against a widely advertised motion picture, "The Birth of a Nation", which is said to furnish a remarkable insight into the methods of the Ku-Klux-Klan, that noble but much maligned band of Southerners who saved half of our country from destruction at the close of the Civil War. THE CONSERVATIVE has not yet witnessed the picture in question, but he has seen both in literary and dramatic form "The Clansman", that stirring, though crude and melodramatic story by Rev. Thomas Dixon, Jr., on which "The Birth of a Nation" is based, and has likewise made a close historical study of the Ku-Klux-Klan, finding as a result of his research nothing but Honour, Chivalry, and Patriotism in the activities of the Invisible Empire. The Klan merely did for the people what the law refused to do, removing the ballot from unfit hands and restoring to the victims of political vindictiveness their natural rights. The alleged lawbreaking of the Klan was committed only by irresponsible miscreants, who, after the dissolution of the Order by its Grand Wizard, Gen. Nathan Bedford Forrest, used its weird masks and terrifying costumes to veil their unorganised villainies.

Race prejudice is a gift of Nature, intended to preserve in purity the various divisions of mankind which the ages have evolved. In comparing this essential instinct of man with political, religious, and national prejudices, Mr. Isaacson commits a serious error of logic.

The CONSERVATIVE dislikes strong language, but he feels that he is not exceeding the bounds of propriety in asserting that the publication of the article entitled "The Greater Courage" is a crime which in a native American of Aryan blood would be deserving of severe legal punishment. This appeal to the people to refuse military service when summoned to their flag is an outrageous attack on the lofty principles of patriotism which have turned this country from a savage wilderness to a mighty band of states; a slur on the honour of our countrymen, who from the time of King Philip's War to the present have been willing to sacrifice their lives for the preservation of their families, their nation, and their institutions. Mr. Isaacson, however, must be excused for his words, since some of his phrases show quite clearly that he is only following the common anarchical fallacy, believing that wars are forced upon the masses by tyrannical rulers. This belief, extremely popular a few months ago, has received a rude blow through the acts of the Italian people in forcing their reluctant government to join the Allies. The socialistic delusion becomes ridiculous when its precepts are thus boldly reversed by facts. Bryan is out of the way at last, and in spite of Mr. Isaacson and his hyphenated fellow-pacifists, the real American people, the descendants of Virginian and New England Christian Protestant colonists, will remain ever faithful to the Stars and Stripes, even though forced to meet enemies at home as well as abroad.

AMATEUR NOTES

Fletcher Otto Baxley's *Alabamian* is assuming an unique and necessary place in the United. Mr. Baxley is devoting his entire time to the encouragement of our poets, who seem rather neglected elsewhere. The amateur world would much appreciate information concerning both the author and translator of the exquisite nature poem "From the Spanish", in the Spring number; though perhaps, like Mrs. Browning's "Sonnets from the Portuguese", this poem is not so foreign as it seems.

In order to satisfy conjecture, THE CONSERVATIVE wishes to state that the peculiar appearance of his preceding issue was wholly unintentional. But for a mistake due to haste and a stupid printer, the paper would have been a conventional 8-page sheet like *The Lake Breeze.*

AN OPEN LETTER

Fellow-amateurs:—

In order that the members of the United may know where I stand upon some of the main questions now before them, I shall take advantage of this opportunity to state briefly my views.

First, I wish it clearly understood that I heartily endorse and approve the movement now well under way to enlist the interest and co-operation of English teachers all over the United States in the work of the

Association. Our present Executive, Miss Hepner, and our able Critic, Mr. Moe, both have done much hard work in this direction, and results are already apparent. I look for a great enlargement of the work of the association by reason of this new and very promising field, which is rich in recruiting material. I hope to see a local branch of the United in every High School of the country. Our association should do more constructive work along these lines. Our official organ should contain articles on story writing and other branches of literary endeavor, written by well known and competent instructors. I believe that such men would gladly furnish such articles without cost after they were informed of the objects we were trying to accomplish. I certainly think that we ought to emphasize the literary features rather than the political and social.

I favour the proposed amendment to the constitution providing for the monthly publication of the official organ, believing that much better results will be obtained and greater interest aroused through a monthly publication than a bi-monthly. The official organ is the tie that binds the members together, and by drawing that tie closer and more frequently we must surely bring the members into closer relations with each other and the work of the association.

I also favour the proposed amendment raising the dues to one dollar per year for applicants as well as for other members, as that is a necessary corollary to the previous amendment for a monthly official organ. This change will increase the expense of publication very materially and as our only sure source of revenue is from dues, it must be plain that the dues will have to be increased.

Let's stretch hands across the seas to those kindred spirits who seek our friendship, by amending the constitution so that we can admit foreign members. Proposed amendment number five also has my support, to place upon the honorary roll all inactive ex-presidents.

Just a word on the question of consolidation. My views upon this subject have become pretty well known by this time, but it may be well to repeat them here. I am firmly opposed to the consolidation of the United with any other organization, and do not consider this matter deserves much attention at this time. I don't think there ever was a real sentiment for consolidation within the United, but the propaganda has been kept alive largely by those whose greatest efforts have been spent in behalf of the National. Our association is too busy doing things worth while to pause and exhaust its energies upon a dead issue. I have no unkind feelings toward those who favour this matter, and especially do

I disclaim any hostility toward the National as an organization, but I cannot see any good reason for the proposed union. Let's all turn in and give our best licks for our own favourite association.

Thanking those members who have persistently urged my candidacy, and assuring them and all the other members of my sincere desire to merit their further confidence and esteem,

I beg to remain, Fraternally yours,

Leo Fritter.

THE CONSERVATIVE

Edited by H. P. Lovecraft in the Interests of the United Amateur Press Association. Office of Publication, 598 Angell St., Providence, R. I.

Sent Gratis to all amateur journalists who may desire it.

THE LINCOLN PRESS

The Conservative, Vol. I, No. III

Providence, R. I., October, 1915

Edited by H. P. Lovecraft

THE STATE OF POETRY

By H. P. Lovecraft

"Non bene junctarum discordia semina rerum".—OVID.

Attend, ye modern bards, who dimly shine
As worthy scions of Mae Flecknoe's line!
Though scarce on Heliconian heights to gleam,
To one still clumsier ye supply a theme:
As meagre stalk from sterile garden climbs,
So springs my trash from your Boeotian rhymes.
In state establish'd on the Dunce's throne,
Hear infant Codrus with the colic moan.
His dreary wail no hint of sense conveys,
But critics hide their ignorance in praise.
Hard by the King, the pale-fac'd Raucus stands,
A ream of witless ballads in his hands.
Metre forgot, he screams his sickly song
In quatrains part too short and part too long.
But ere he stops, Agrestis fills the air
With dainty accents, and illusions rare.
How might we praise the lines so soft and sweet,
Were they not lame in their poetic feet!
Just as the reader's heart bursts into flame,
The fire is quenched by rhyming "gain" with "name",

And ecstacy becomes no easy task
When fields of "grass" in Sol's bright radiance "bask"!
To Durus now our keen attention turns,
Whose rugged page with manly passion burns.
Would that his apt expressions did not lie
Where syllable and tone must go awry;
A lesser sentiment we needs must feel
If "re-al" love be mispronounced as "reel";
While far from his loose line we long to roam,
When stately "po-em" masquerades as "pome"!
Next Hodiernus with his lyre appears,
And glads the modern critic's Midas-ears.
Upon his shelves neglected classics rest,
Whilst he reads Kipling, and proclaims him best.
The well-turn'd verse, the choice, harmonious phrase,
Are foreign to his new, corrupted ways.
Form is an error, elegance a crime,
To him who courts the plaudits of the time.
Ablest is he who can in rhyming reach
The lofty coarseness of a Cockney's speech.
No name we give to yon degen'rate swine
That apes the filthy Whitman's vulgar line.
The stamm'ring sound, the tainted atmosphere,
The blank confusion, and the prospect drear,
So much repel the mind of decent grade,
That author's lost 'mid Chaos he hath made!
Mark now Mundanus, who with sordid mind
Dwells on our joys and ills of meaner kind.
For him no grassy slopes of Tempe wait,
Nor does his Muse Arcadian bliss relate:
Strephon and Chloe, all the shepherd train,
Excite his wrath, and summon his disdain.
Saturnian days no thought of his engage,
But all the world's to him an Iron Age.
His earthy fancy never mounts the sky,
But draws its source from kennel, barn, or sty.
No sylvan scenes, nor reed-fring'd brooks in June,
But mills, and mines, and shops inspire his tune.
Almighty Dullness! See the empire rise,

The pure to stain, the strong to paralyse:
Destructive Commerce! Thy all-blighting pow'rs
Pollute our lines, and crush Thought's fairest flow'rs.
Can Art survive in a degraded age
When none but boors and cynics hold the stage?
When verse ideal brings the vulgar smile,
And honest words are slighted for the vile?
He who would light again the poet's fire.
Must straight to some secluded spot retire;
Where, pond'ring on the happier days of yore,
His fancy may the ancient times restore;
Where, as of old, kind Nature's voice is heard,
To raise the mind, and prompt the written word.
There may we find the Golden Age anew,
Where thoughts are simple, and our dreamings true;
In such blest scenes we may rehearse again
The classic grandeur of Eliza's reign,
In Shakespeare's fashion move the anxious heart,
Or charm the woodland nymphs with Jonson's art.
But let me cease! No such expanding hope
Can stir my pencil from the style of Pope,
The sounding line, which neither breaks nor halts,
Is needful to conceal my graver faults!

THE ALLOWABLE RHYME

By H. P. Lovecraft

"Sed ubi plura nitent in carmine, non ego paucis
Offendar maculis".
—Horace

The poetical tendency of the present and of the preceding century has been divided in a manner singularly curious. One loud and conspicuous faction of bards, giving way to the corrupt influences of a decaying general culture, seems to have abandoned all the proprieties of versification and reason in its mad scramble after sensational novelty;

whilst the other and quieter school, constituting a more logical evolution from the poesy of the Georgian period, demands an accuracy of rhyme and metre unknown even to the polished artists of the age of Pope.

The rational contemporary disciple of the Nine, justly ignoring the dissonant shrieks of the radicals, is therefore confronted with a grave choice of technique. May he retain the liberties of imperfect or "allowable" rhyming which were enjoyed by his ancestors, or must he conform to the new ideals of perfection evolved during the past century? The writer of this article is frankly an archaist in verse. He has not scrupled to rhyme "toss'd" with "coast", "come" with "Rome", or "home" with "gloom" in his very latest published efforts, thereby proclaiming his maintenance of the old-fashioned poets as models; but sound modern criticism, proceeding from Mr. Rheinhart Kleiner and from other sources which must needs command respect, has impelled him here to rehearse the question for public benefit, and particularly to present his own side, attempting to justify his adherence to the style of two centuries ago.

The earliest English attempts at rhyming probably included words whose agreement is so slight that it deserves the name of mere "assonance" rather than that of actual rhyme. Thus in the original ballad of "Chevy-Chase", we encounter "King" and "within" supposedly rhymed, whilst in the similar "Battle of Otterbourne" we behold "long" rhymed with "down", "ground" with "Agurstonne", and "name" with "again". In the ballad of "Sir Patrick Spense", "morn" and "storm", and "deep" and "feet" are rhymed. But the infelicities were obviously the result not of artistic negligence, but of plebeian ignorance, since the old ballads were undoubtedly the careless products of a peasant minstrelsy. In Chaucer, a poet of the Court, the allowable rhyme is but infrequently discovered, hence we may assume that the original ideal in English verse was the perfect rhyming sound.

Spenser uses allowable rhymes, giving in one of his characteristic stanzas the three distinct sounds of "Lord", "ador'd", and "word", all supposed to rhyme; but of his pronunciation we know little, and may justly guess that to the ears of his contemporaries the sounds were not conspicuously different. Ben Jonson's employment of imperfect rhyming was much like Spenser's; moderate, and partially to be excused on account of a chaotic pronunciation. The better poets of the Restoration were also sparing of allowable rhymes; Cowley, Waller, Marvell, and many others being quite regular in this respect.

It was therefore upon a world unprepared that Samuel Butler burst forth with his immortal "Hudibras", whose comical familiarity of diction is in grotesqueness surpassed only by its clever licentiousness of rhyming. Butler's well-known double rhymes are of necessity forced and inexact, and in ordinary single rhymes he seems to have had no more regard for precision. "Vow'd" and "would", "talisman" and "slain", "restores" and "devours" are a few specimens selected at random.

Close after Butler came John Oldam, a satirist whose force and brilliancy gained him universal praise, and whose enormous crudity both in rhyme and in metre was forgotten amidst the splendor of his attacks. Oldham was almost absolutely ungoverned by the demands of the ear, and perpetrated such atrocious rhymes as "heads" and "besides", "devise" and "this", "again" and "sin", tool" and "foul", "end" and "design'd", and even "prays" and "cause".

The glorious Dryden, refiner and purifier of English verse, did less for rhyme than he did for metre. Though nowhere attaining the extravagances of his friend Oldham, he lent the sanction of his great authority to rhymes which Dr. Johnson admits are "open to objection". But one vast difference betwixt Dryden and his loose predecessors must be observed. Dryden had so far improved metrical cadence, that the final syllables of heroic couplets stood out in especial eminence, displaying and emphasizing every possible similarity of sound; that is, lending to sounds in the first place approximately similar, the added similarity caused by the new prominence of their perfectly corresponding positions in their respective lines.

It were needless to dwell upon the rhetorical polish of the age immediately succeeding Dryden's. So far as English versification is concerned, Pope was the world, and all the world was Pope. Dryden had founded a new school of verse, but the development and ultimate perfection of this art remained for the sickly lad who before the age of twelve begged to be taken to Will's Coffee-House, that he might obtain one personal view of the aged Dryden, his idol and model. Delicately attuned to the subtlest harmonies of poetical construction, Alexander Pope brought English prosody to its zenith, and still stands alone on the heights. Yet he, exquisite master of verse that he was, frowned not upon imperfect rhymes, provided they were set in faultless metre. Though most of his allowable rhymes are merely variations in the breadth and nature of vowel sounds, he in one instance departs far enough from rigid perfection to rhyme the words "vice" and "destroys". Yet who can take offence? The unvarying ebb and flow of the refined metrical impulse conceals and condones all else.

Every argument by which English blank verse or Spanish assonant verse is sustained, may with greater force be applied to the allowable rhyme. Metre is the real essential of poetical technique, and when two sounds of substantial resemblance are so placed that one follows the other in a certain measured relation, the normal ear cannot without cavilling find fault with a slight want of identity in the respective dominant vowels. The rhyming of a long vowel with a short one is common in all the Georgian poets, and when well recited cannot but be overlooked amidst the general flow of the verse; as, for instance, the following from Pope:

> But thinks, admitted to that equal SKY,
> His faithful dog shall bear him COMPANY.

Of like nature is the rhyming of actually different vowels whose sounds are, when pronounced in animated oration, by no means dissimilar. Out of verse, such words as "join" and "line" are quite unlike, but Pope well rhymes them when he writes:

> While expletives their feeble aid do JOIN,
> And ten low words oft creep in one dull LINE.

It is the final consonantal sound in rhyming which can never vary. This, above all else, gives the desired similarity. Syllables which agree in vowels but not in final consonants are not rhymes at all, but simply assonants. Yet such is the inconsistent carelessness of the average modern writer, that he often uses these mere assonants to a greater extent than his fathers ever employed actually allowable rhymes. The writer, in his critical duties, has more than once been forced to point out the attempted rhyming of such words as "fame" and "lane", "task" and "glass", or "feels" and "yields" and in view of these impossible combinations he cannot blame himself very seriously for rhyming "art" and "shot" in the March CONSERVATIVE; for this pair of words have at least identical consonants at the end.

That allowable rhymes have real advantages of a positive sort is an opinion by no means lightly to be denied. The monotony of a long heroic poem may often be pleasantly relieved by judicious interruptions in the perfect succession of rhymes, just as the metre may sometimes be adorned with occasional triplets and Alexandrines. Another advantage is the greater latitude allowed for the expression of thought. How numerous are the writers who, from restriction to perfect rhyming, are frequently compelled to abandon a neat epigram or brilliant antithesis, which allowable rhyme would easily permit, or else to introduce a dull expletive merely to supply a desired rhyme!

But a return to historical considerations shows us only too clearly the logical trend of taste, and the reason Mr. Kleiner's demand for absolute perfection is no idle cry. In Oliver Goldsmith there arose one who, though retaining the familiar classical diction of Pope, yet advanced further still toward what he deemed ideal polish by virtually abandoning the allowable rhyme. In unvaried exactitude run the couplets of "The Traveller" and of "The Deserted Village", and none can deny to them a certain urbanity which pleases the critical ear. With but little less precision are moulded the simple rhymes of Cowper, whilst the pompous Erasmus Darwin likewise shows more attention to identity of sound than do the Queen Anne bards. Gifford's translations of Juvenal and Persius show to an almost equal degree the tendency of the age, and Campbell, Crabbs, Wordsworth, Byron, Keats, and Thomas Moore are all inclined to refrain from the liberties practiced by those of former times. To deny the importance of such a widespread change of technique is fruitless, for its existence argues for its naturalness. The best critics of the nineteenth and twentieth centuries demand perfect rhyming, and no aspirant for fame can afford to depart from a standard so universal. It is evidently the true goal of the English, as well as of the French bard; the goal from which we were but temporarily deflected during the preceding age.

But exceptions should and must be made in the case of a few who have somehow absorbed the atmosphere of other days, and who long in their hearts for the stately sound of the old classic cadences. Well may their predilection for imperfect rhyming be discouraged to a limited extent, but to chain them wholly to modern rules would be barbarous. Every individual mind demands a certain freedom of expression, and the man who cannot express himself satisfactorily without the stimulation derived from the spirited mode of two centuries ago should certainly be permitted to follow without undue restraint a practice at once so harmless, so free from essential error, and so sanctioned by precedent, as that of employing in his poetical compositions the smooth and inoffensive allowable rhyme.

EDITORIAL

Weak and pliant indeed is he who maketh no enemies. Ever since The CONSERVATIVE commenced his series of frank criticisms and unvarnished comments, his heels have been annoyed by the vindictive snappings of a dozen or more vituperative little curs whose bristles he seems to have brushed the wrong way as he passed by them. Not all of these have yet expressed themselves in print, but from the gifted Charles D. Isaacson down to the wretched, sneaking mongrel "Bab Bell", they have each taken their "little fling" at the newcomer. Now the CONSERVATIVE has no wish to trample the under dog, nor even to stifle the feeble yelps that assail this paper; wherefore he extends herewith an invitation for every hostile amateur journalist, human, Nationalite, or "Bab Bell", to submit for publication herein any and all sneers, attacks, or insults which he may have prepared against the CONSERVATIVE. Reasonable brevity will insure publication without deletion. The CONSERVATIVE believes that no one possesses the right to attack him unless willing to have that attack printed with original spelling, style, and grammar, in these pages, directly beside the articles whose tone he is denouncing. The public may then be able intelligently to compare the reasoning and attainments of the CONSERVATIVE and his critics. It is to be hoped that these critical canines and insulting insects will by next issue have furnished the CONSERVATIVE with sufficient venom to start a new column, to be entitled "From the Enemy's Camp".

It scarcely need be remarked that the above has no reference to those persons of intelligence and good manners who conscientiously disagree with the CONSERVATIVE in gentlemanly fashion. These critics and dissenters are but to be praised for their sturdy independence of thought, and their admirable restraint of expression. For them is reserved the friendly answer, and, when possible, the apologetic recantation. It may be noticed that in this issue the CONSERVATIVE has conceded practically all points to Mr. Kleiner in the discussion concerning allowable rhymes.

THE CONSERVATIVE AND HIS CRITICS

"Melius non tangere, clamo"!
—Horace

It appears that the CONSERVATIVE's review of Charles D. Isaacson's recent paper was not accepted in the honestly critical spirit intended, and that Mr. Isaacson is preparing to wreak summary verbal vengeance upon the crude barbarian who cannot appreciate the loathsome Walt Whitman, cannot lose his self-respect as a white man, and cannot endorse a treasonable propaganda designed to deliver these United States as easy victims to the first hostile power who cares to conquer them. In view of the CONSERVATIVE'S frank and explicit recognition of Mr. Isaacson's unusual talent, the predicted reprisal seems scarcely necessary, yet if it must come, it will find its object, as usual, not unwilling to deliver blow for blow. The CONSERVATIVE possesses very definite opinions on the questions involved, and has by no means exhausted all his armory of darts in their defense. Owing to the uncertainties of the press, Mr. Isaacson's contemplated screed may have appeared ere this; in any case the CONSERVATIVE may with propriety announce his attitude in the words which Colley Cibber, reviser of Shakespeare, puts into the mouth of King Richard:

Hark! the shrill trumpet sounds, to horse, away,
My soul's in arms, and eager for the fray!

GEMS FROM "IN A MINOR KEY"

(with Remarks by The Conservative.)

"— mentally unpalatable, even as are the words of George Sylvester Vierick to the great (no kidding) English People".

—W. H. Goodwin.

No kidding, Goodwin, you with wisdom say
That England likes not George Sylvester's way:
The honest truth poor Vierick ne'er could speak,
And Britons hate a liar and a sneak!

"—Germans, and all *persecuted* peoples".
—Charles D. Isaacson.

Heav'n help the Prussian, fragile and oppress'd,
Whose injur'd feelings lacerate his breast.
O Cruel World! This peaceful creature spare,
That he may ravage land, and sea, and air!

"We will not fight. We will not march to war".
—Charles D. Isaacson.

Horatius at the bridge intrepid stands,
A branch of olive in his gentle hands.
Th' Etruscan host draws nearer, and with *pride*
The manly hero bows and steps aside!

THE RENAISSANCE OF MANHOOD

After the degrading debauch of craven pacificism through which our sodden and feminised public has lately floundered, a slight sense of shame seems to be appearing, and the outcries of peace-at-any-price maniacs are less violent than they were a few months ago. Military training for business and professional men has been provided at Plattsburg, N. Y., and the high schools of Providence, R. I., have established, and despite the wails of the unwarlike, efficient courses in martial instruction and drilling.

Why any sane human being can believe in the possibility of universal peace is more than the CONSERVATIVE can fathom. The essential pugnacity and treachery of mankind is only too evident; and that every nation, even though pledged, would actually abolish means of warfare is absolutely unthinkable. Should the entire civilised world agree simultaneously to disarm, one or more nations would undoubtedly retain secret armaments and at the proper time take advantage of their more altruistic and less astute contemporaries in a wild career of conquest against unarmed victims. To say that higher culture would reason away the causes of war is complete idiocy. Germany, generally conceded to have been the world's most philosophical and intellectual nation, has achieved an equal fame in martial cruelty and bestiality. No country is, or ever can be "above" warfare, until the basic impulses of the human animal shall have miraculously changed.

Aversion to just war can arise from one of four causes; (1) unconscious physical cowardice engendered by long years of peace, (2) hysterical idealism produced from incomplete training in pure science, (3) mental bias derived from an erratic, temperamental intellect, and (4) that plain, obtuse servility which copies and spreads the opinions of others. Under the first head of unconscious physical cowards we must group the sobbing sisterhood who sigh forth in melody of questionable musical and poetical value that "They Didn't Raise Their Boys to be Soldiers". Physical cowardice is not always for one's self; it may be sympathetic cowardice for others; but its unfailing sign is the exaggerated importance and gravity of human suffering. This "cowardice" may sometimes do immense good in lessening the minor discomforts of life, but it must not be allowed to exceed its province and sap the virile vigour of a nation. Among the hysterical idealists we may group the well-meaning clergyman who, in spite of Martin Luther's defense of the soldier, declares that "war is un-Christian"; as well as the ethical enthusiast who tells us that "man has outgrown war". Quite as hysterical is the socialist or anarchist who in his beer-barrel declamation screams out that "war is only the tool of rulers to aggrandise themselves at the expense of the masses". The Quakers are an organised embodiment of this erratic idealism. The third or mentally biased class of pacificist is seldom to be distinguished from the idealist; perhaps idealism itself is a form of mental bias; but the line must be drawn to distinguish betwixt those whose idealism comes from defective education and those who are idealists from defective comprehension. Class four, the copyist element, is probably the most abundant of all. It embraces every part of our lower orders, and could be turned into a fiery, militaristic body if the suitable demagogue were provided.

In the opinion of the CONSERVATIVE, Theodore Roosevelt's famous speech of August 25, 1915, marks a momentous change in American public sentiment. It is the beginning of the end of supine submissiveness and womanish ideals on the part of the majority. Americans will henceforth be less eager to drug themselves with arguments and theories; they will prefer to face bare Truth, and to know that men must fight to keep what they have; that in this world of sin nothing exists unless there exists behind it the stern physical power to defend and preserve it.

LIQUOR AND ITS FRIENDS

While a cynical press, disgusted at the political acts of Mr. William J. Bryan, applaud in servile glee each motion of his successor, Robert Lansing, Prime Minister of the United States, and presumably a man desirous of bettering our country, has just restored the disgusting presence of liquor at American state dinners. As though to aggravate the offense, Mrs. Lansing has given out the statement: "Mr. Lansing and I are not extremists in the advocacy of Temperance"! William Jennings Bryan was a bungler in politics and a stranger to dignity; a simple creature who sought to apply impossible theories to the government of a great nation; very obviously the intellectual inferior of Robert Lansing. But he was an honest man, bent on the victory of what he deemed right, and bowing before no vicious custom, however long established in good society. Bryan, with the same will that made our administration ridiculous in its foreign policy, made it glorious in its freedom from vicious intemperance. His abolition of wine from tables of state was the first toward giving the American people a high governmental example of decency. What all decent men had preached for nearly a century, he and he alone established where all might view it in exalted practice. His was the only true logic: the government attempts to keep the people to the law; liquor attempts to stir the people against the law; therefore the purposes of government and liquor are forever opposed. No government can afford to demand virtue when all its members conspicuously violate it. But our thoughtless masses and unprincipled newspapers failed to grasp the significance of the act. The superficial satirical phrase "grape-juice diplomacy" is a tremendously forceful epitome of the brainless estimate which confounded Mr. Bryan's sound ideas on Temperance with his unsound ideas on peace and politics. Thus with the spectacular departure of the ex-Secretary from Washington there was also a departure of his virtuous principles, and Robert Lansing "is not an extremist in the advocacy of Temperance". In repeating the assertion that Mr. Bryan is intellectually inferior to Mr. Lansing, the CONSERVATIVE must therefore add a further comparison, and state with equal emphasis that as a *man* and a *moralist,* the "grape-juice diplomist" presents a figure which dwarfs into pettiness his wine-bibbing, time-serving, vice-sanctioning successor. Robert Lansing is a gentleman and a real statesman, but so far as a moral example is concerned, he stands on a level with the distiller, the brewer, and the bartender. If the United States government really desires order and virtue amongst its inhabitants, it will promptly require that the most noxious evil of human life be not publicly sanctioned and flaunted in the very shadow of the Capitol's dome, or within the White House itself. True reformation, contrary to the general idea, begins at the top and works downward as if through gravity.

Not long ago one of Mr. Lansing's fellow-drinkers and possible admirers, E. J. Gray by name and beer salesman by profession, also contributed his mite toward the cause of vice and moral delinquency. At Onset, Massachusetts, during a Temperance speech delivered by ex-Governor Foss, Mr. Gray interrupted the speaker in one of his anti-liquor arguments by rising and bawling: "You're a liar"! After this the red-faced liquor-advocate proudly volunteered the information that "he had drunk whiskey and seltzer for twenty-five years", to which Gov. Foss very justly and aptly retorted: "You look it"!

While the vulgar Gray incident may outwardly seem quite different from the conservative decision of Secretary and Mrs. Robert Lansing to serve wine at all their diplomatic banquets, the same bestial demon lurks equally beneath both. In each is there a conscious disregard for natural law and moral rectitude; a hideous disregard which will eventually wreck civilisation.

THE YOUTH OF TODAY

The aggressive intellectual tone of the rising generation is indeed refreshing. Without the encumbering polish of former ages, the schoolboys of today fear not to speak as they think, and to attack dissenting opinion whenever and wherever they encounter it. Seldom has the CONSERVATIVE enjoyed a livelier or more unexpected pleasure than that which followed the sending of his first issue to a youthful United recruit, Master David H. Whittier, who has just graduated from a prominent Boston high school. Master Whittier, like his famous poetical relative, pounces virtuously upon unorthodox ideas wherever he may find them, hence he sent the CONSERVATIVE a long, bitter, and unsolicited criticism of the (March) article on pan-Teutonism as soon as he had read it. Being not particularly designed for the Bostonian type of involved intellect, "The Crime of the Century" failed to appeal to Mr. Whittier's refined taste, wherefore the young man admitted frankly that he did not like it, stated that the CONSERVATIVE is a superficial, unscientific, and prejudiced reasoner; and accounted for his own violent opposition on the grounds that the CONSERVATIVE's point of view "so revolted him"! Mr. Whittier has requested permission to use in print certain portions of the CONSERVATIVE's letters to him. This permission is hereby granted with extreme pleasure, since no pursuit is more gratifying than that of helping a worthy youth to shake off his natural timidity, and to come forth fearlessly into the United's public eye as a controversial giant. So long as the CONSERVATIVE shall exist, Mr. Whittier need never want a victim for his bold sallies. Edgar Ralph Cheyney, in the May *New Member,* calls upon adolescence to express itself. Let him look Bostonward, for in David H. Whittier he may behold such expression at most exquisitely developed pitch

AN IMPARTIAL SPECTATOR

Mr. John Russell, the United's clever satirist, has composed the following lines concerning the controversy over regular metre lately waged through the pages of *The Looking Glass, The Lake Breeze,* and the CONSERVATIVE:

METRICAL REGULARITY;
or, Broken Metre.

Dear Youth, if you would be a poet,

Pray study this, and see you know it:
With careful rhyme and one smooth metre,
Your poem can't but be much neater.
Should you prefer to rhyme in anapaest,
Convinc'd that such conveys your fancy best,
Change not the form, nor try heroic lines,
Howe'er your fleeting mood your pen inclines.
Just see that you hold to the same old refrain,
For if you change once, sure you'll change it again.
And the critics (confound them) will haughtily say
'Tis the worst thing they've seen for full many a day.
And now, in conclusion, pray shun the illusion
That all you've to do is to write:
If you study your rhymes; feet, metre and times,
You'll a masterpiece some day indite!

—J. R.

While Mr. Russell's words seem to constitute a very keen thrust at the CONSERVATIVE, his cleverly varied metre satirizes with equal keenness the other side of the discussion; wherefore he must be classified by means of that much abused hypothetical term, "neutral".

SYMPHONY AND STRESS

A recent article in *The Symphony,* entitled "Buzzards", condemns the man of "negative" characteristics, incidentally denouncing the critic and the reformer. The psychological characteristics thus revealed in the anonymous author are of even greater interest than the unusual theories displayed. *The Symphony* is the product of a small circle of cultured ladies, most of them United members, exempt from contact with the world and its sordidness. They agree with the utterance of the author, that in promoting virtue it is best for each person to make himself virtuous, letting his brothers, under the stimulus of mutual encouragement and inspiration, do likewise, rather than to interfere with the habits of others from the outside. As they say, "it's better to begin on the inside and work out"! But have the Family of Symphonies ever pondered on the condition of their inferiors; the sluggish-brained, morally weak lower class of drunkards and degenerates? Symphony may undoubtedly keep themselves on a high plane through their exalted system of Positive Ideals, but are they satisfied to look down upon a populace steeped in vice, and lacking the intellect to raise itself? Before condemning the reformer, they might well look upon the clean, virile personality of Andrew Francis Lockhart of Milbank, South Dakota, who has succeeded in driving the evils of Rum from his native city. This man has Positive Ideals, ideals as positive in their righteousness as those of any Symphonic, but he has the negative element as well. He not only preaches and practices virtue; he is actively engaged in its extension through the destruction of vice. Threats of death and murderous assaults upon his person are as nothing to him. He sees his duty, and follows it as best he understands it. He has made South Dakota a better state wherein to live; indeed, where could pure-minded idealists live in security, were there not a few vigorous, negative souls who dare to attack corruption and clear the way for decency? No, Andrew Francis Lockhart is a reformer, but he is not a "buzzard".

The Symphony is one of the most beautiful of all the semi-professional papers issued by United members. Each issue is perused with the keenest interest and delight by the CONSERVATIVE, who feels strongly its uplifting influence, and appreciates the uniformly delicate artistry of its tone. But the CONSERVATIVE also reads another semi-professional journal issued by a United member; Lockhart's *Chain Lightning.* Here all is different. We read not of happy souls re-purified through wholesome thought, but of drugged, soulless bodies depraved through drink and debauchery, of law bought by depraved criminals, of vice made a municipal institution, of all that fills the mind with aversion and disgust. No elaborate, musical sentences here delight the ear; instead, a fierce, tense, colloquialism drives home the ugly truths which we are reluctant to hear, but which, without hearing, we may never comprehend or remedy. Most of these horrors are utterly beyond the realization of the sheltered Symphonies, many of them are beyond the realization of the secluded CONSERVATIVE; but that they exist, the burning indignation and sincerity of Mr. Lockhart forbid us to doubt. This is a world of wonderful good and unspeakable evil. Let the Family of Symphonies extend throughout the upper realm which gave it birth, but let it forbear too hastily to frown on those noble reforming souls who are willing to imperil their lives, sacrifice their illusions, abandon their happiness, and walk among the vicious and the lowly, even as did one Man nineteen hundred years ago.

William J. Dowdell, in transforming his *Bearcat* into a 7 x 10 journal of high and conservative ideals, is demonstrating very forcibly the fine quality of truly ambitious youth. Let the National rail about our young members if it so chooses; they are certainly doing better than most of the National's *old* members! Mr. Dowdell's new policy is one of sense and soundness, and his paper will soon attain an envied position through the dignified tone of its contents, both contributed and editorial. During the present year Mr. Dowdell has printed articles by some of our most gifted members. This condition will undoubtedly continue, and the improved aspect of the publication will attract even more amateurs of prominence to its pages.

The CONSERVATIVE desires very sincerely to felicitate Mr. William T. Harrington on his latest *Coyote.* The transition from the March standard is almost startling, and the whole present atmosphere of the periodical prophesies future improvement at no tardy rate.

Having learned of the adoption of amateur journalism by an inmate of the Columbus penitentiary, the CONSERVATIVE is impelled to reflect that a good many other amateurs, particularly in the National, ought to be in gaol as well.

The editor *of The Tryout,* a National paper, takes issue with *The Lake Breeze* concerning the status of "the small boy with a printing press" in amateur journalism. Mr. Smith declares that upon this same boy the whole past, present, and future of amateur journalism depends; but the

CONSERVATIVE is of a different opinion, being unable to see why the typesetter or pressman is so essentially affiliated with the art of literature. True, some of the best amateurs have also been printers, as attested by Messrs. Dowdell, Sandusky, Porter, Macauley, and the formerly active genius Edward Cole, but these cases by no means prove that the pen and the type-stick are kindred implements. If the claim of Mr. Smith be true, why does not his beloved National choose eminent master printers for Laureate Judges in Poetry?

When Victor L. Basinet's new paper, *The Rebel,* shall appear, the amateur public will have an opportunity to behold the workings of a very extraordinary mind. Mr. Basinet is in some respects a true genius, blessed with an almost instinctive perception of the delicate and the artistic, and possessing a rhetorical style of remarkable vigour. But superadded to these qualities is such a strange point of view on social problems and systems, that the rational reader will stand aghast at the thoughts revealed. How Mr. Basinet became successively a socialist and a confessed anarchist is more than the CONSERVATIVE can say, though he has met the gentleman personally. Utter disregard of the fundamental failings of humanity seems to be the keynote, however, since this dreamer refuses to believe that mankind cannot live forever in brotherhood under the Golden Rule, once that happy state of affairs is established. But his own arguments ought to correct his beliefs. He tells us that capitalists should be dethroned, since they abuse their privileges and oppress their brothers, etc. etc. But, he adds, all men are equal. Then how can he say that his proposed earth-wide brotherhood will not be marred with strife more hideous and universal than any yet known? It is all in the education, he says. But are not his hated capitalists taught the Golden Rule also? The world would like to live just as Mr. Basinet would have it, but fortunately most of us are conservative enough not to tear down our present system of society when we know of no better one to supersede it.

Another amateur whom the CONSERVATIVE has met several times in person is Mr. John T. Dunn, the Irish Patriot. Mr. Dunn is a man of undoubted talent, being now editor of *The Providence Amateur,* yet his anti-English views are such that they call for correction. The CONSERVATIVE has no particular antipathy toward the Green Isle and its people, yet he must protest at the rebellious, seditious and treasonable attitude which some maintain toward that stronger race which governs them. England has admittedly been neglectful of Ireland's interests in the past, but that such old scores should be transmitted to the present well-treated generation of Irish and Irish-Americans is anomalous. Through Britannia will come Hibernia's greatest days of glory, yet an ungrateful, revengeful few will do their best to obstruct progress, bite the hand that feeds them, and calumniate the loyal Irish People who are faithful to England. Ireland is now an equal and integral part of the British Empire, and he who slanders that Empire indirectly slanders Ould Oireland herself.

That metrical precision is still appreciated by the sounder school of critics is well shown by the awarding of poetical honours in the United this year. Our new Laureate, justly enough, is Mr. Rheinhart Kleiner, supreme master of perfect rhyme and metre, and the poem on which the award was based is "The Evening Prayer", a chastely lustrous gem of thought whose devout and delicate atmosphere is adorned with a technical finish beyond reproach. What radical is so extreme, that he would wish to see this faultless jewel marred by irregular cutting or splintered by the mallet of "liberalism"?

The inferior award, proudly flaunted by the CONSERVATIVE, is certainly a triumph of technique, since his "poem" in the *Official Quarterly* contains little merit indeed beyond having exactly ten syllables in each line.

The August *United Amateur* is indeed a credit to our new Official Editor. The list of members shows considerable change, and reveals the regrettable fact that our two latest ex-Presidents have retired to honorary membership, leaving the Official Editor himself as our only active ex-President. If this is to happen in the future, and the Presidency is to be considered only as a step toward retirement, we shall be tempted to become a monarchy, with our present Executive as King Leo I.

SOCIALISM

By John Russell

Now just a word between us two:
What truly is the end in view?
Must we all share and share alike,
From Algy down to Irish Mike?
Must the skill'd doctor, with his brains,
Be satisfy'd with such small gains
As his who wields the lowly pick,
Or carries hods of lime and brick?
And must the man who can invent,
With equal profit be content
To his who labours on the street,
Or in the meadows mows the wheat?
Won't some be rich and others poor,
And human nature still endure?
Or must within one stagnant "pool"
Go wage of wise man and of fool;
And with the same fix'd wage be paid
The skill'd stenographer and maid?
And what about the leaders then:
Will they share with the working men?
I rather think these worthies would
Prefer to grab the most they could!
I'm sure that this is not the plan
To benefit the working man.
As for myself, I frankly say:
Just give me work and decent pay,
And dreamers will in vain insist
That I become a socialist.

The Conservative

Edited by H. P. Lovecraft on the Interests of the United Amateur Press Association. Office of Publication, 598 Angell Street, Providence, R. I., U. S. A. For circulation amongst Lovers of Literature.

THE LINCOLN PRESS

The Conservative, Vol. I, No. IV

Contributors Number

Providence, R. I., January, 1916

Edited by H. P. Lovecraft

SONG OF THE NORTH WIND

From whence I come or where I dwell
  Is never for you to know,
Be it height of heaven, depth of hell,
  I hold you in my throe;
But before I come men signal me—
  Red rag and rocket flare—
And I send my calm from over sea
  To say I will be there.

Sired was I ere the world was born,
  Old when the world was young,
An alien I from space outworn,
  My shriek the first song sung:
Old was I ere thought was hurl'd
  As fire by whirling pow'rs;
My cold breath iced a molten world
  As play in dead-year'd hours.

When life, a weakling, writh'd in earth,
  I held my chilling breath,
And mountains, rivers, men had birth
  In the breast of unconscious death;

And I gave to earth, from out my side,
My children, changelings three:
The bacchic blood of my amorous bride
Flows in them measureless, free.

My beacon light is the setless star,
I roar in the Arctic track,
My breath, as a cyclone, rages afar,
I sing,—and mountains crack;
I smile, and the lure is deathless fame
And the sail of the iron ship;
I frown, and naked is stripp'd its frame,
And crunch'd in my crushing grip.

I lay in waste the fertile land,
I strike the flowers heart
I barren the yield wherever plann'd
As I blight the bud at start;
I strip the tree of leaf and bough,
However my fancies stray,
I fling disaster into the Now
From a thousand miles away.

I lust the sea with hellish roar,
I storm its portals round,
I strew with wrecks its rock-sunk shore
From Open to the Sound;
I whirl and rip on the steamer's deck
Till they hammer the hatches down,
I mock and flaunt ere I taste the wreck—
Before they sink to drown.

From whence I come or where I dwell
Is never for you to know,
Be it height of heaven, depth of hell,
I hold you in my throe;
But before I come men signal me—
Red rag and rocket flare—

And I send my calm from over sea
To say I will be there.

—WINIFRED VIRGINIA JORDAN.

INTRODUCING MR. JAMES PYKE

Of the many gifted poets entering The United Amateur Press Association during the present period of improved literary standards, few can bear comparison with the one who now makes his first appearance in these pages, Mr. James T. Pyke of Riverside, East Providence, R. I.

Mr. Pyke is a gentleman blessed equally with the advantages of highest culture and of highest intellectual endowments. He is graduate both of Brown University and of Andover Theological Seminary, having been Class Poet at the latter institution. Upon his graduation from Andover, Mr. Pyke was ordained to the Congregational ministry, to which profession he lent all the remarkable genius with which favouring fortune has invested him; but the tremendous strain of pastoral activity on a delicate constitution at last proved excessive, and he has now retired to a quiet life of letters, cultivating the Muses in his cottage at Riverside, overlooking the sparkling reaches of Narragansett Bay.

The unusual modesty of Mr. Pyke has veiled a poetical genius which will now blaze out all the more resplendently because of its previous concealment. His first efforts were made in boyhood, and specimens written at the age of seventeen show all the inspiration and polish to be expected from a man of mature years. But these were no more than the faint promise of future excellence. His poems of manhood are infinitely moving and beautiful. Nature, viewed through the medium of his sonnets, takes on new and lovelier aspects, whilst his longer poems cover every phase of human life and aspiration. "The Conservative's" lines in the "United Official Quarterly" for November, 1914, were an endeavor to convey some idea of their grace and loftiness.

Mr. Pyke's particular models in verse have ever been the New England poets, and to the classic coterie of the preceding century he may be justly deemed a legitimate successor.

It is not often that an organisation of amateurs can boast the membership of a genius of Mr. Pyke's type and "The Conservative" has scant need to say that he is vastly proud to have been the means of bringing Mr. Pyke into his beloved United Amateur Press Association.

CONSOLATION

Oh, grieve not if the gentle glance
That spoke to yours so shyly
But yesterday, now looks askance
On you, who hold it highly!

And do not sigh, if lips and hands
That once were kind and willing
Obey no more love's sweet demands,
When love has lost its thrilling!

If Jane's or Agnes' heart will roam
To fresher fields and fairer,
So yours has often stray'd from home,
In quest of pastures rarer!

For love may stay or haste away;
Love knows no time, nor season;
For each unrest and change of nest,
Love has its own sweet reason!

—RHEINHART KLEINER

THE HORIZON OF DREAMS

Afar on the rim and the edge of things,
Where the pearl seeds float and weep;

Where the wee cloud-mothers, with delicate wings
  Flit over the mountains of sleep;
Afar down the valley where fancies drift
  When the sun has shot his last beam
There lies a sweet realm just over the lift
  Of the wave and the wonder of dream.

Afar on the rim and the edge of the moon
  When the twilight has scatter'd her sheep,
When the tears of the night are found too soon
  Just there where the dew drops deep:
Afar where the boats of children lie
  And lazily rest on the tide,
And lazily swing when the dusk is nigh,
  Is the place where the dream-children hide.
Afar down the slope of the pale moon's rays
  Where she scatter'd her jewels abroad,
Where all of your dreams were lost in the blaze
  When she lifted herself from her load:
Afar down the stretch of the wonderful sea
  Where the gold is a part of its gleam,
Lies the land of enchantment for you and for me
  On the low sweet Horizon of Dream.

—ANNE TILLERY RENSHAW

ON RECEIVING A PICTURE OF SWANS

With pensive grace the melancholy Swan
Mourns o'er the tomb of luckless Phaeton;
On grassy banks the weeping poplars wave,
And guard with tender care the wat'ry grave.
Would that I might, should I too proudly claim
An heav'nly parent, or a god-like fame,
When, flown too high, and dash'd to depths below,
Receive such tribute as a Cygnus' woe.

The faithful bird, that dumbly floats along,
Sighs all the deeper for his want of song!

—H. P. LOVECRAFT.

GALILEO AND SWAMMERDAM

One look'd into celestial light,
Saw moon and stars in th' infinite;
Their beauty stirr'd his heart.
The telescope came to his eyes,
And harmonies, set in the skies,
Became of life a part.

The other lov'd the creeping things,
The atoms small, the world of wings,
The puny stir of breath.
The microscope show'd earth at war;
Devouring Nature's doling law;
And his love brought him death.

—WINIFRED VIRGINIA JORDAN

MAIA

Thou comest in the May-time
To star the earth with flow'rs,
To usher in the play-time
After laborious hours.

The myriad blooms acclaim thee
With petal-lips aglow,

While birds and rills but name thee
    In all their flight and flow.

Speed on thy joyous mission
    With wonder-blossoms clad,
Of life the sweet magician
    To make our sad hearts glad.

—JAMES T. PYKE

THE POET

The poet is Protean, and is pleas'd
To venture forth as other than himself;
For in the character of fay, or elf,
Or what not, pray, his heart is greatly eas'd.
Therefore look not for self-disclosures true
In all he says and does in variant mood.
Is he Jack Robinson or Robin Hood
Because he wakes the glen with loud halloo?
So would you sense a black streak in his heart
Because he knows all motives to all sin?
Judgment in inferences is akin
To purposes of low Satanic art:
The poet quickly feels the heat of strife,
Yet knows that life is love and love is life.

—JAMES T. PYKE

DEPARTED

By Maude Kingsbury Barton

I wander out into the fields, I linger under trees
I hear the songs of lovely birds, and drowsing of the bees.
I glance up to the cloudless sky, such glory there I see!
But still I find no happiness is left on earth for me.

The streamlets are as sparkling, and the sky is just as blue
As the day that you departed. I wonder if you know,
As your spirit soar'd on upward, and left me here below,
That my heart was breaking, breaking, that you were call'd to go?

The autumn leaves are falling, there's a ling'ring bud or two
In my garden of the roses, I see you flitting through.
I ever hear your laughing voice, I see your golden hair,
The sunlight shining on it, and your eyes beyond compare.

The moon is shining brightly, O the silver moon so white.
But to me the earth is gloomy since you are not here tonight.
I wonder if in Paradise, where all the angels are,
You can look down upon this earth and see me from afar?

My soul, my soul is fainting with a longing for the time
When I'll be call'd from this green earth to yonder Heav'nly clime.
When your sweet spirit mine can meet, never again to part,
In Paradise's garden, hand in hand and heart to heart.

TO CELIA

This kindness, had it come when first I thought
To win your heart's regard and true esteem,
Would not, as now, since 'tis no longer sought,
Have seem'd the ling'ring phantom of a dream.

For all your glance, and smile, and touch, betray,
I yearn'd in vain, in other hopeless times;
Had counted that dear treasure, which, today,
You give from your affection's ardent climes.

But now this new and sudden sympathy,
This tardy warmth, that follows old neglect,
Leave me unmov'd, who once so willingly
Had welcomed love, to shelter and protect;—

Love in such guise of beauty and delight,
As you, perhaps, had taught my heart to know;
Such sweetness and such tenderness and might,
As only soul to soul can ever show!

And since that dream has died, my heart must mourn
To know that yours, too late, has learn'd to care;
For, long ago, the rue and wounding thorn
Of that old love, were plucked for one more fair!

—RHEINHART KLEINER.

THE CONSERVATIVE

Edited by H. P. Lovecraft in the Interests of the United Amateur Press Association. Office of Publication, 598 Angell St., Providence, R. I., U. S. A. For circulation amongst Lovers of Literature.

THE LINCOLN PRESS

The Conservative, Vol. II, No. I

Providence, R. I., April, 1916

Edited by H. P. Lovecraft

BENEDICTION

The sun has sunk down, and a ling'ring trace
Of burnish'd gold tints the hills of grey;
And across the evening's pearl-scarr'd face
A lone loon wings his unheeded way.

The shadows are deep round the shelter'd lake,
And the swamp is hid in a vapour veil
That rises and falls o'er the wild rice brake,
And wavers and floats like a phantom sail.

A star burns clear in the folds of night,
And through the deep thicket that lines the shore
Shines a flickering fleck of crimson light,
That glows from a distant cottage door.

The day is done, and o'er Earth's broad span
A sweet, solemn silence gently falls,
And peace caresses the sons of Man,
In the peasant's cot and the Baron's walls.

—ANDREW FRANCIS LOCKHART

ANOTHER ENDLESS DAY

Another endless day;
  A night that flies too soon;
Unwilling toil, half-hearted play,
  From new to waning moon!

No joy, nor heart to laugh;
  No hope where once 'twas high;
The cup I've but begun to quaff
  Is stale—the fountain dry!

Oh, for a cause to fight;
  A passion or a pang;
A love to thrill with new delight;
  A grief I never sang!

Something to stir my soul
  As not in life before;
To make the weary spirit whole,
  And bless the day once more!

—RHEINHART KLEINER

APRIL

  Winter's sway
  Pass'd away
'Neath a blue sky's leaven;
  In its place
  Out of space
Dropp'd a golden heaven!

Soft and low,
Sweet and slow,
Singing in the hollow;
Sun and rain
Back again,
Blithesome blooms a-follow!

Robins preen
'Mid the green
Draping Nature's altar;
In the mead
Happy reed
Lifts from dream-bound psalter.

Hopes and fears,
Smiles and tears,
In each gleam or shower;
Laugh and weep,
Sow and reap,
April's in her bower!

—WINIFRED VIRGINIA JORDAN

IN MORVEN'S MEAD

In Morven's Mead I heard a cry
And sound of glad wings passing by;

And searching softly o'er the ground,
A smiling, star-fac'd flower found!

—WINIFRED V. JORDAN

THE NIGHT WIND BARED MY HEART

The Night Wind bared my heart;
I felt the old, keen smart
Of grief: cold Mem'ry's eyes
Her subtle misery plies
With art!

The Day Wind heal'd the smart
That fasten'd on my heart;
But, Oh, from grief was prest
The joys that from my breast
Depart!

—WINIFRED VIRGINIA JORDAN

R. KLEINER, LAUREATUS. IN HELICONEM

Blest by Apollo and th' admiring Nine,
On Helicon see tuneful KLEINER shine.
Euterpe close his piping lay attends,
And with his notes her own in concord blends.
Fleet Pegasus th' enchanting music hears,
And beats his pinions, and pricks up his ears;
Whilst the skill'd Erato, with sacred lyre,
Joins in the strain, and feels the noble fire.
Melpomene forgets her dark alarms,
And Polyhymnia lays aside her psalms:
The fair Thalia smiles with brighter grace,
And gay Terpsichore suspends her pace:
Calliope and Clio rest their quills,
As wise Urania at the chorus thrills.
The mighty Phoebus trembles on his throne,
For KLEINER's chords are sweeter than his own!

—H. P. LOVECRAFT

THE BEST WINE

Weary of Care, I went in search of Joy,
And drank, my greedy fill of Pleasure's Wine,
Until, soul-sick, I knew the Grim Decoy;
The Bitter Dregs of Discontent were mine.

'Twas then a ragged urchin by the way
Held out his little hand—and I confess
That in the Joy I gave to him that day
I found the Dregless Wine of Happiness!

—WILLIAM DE RYEE.

YE BALLADE OF PATRICK VON FLYNN

Or, The Hibernio-German-American England-Hater

By Lewis Theobald, Jun.

"Germanis ipsis Germaniores"

Attind ye all me wonthrous tale, an' Oi will tell to you,
Of how an honest Oirishman into a Proosian grew.
'Twas nigh on twinty year' ago Oi lift me native bog
To seek in these majestic States a place to earn me grog.
Sure, wurrk was aisy found fur me, fer Oi'm a clever man;
Oi earnt so much Oi soon cud buy me whiskey by the can.
Wid half a dozen other Micks, a merry, dhrinkin' crew,
Oi used to hang around shebeens an' currse Ould England blue!
Jist why Oi hate the Englishmen, Oi don't remimber quoite,
But Jimmy Dugan's grand-dad says they've ne'er used Oireland roight.
Sure all they iver done fer us was civilise our land,
An' we've no use fer sober laws, but all fer fraydom shtand!

How glad will be the fateful day whin England last draws breath,
An' good Ould Oireland shall be free—to dhrink hersilf ter death!
Now comes the cruel, cruel, warr, wid German's runnin' loose.
Sure, here's the toiem to make a shtir, an' give some more abuse!
Us Oirish have no love fer Dutch, but side wid Germany
Because she hates Ould England most as fiendishly as we!
We know der Kaiser'd treat us wurrse thin England iver done,
But sure, if we used England roight we'd lose our sweetest fun!
There's somethin' in the Oirish hearrt thot niver bows to rules;
At jooty's call we tache our sons sedition in the schools.
Last night the Germans hereabouts all gather'd in a hall,
Wid German flags above the stage, an' Kaisers on the wall.
Oi don't know what they wanted, but so far as Oi cud see,
They mere hoched der Kaiser and enjoind "noothrality."
They all denounc'd the Prisident an' currs'd the Yankee laws
Fer bein' too un-noothral loike to hilp the German cause.
Thin they shtarted afther England, an' me hearrt bate quick wid proide
As about "foul British perfidy" they babbled an' they lied.
Oi thought we Oirish cud invint the rankest Billingsgate,
But wonthrous arre the fishy yarrns thim Dutchmen kin relate!
Me frinds what had come wid me was so mov'd wid martial ire,
They cluster'd round the rusty shtove to argue an' perspire.
Oi grew so pathriotic thot I tuk me hat in hand
An' shouted "Hoch der Kaiser, und das dear ould Vaterland!"
Bedad, we'll lick thim Britishers within a fortnight sharrp,
An' jine on one thriumphant flag the aigle an' the harrp!
Thin all began to fraternise; McNulty and von Bohn—
O'Donovan and Munsterberg, von Bulow an' Malone.
In Baccic bonds our pact we seal'd; in harrmony serayne
We sang at once "Die Wacht am Rhein" an' "Wearin' av the Grane."
Old von der Goltz pick'd up a brogue; in Dutch young Dooley sang;
Mid Prussian an' Hibernian shtrains the ancient rafthers rang!
Now all at once a magic seem'd to creep into me bones—
Me whiskey-mellow'd Oirish voice burst forth in Prussian tones!
Oi felt a sthrange sinsation, and in fancy seem'd to see
Instad of dear ould Shannon's banks, the gently rippling Spree—
No, not the Spree ye think Oi mane, but that which softly flows
Through glorious Deutschland's grassy leas, where warr an' kultur grows.
Ochone! Ochone! Where am Oi now? What conflict am Oi in?

Do Oi belong in Dublin town or back in Ould Berlin?
A week ago me son was borrn; his christ'nin's not far off;
Oi wonther will I call him Mike, or Friedrich Wilhelm Hoff?
'Tis hard indade fer one loike me to know jist where he's at;
Oi wonther if me name is Hans or if it shtill is Pat?
But let me bore ye all no more; the proper course is clear.
Oi'll slanther England all Oi dare, an' rayson niver hear.
A loyal, "noothral" Oi shal be in all me wurrds an' worrk,
An' niver shpake excipt to praise the Dutchman an' the Turrk!

The Conservative

Edited by H. P. Lovecraft in the Interests of the United Amateur Press Association. Office of Publication, 598 Angell St., Providence, R. I., U. S. A. For Circulation among Lovers of Literature.

The Lincoln Press

The Conservative, Vol. II, No. II

Providence, R. I., July, 1916

EDITED BY H. P. LOVECRAFT

THE AMERICAN PROLETARIAT VERSUS ENGLAND

By Henry Clapham McGavack

A large number of Americans have no use for England. They despise her and all she stands for. In spite of the fact that they constitute the most thoughtless and most ignorant section of our people, they are rather powerful politically and are, therefore, not to be ignored in matters which affect international amity.

To them England is the tyrant who taxes without the consent of the taxed. They do not understand the Revolutionary War.

To them England is the barbarian power who respects no other's rights at sea. They do not understand the War of 1812.

To them England is the cruel overlord of Ireland. She is also the home of Monarchy and Aristocracy—fearful cancers. They do not understand English political and social institutions.

Deadly ignorance is the mother of rank prejudice.

To attempt in a short sketch a clear presentation of the truth regarding England and the English in the several connections mentioned above is undertaking the impossible. But it is possible to *indicate,* in a more or less hazy manner, the most striking facts, leaving to any interested reader the task of making a more complete study for himself.

Three or more articles are here squeezed into one, with the hope of impressing on the American Anglophobe a realization of just how wrong and unjust his conceptions of the great Motherland have been.

Now, the War of 1812 was a commercial one on our part, in which we failed to get recognition for our point of view. So far as England was concerned it was an outgrowth of the Napoleonic Wars, being caused largely by undue eagerness in ferreting out contraband. Her feeling toward us was one of indifference, more or less, rather than one of haughty overlordship. Her methods were not overscrupulous, perhaps; but Napoleon was her object, not the United States.

At the present time, affairs are somewhat analogous to the conditions in 1812. There is no difference to our viewpoint, however. England is actuated by motives of real concern for the proper treatment of American interests at sea so far as is consistent with her own safety. Her attitude has been constantly just, even forbearing. But space does not permit of its discussion here, as it is not relevant to the theme. Suffice it to say that a genuine comprehension of England and the English on the part of Americans is the surest way to an understanding of the true aim of English policy. That these aims are prejudicial to the United States, no one can even attempt to prove.

But the trouble really started in 1776.

The Revolutionary War was George the Third's own private and particular war. With practically the whole English nation against him, he persisted in that policy of personal government for the Colonies which culminated in the Declaration of Independence. Chatham opposed him and spoke for the Americans. Likewise did Burke and Charles James Fox. The Marquis of Cornwall, Lord Admiral Howe accepted their commissions reluctantly and fought only because they considered military duty above personal opinions. Admiral Keppel flatly refused to fight the Colonies. Nor would Sir Geoffrey Amherst, one of the greatest commanders of his day, though the King personally entreated him to take an army. Furthermore, the English people themselves refused to enlist, thus forcing the government to hire those Hessians who are the objects of so much American scorn.

In the face of all this, it is preposterous to assert that we whipped England. We did little more than subdue George the Third—with the aid of France. It is rank prejudice to indict the English nation for the stupid policy of one of its kings. It is insensate folly to cherish spite and venom against that nation one hundred and forty years *after* the event.

Yet we do just that.

To most of us, England is the arch-representative of basest tyranny. This in spite of the Magna Charta and the Bill of Rights and the fact that Parliament is older than the Austrian monarchy of the Hapsburgs.

After the Revolutionary War came ministerial responsibility. George the Third found himself shorn of real power. Henceforth, by and with the advice of his ministers, must the king govern in fact as well as in theory. Today, the ministers are responsible to Parliament for all acts of the executive, and only during Parliament's pleasure do they remain in office. How absurd, then, to speak of tyranny.

On the other hand, the kingship is full of deep meaning and sentiment to the people of the "Tight little Island."

For one thousand years there has been a King of England. He is part and parcel of her constituted existence, a co-ordinate member of her government. Today, although his power does rest with an executive ministry, his presence, through hereditary descent by law established, is truly representative of the eternal majesty of the British people. He links the past with the present and the future. As Emperor of India, he is standard bearer for grander dominion than that of Rome. Naturally, then, the English revere their monarchy. They recognize its symbolic mission, perceiving in its stately pomp and pageantry the reflection of a glorious national history.

It is a monarchy, furthermore, which weighs but lightly on the taxpayer. The crown revenues are derived from estates once belonging to the Royal Family, which were turned over to the state by George the Third, who accepted in lieu thereof a fixed Civil List. As the revenues from the Crown Lands exceed the Civil List, the nation is decidedly the gainer by the arrangement.

Moreover, the King of England is a hardworking, pains-taking public servant whose daily round of arduous duties is no less wearisome and exacting than that of any great man of business. His recent gift to the nation of nearly five hundred thousand dollars (almost the entire Civil List) shows that he is not lacking in patriotic self-denial. The direct power of the Crown is limited, but the personal influence of its wearer is very great. That this has been aught but a good influence since the days of William the Fourth no one can truthfully assert.

Space does not here permit an extended discussion of the British aristocracy. A few words relative thereto, however, may serve to dispel some American misconceptions with regard to it.

According to Continental standards, it is not an aristocracy at all. In Germany, Austria, Spain and Italy, every son of a noble is a noble. The titled class is very large, as a rule very worthless, and possesses numerous privileges subversive to the rights of so-called inferior men. In Great

Britain only the head of the titled family is noble. His sons are commoners in the eyes of the law and remain such until the eldest succeeds to his father's place, or until any one (or all of them) secures a peerage in his own right through some contribution to the advancement of the country deemed worthy of notice by the Crown. Younger sons, as a rule, must scramble for themselves. Consequently, the race retains its push and initiative, the middle classes constantly receive infusions of the best blood, while titular distinctions remain open to anyone with the brains, ambition and worth to earn them.

A great scientist, for instance, becomes Lord Kelvin; a great poet Lord Tennyson; a great statesman Lord Beaconsfield; a great soldier Lord Kitchener. Attain success and the King registers it for all time.

On the other hand there are some very, very old families in England—many of them without titles, but none the less noble for that. They are not decrepit, bloodless, decayed old families either.

Thomas Fitzalan-Howard, for instance, is fifteenth Duke of Norfolk of the second creation. He would be the nineteenth Duke were it not for an act of attainder passed against one of his ancestors which caused a cessation of the title through four lives. Furthermore, he is descended from the Fitzalans who were Earls of Arundel way back in the time of the first Edwards. So be it. Thomas Fitzalan-Howard is a very old man of a very old family and a decidedly active, public-spirited, hardworking old man none the less. Ancestry, in making of him a fine gentleman, has not deprived his country of a most efficient citizen.

Then there is the Earl Curzon of Kedleston, son of the fourth Baron Scarsdale, who entered the House of Commons, made a name for himself, became Viceroy of India and took his seat in the House of Lords on merit alone before the death of his father of whom he was the heir. That father was himself a remarkable man—Clergyman in the Church of England, Judge of the County Court, large landed proprietor, a universally loved and respected person. He died in March of this year, considerably over eighty years of age.

It's a great breed, the British Nobility. A noble history it has, too. Americans should remember that it was the Barons who wrested the Magna Charta from King John; the great Whig Nobles who destroyed the Stuart tyranny and brought over the Houses of Orange and Brunswick-Luneburg.

Ireland has always been a mighty factor in American Anglophobia. At present the Irish irreconcilables and the Germans are doing all they can to heighten the diseases. They have created a vast amount of maudlin sympathy for the leaders of the latest Sinn Fein outbreak so promptly and properly executed by the British government. Their success in this regard argues little for American possession of the judicial temperament.

Now, the Irish question, like all other questions, is two-sided. England has not always been on the right side. On the other hand, she has not always been in the wrong although she would suppose so who judged from the sentiment largely expressed in this country.

One who would correctly inform himself of Irish affairs should read the authorities on both sides and strike the middle ground. To anyone pressed for time, I would recommend a perusal of Professor Patrick W. Royce's very fair and very lucid history. Professor Royce was both Irish and Catholic; but under no circumstances does he lose the judicial, impartial attitude, at no time does he give way to passion; always does he recognize the relativity of facts and circumstances, never does he fail to judge in the light of the spirit of the times. It would be well were the perfervid, harebrained Irish enthusiasts of the present generation to acquire a modicum of his calm and unruffled composure. More weight, at least, would attach to them.

Ireland has, in the past, been terribly misgoverned; but very probably not more so than the average subject race of bygone times and certainly not one whit more cruelly than the Prussian Poles and Danes are ruled today by Casement's dear friend, Germany. On the other hand, within the last two or three generations, England has been doing all in her power to better conditions in Ireland—and has succeeded wonderfully well. Manufacturing and commerce is being encouraged and the fertile soil of the country is being opened to the small cultivator by the wholesale parceling of great estates. The result has been to place the Irish farmer in a much better economic position than is possessed by his brother in England.

Home Rule, too, is on the statute books, awaiting only the end of the war to be put in force. A very liberal form of Home Rule it is to be.

It should further be observed that Irishmen have never, in the whole course of their history, been united among themselves with regard to just what they expected of England. That, upon many occasions, England should have chosen her own course, regardless, is, therefore, not strange.

Today we have Ulster standing out against Home Rule, preferring to be governed from London rather than from Dublin. New Ulstermen are Irish—they lay claim to no other nationality. They are a minority of the

Irish population, to be sure; but a very large minority, certainly too large to be ignored. To England comes the difficult matter of adjusting the differences between the two factions of the Irish nation. It is a problem which revolts do not even begin to solve. It is a problem which people separated from the scene by three thousand miles of sea would be wise to let alone.

The Irish in this country are, for the most part, descendants of those who lived under the old order of things. Their prejudice runs away with them. Their ignorance obscures to them the truth. They glory in an attempt to stab England in the back because their patriotism is a blind insanity. But the worst feature of their existence is the fact that they instil into many gullible American minds a feeling of rancor against England which is not justified by the realities. They are enemies of the United States as well as of England. For, much depends upon good feeling between this country and the British Empire.

Good feeling is based upon knowledge.

In short, we Americans should strive to learn more of England, what she is, what she stands for. Certainly three thousand miles of undefended Canadian boundary should prove to us that there is no menace in her Empire. Her correct behavior during the Civil War and when we fought Spain should be remembered in her favor. It would be unwise to forget that financially and industrially she leads the world; that politically she is the most advanced of any state known to history—an inexhaustible source for study, reflection and admiration.

Nor does it take deep delving to convince one that Lord Curzon was nearer right than wrong when he declared that "The British Empire is, under Providence, the greatest force for good that the world has ever seen."

England made the Empire.

THE CONSERVATIVE

Published in the interest of the United Amateur Press Association, and sent free to all Lovers of Literature, and others who desire it, at 598 Angell St., Providence, R. I., by Howard P. Lovecraft.

The Conservative, Vol. II, No. III

Providence, R. I., October, 1916

EDITED BY H. P. LOVECRAFT

THE MOCKING BIRD

When Southern moonlight softly falls,
When Day has died and stars unfold,
From jasmine-scented groves—Oh, Love!
A Mocking-bird with Lyre of Gold!

All of your tears, all of your sighs;
All of Life's joys that thrill you through;
God's benediction and His love—
Are speaking in those notes to you.

All that you long'd and meant to be;
Your pray'rs, your dreams—(Oh, earthly bars!)
Are mounting, mounting, with that voice,
Straight up God's stairway to the stars!

—OLIVE G. OWEN

OLD ENGLAND AND THE "HYPHEN"

By H. P. Lovecraft

Of the various intentional fallacies exhaled like miasmic vapours from the rotting cosmopolitanism of vitiated American politics, and doubly rife during these days of European conflict, none is more disgusting than that contemptible subterfuge of certain foreign elements whereby the legitimate zeal of the genuine native stock for England's cause is denounced and compared to the unpatriotic disaffection of those working in behalf of England's enemies. The Prussian propagandists and Irish irresponsibles, failing in their clumsy efforts to use the United States as a tool of vengeance upon the Mistress of the Seas, have seized with ingenious and unexpected eagerness on a current slogan coined to counteract their own traitorous machinations, and have begun to fling the trite demand "America first" in the face of every American who is unable to share their puerile hatred of the British Empire. In demanding that American citizens impartially withhold love and allegiance from any government save their own, thereby binding themselves to a policy of rigid coldness in considering the fortunes of their Mother Country, the Prusso-Hibernian herd have the sole apparent advantage of outward technical justification. If the United States were truly the radical, aloof, mongrelised nation into which they idealise it, their plea might possibly be more appropriate. But in comparing the lingering loyalty of a German-American for Germany, or of an Irish-American for Ireland, with that of a native American for England, these politicians make their fundamental psychological error.

England, despite the contentions of trifling theorists, is not and never will be a really foreign country; nor is a true love of America possible without a corresponding love for the British race and ideals that created America. The difficulties which caused the severance of the American Colonies from the rest of the Empire were essentially internal ones, and have no moral bearing on this country's attitude toward the parent land in its relations with alien civilisations. Just as Robert Edward Lee chose to follow the government of Virginia rather than that of the Federal Union in 1861, so did the Anglo-American Revolutionary leaders choose local to central allegiance in 1775. Their rebellion was in itself a characteristically English act, and could in no manner annul the purely English origin and nature of the new republic. American history before the conflict of 1775-1783 is English history, and we are lawful heirs of the unnumbered glories of the Saxon line. Shakespeare and Milton, Dryden and Pope, Young and Thomson, Johnson and Goldsmith, are our own poets; William the Conqueror, Edward the Black Prince, Elizabeth, and William of Nassau are our own royalty; Crecy, Poitiers, and Agincourt are our own victories; Lord Bacon, Sir Isaac Newton, Hobbes, Locke, Sir Robert Boyle, and Sir William Herschel are our own philosophers and scientists; what true American lives, who would wish, by rejecting an Englishman's heritage, to despoil his country of such racial laurels? Let those men be silent, who would, in envy, deny to the citizens of the United States the right to cherish and revere the ancestral honours that are theirs, and to remain faithful to the Anglo-Saxon ideals of their English forefathers!

Since the establishment of a republic by the Englishmen of the American Colonies, millions of non-British persons have been admitted to share the liberty which English hands created. In many cases, these immigrants have proved valuable accessions, and when accepting fully the ideals of the Anglo-American culture, those of them who are of North European blood have become completely amalgamated with the American people. Germans, in particular, being of identical racial stock, are able to fuse quickly and wholly into the Colonial population. But as they become Americans, so must they also, in a sense, become Englishmen. When the Elector of Hanover, a thorough German, acceded to the English throne, it was his duty to become an English monarch; and in a similar way it is an obligation of all other non-English individuals, princes or peasants, to adopt Anglo-Saxon ideals when they come to reap the advantages of an Anglo-Saxon nation. That millions of virile Germans have done so, is a gratifying fact to consider.

But since alien immigration has far exceeded normal proportions, it is but natural that we have among us an alarmingly vast body of foreigners from various countries who are totally unable to appreciate Anglo-American traditions. If not still attached to their respective nations, they are at least prone to regard the United States as a sort of spontaneously evolved territory without previous history or ancestry. Forgetting the Saxon inheritance that gave us language, laws, and liberty, they speak of America as a composite nation whose civilisation is a compound of all existing cultures; a melting pot of mongrelism wherein it is a crime for a man to know his own grandfather's name. They prate of Americanism as something of autochthonous growth, neglecting or unwilling to assign

England the credit for its origin; and presuming to blame any citizen who is more just than they in his appreciation of the Mother Land.

More guileful immigrants use their "Americanism" as a blind for treason. Leaving their own countries in dissatisfaction, they assume the cloak of American citizenship; organise and finance conspiracies with American money; and finally, with an audacity almost ironical, call upon the United States for help when overtaken by justice! Half the detestable violence of the Irish "Fenians" and "Sinn Fein" ruffians was hatched in America by those who dare drivel about such a thing as "neutrality"! Others continue to serve their own countries under the all-enveloping American mantle. Prussian-American patriots deep in the sanctimonious circles of "Americanism" and "pacifism" are at the same time secretly destroying American property for the benefit of the Prussian cause. And these are the sort of worthies who compare their treacherous anti-American acts with the traditional affection of a real American of the land which gave birth to the American nation!

The very small surviving flock of native Fourth-of-July England-haters must not be charged with that moral delinquency which attaches to the foreign agitators. These belated Revolutionists mean well, and are to be tolerated with kindness. They head that amusing element which applauds every Englishman who becomes naturalised in the United States, but which denounces with unmerciful inconsistency every American who, like the late Henry James, renews ancestral ties with Great Britain.

Summing up, we may well declare it folly to taunt the American lover of Old England with the cry of "Hyphenate!" His passion is not, like that of the Prussian or Irish "hyphenate", based exclusively on personal ancestry; in his affection for the parent Kingdom he is but reiterating his devotion to the ideals of the daughter Republic; he is giving to his country a double loyalty!

INSOMNIA

The Thing, am I, that rides the Night,
That clips the wings of Sleep;
The Thing, am I, in sunshine bright

That goads, with hag-mind, deep;
The Thing, am I, with forked knife
That prods the weary brain,
And snarls when Pleasure strives for life
Within my haunts of Pain.

I laugh: Ha! Ha! Ho! Ho! Hoo! Hoo!
When all the house is still;
I quaff: Ha! Ha! Ho! Ho! Hoo! Hoo!
When ghost-sheep run up hill!
My slaves count hundreds—fives and tens,
Till shadows stab their eyes!
They jump ten thousand sheep in pens
Until their counting lies!

Their music is a fun'ral march;
They see the wreath'd flow'rs fair;
They see their robes, as white as starch,
They feel the Eyes that stare.
They tramp the path of Fear and Flame
That narrows to four walls,
With minds red-hot with Curse and Shame,
Above the Pray'r that falls.

And then, I stage anew the trick
That brought me hell-curs'd gold;
I spread the reek of hunger thick
Upon a white-fac'd fold!
And Mem'ry, loath to serve my ends,
I heckle at the throat,
Till she her Province far extends
Beyond her hate-black moat.

And then—my Slaves will laugh, "Ha! Ha!"
And count sheep white and grey,
And moan in numbers mumblings mar,
Through night, through dawn, through day;
While lips that quiver pray for rest,
And dear hearts crucify,

Till those that dare, 'neath Pity's breast,
In frenzy beg to die!

THE THING, AM I, THAT RIDES THE NIGHT,
THAT CLIPS THE WINGS OF SLEEP;
THE THING, AM I, IN SUNSHINE BRIGHT
THAT GOADS, WITH HAG-MIND DEEP;
THE THING, AM I, WITH FORKED KNIFE
THAT PRODS THE WEARY BRAIN,
AND SNARLS WHEN PLEASURE STRIVES FOR LIFE
WITHIN MY HAUNTS OF PAIN.

—WINIFRED VIRGINIA JORDAN

PRUSSIANISM

By William Thomas Harrington

That the present conflict of nations was originated by an overbearing Prussian military autocracy, joined to a ravenous Prussian commercial ambition; and that its object was to achieve for Prussia in one superhuman effort the military and economic control of Europe, and the practical domination of the world; is today the general verdict of mankind. Ever since its foundation in the hour of victory over Louis Napoleon, the German Empire has been filled with the literature of war. The business of war has been taught, preached, fastened, and inculcated in every conceivable way; firearms have, figuratively speaking, been displayed in the front windows, whilst on every frontier the machinery of war has rattled its ominous challenge. Never was a nation so diligently prepared and so efficiently equipped for war, years in advance of all its possible adversaries. And when this marvellous mechanism was unloosed, its one aim was nothing less than the supremacy of the world.

The brutal acts of Germany in her headlong rush through Belgium toward Paris can never be justified or disavowed. The orders came from Berlin, and German officials upheld and encouraged crimes of the most outrageous sort, in which every law of civilised warfare and every principle of human ethics were flagrantly violated. But the world was to hear of outrages still more atrocious. In the sinking of the Lusitania, Prussian officialdom cunningly planned and executed one of the most revolting crimes in history. Citizens of the neutral nations had hitherto been content to rest in an attitude of silent disapproval; but now, when the German vulture waved her bloody plumes over the corpses of their own wives, sisters, mothers, children, and unoffending civilian countrymen in ghastly premeditated murder, they forgot their formal, cold-blooded "neutrality," and felt that the indescribable Crime of Crimes fairly shrieked for requital.

By acts such as these, Germany has become the Ishmael of the nations. With her hand against every man now, every man's hand will be against her in the years to come. How, after the war, will she cope with the righteous indignation of the world in her efforts to reconstruct her lost foreign commerce? Unhappily, the guilty will not suffer alone; for there are in America many honest and innocent persons of German descent, who will feel cruelly the universal condemnation of all that attaches to the German name.

Had she but preserved peace, Germany might have become a fairly close second to England in power; but through her silliness in maintaining the notion of a racial superiority that must be demonstrated by powder, she is doomed to be ruined by her own strength. As to the future; the ultimate and inevitable defeat of the Central Powers may restore to the world that nobler Germany we knew before she went insane. Had she conquered Europe and seized vast territories, she would undoubtedly have experienced that racial and spiritual degeneration and final ruin, which befell Imperial Rome. Having caused years of misery for others, she would have dragged herself down with them into a grave of lost civilisation.

The present vaunted unity of the German Empire is nothing more or less than a slavery of all the lesser States under Prussia. Prussia not only regards the more desirable type of Germans as mere vassals; but suppresses liberty of every sort amongst them, including that of the press. It is under compulsion that the people of the other German States are fighting Prussia's infamous battles, and dying for her shameful cause.

When Germany declared war on Russia and France, it was her intention to seize France at once, for use as an indemnity to defray the cost of the war. With the failure of this attempt, and with the wholly unexpected prolongation of hostilities, German thinkers have come to see bankruptcy staring them in the face. Since it has been proven that German treaties cannot be relied upon, even those nations not actually allied against Prussia know that she must be thoroughly crushed. What guarantee of stable peace, they ask, can be obtained from treating with Kaiser Wilhelm; or in case of his death, with his successor, the present Crown Prince? This precious pair and their ilk are too well known to be trusted. In full self- government by the German people lies the only hope of a permanent pacific adjustment. But the end cannot be far off. The ruling element of Germany know that they have thrown the last great group, the volunteers, into the maelstrom of battle, and that nothing more remains. They know that lacking a miracle, England and her brave Allies have won. British, French, and Russian generals are not fighting for empty geographical progress; they are fighting to kill men, the human serpents that have been arrayed against civilisation; and before the present great offensive movement shall have attained its climax, they will have killed more Germans than Germany can spare. The Kaiser and his satellites will be more than ready to make peace before the inevitable collapse begins. They desire to save appearances before their subjects, whose independent will they have come to fear. As a whole, this war can mean to Germany but one thing; the dawn of a new liberty for the people; for the majority of Germans will no longer tolerate a Prussian dictator who values them only as "kanone-futter."

TWILIGHT

The ruddy sun, his garish lustre shed,
With milder radiance lights the vesper scene;
Big-looming o'er his hilly western bed,
He beams a benediction on the green.

'Tis then my spirit sweetest comfort knows;
Then that my heart has respite from its pain:
Those cares are soften'd at the day's glad close,
That burn'd, when noon's hot ardour parch'd the main.

Yon purple peaks, and lines of dark'ning hills,

An equal peace at touch of evening own;
Departing Phoebus with affection thrills,
And soothes the heights he soon must leave alone.

Adown the valley, and across the mead,
The welcome shades of gentle dusk unfold;
The lullabies of brook and crooning reed
My weary thoughts in dreamy rapture hold.

In vap'rous bow'r, just o'er th' horizon's edge,
The sun and sky enjoy a last embrace;
Recounting each, with many a solemn pledge,
Fair deeds perform'd to light the world with grace.

Then falls the blessed boon of eventide;
The fresh'ning dew a drooping earth restores;
The loveliest moments with the shadows glide;
The mortal soul in loftiest ether soars.

Now may fond Retrospection reign supreme;
Dear mem'ries surge amid the fading light;
Till the first star's uncertain, twinkling beam
Leads on th' unnumbered glories of the night.

—CHESTER PIERCE MUNROE

THE BOND INVINCIBLE

By David H. Whittier

The laws of Infinite Goodness are not always manifested in those accustomed ways which we deem so inevitable, nor are their noblest operations always to be sought amidst those scenes of splendour where the tide of life flows with greatest strength and swiftness. Their deepest truths are oftentimes set forth among the humblest of men; for verily, they are no respecters of persons.

In a little town there once lived a youth and a maid who bore a mutual affection so strange and so intense, that not only did their neighbours marvel, but they themselves could scarce comprehend its singular and engrossing nature. From infancy the two had grown up side by side; every day drawing closer together, and becoming more and more occupied with thoughts of each other, till at length their fondness excluded many seemingly more important, and certainly more material needs and interests. Each was widely noted for a certain quiet goodness of heart, and each deserved the reputation; for all their thoughts and acts were pure beyond the common standards of mankind. They lived only for each other, and their thoughts were only of each other.

But one day a malignant demon interfered, where all before had been in the hands of God. The maid, stricken with a malady which defied the efforts of rural healers, declined with fatal rapidity toward the valley of shadows. Shortly before the end her lover reached her side, sinking by the deathbed with a silent apparent calm which revealed but little the inward fear and utter vacancy brought to his sensitive spirit by the dire calamity. He held her in his arms as her soul prepared to leave him, and as she crossed the portal of this world she whispered of her devotion, vowing that nothing in the land beyond might have power to divide them, or to draw them farther apart than they had ever been. He kissed her lips for the last time, and then the shadow fell, leaving him alone, utterly alone in space; for the world of men had never been with him, and he had lost the only world that was truly his.

They laid the maiden to rest beneath the green grasses of the hillside, whilst the youth wandered aimlessly through the village and the woods and fields nearby, in a strangely vacant mood which never seemed to lift. The good folk of the town often tried to speak to him, but their well-meant words caused only annoyance, and they were always repulsed; though never with roughness, for his sorrow had mellowed his nature, and made his kind heart even kinder than it had been before. His thoughts were ever outside the things about him; and though he seemed to talk sometimes, and even to try to smile, his inmost being held no real communion with those of this world. His mind was with the other, so far away, and yet so near to him in his hours of pensive solitude. His only peace came when he was alone, and thinking of her; so ere long he withdrew from the village to lead a hermit's life in the neighbouring wood.

For many years his existence was a strange one. He ate, and slept, and thought; but of these three things he thought the most, eating and sleeping only that he might think the better. He lived in a sphere of his own, above and beyond the world in which he seemed to live. The few who passed by his sylvan abode would sometimes behold him, walking slowly and calmly, with a strange, inscrutable smile of expectation on his lips; and they would wonder what it was that he expected, for to them his life seemed a blighted, wasted thing, and his mind, almost a blank. They knew, as did most of the villagers, that always he was helping others, and that many owed to him all their happiness in life. Sufferers, oppressed by lack of money or of some less material comfort, found in him a source from which seemed to flow the love and solace of God. In numbers they flocked to him, yet was none turned away. For himself he appeared to do nothing. His life was lived for others, yet he smiled and seemed to have hope of that peace which goodness brings to all who are able to rise to the heights of ascetic self-abnegation.

One day there came within the wood a caravan of wandering gypsies, who encamped as though for a long sojourn. Among their number was a girl of very singular characteristics; so young that she seemed scarce grown to that age when the mind reflects upon things unseen, yet withal so much given to deep musing, that she would frequently detach herself from the others, and sit for hours in silent, thoughtful solitude. Whenever the band made camp, this girl would withdraw from the scene of noise and bustle, for activity wearied and sickened her, imparting a strange loneliness as though some vital part of her, close to the heart, were missing. The gypsies respected her moods and feebleness, and never demanded from her that labour which falls to the lot of most gypsy women. They thought her strange, and even mad, though no one had the cruelty to say so openly; for in their rough way they loved her much, and were loath to wound her sensibilities.

This night the gypsy maid wandered forth as always from the busy tribe as they prepared their encampment; but her slow and aimless steps were not quite as of yore, nor did she feel that sense of pain which was wont to harass her so poignantly. It rather seemed to her that all was but a blank, and she a phantom looking upon vacancy and seeing all in nothing. At length the sky grew dark, and many clouds, as though gathered from all quarters of the heavens, hung black and low over the wood. The girl, hardly able to guide her footsteps in the feeble light, seated herself upon a boulder and became lost in meaningless meditations. The wind now arose, increasing in violence till a veritable torrent of rushing air tore its way through the trees with a din whose weirdly wonderful cadences spoke a terrible intensity and soul-stultifying meaning. And as the wind waxed in fury, so waxed some vital spark within the frail breast of the gypsy. Her heart was filled with a strange and fathomless longing, and she was irresistibly forced to rise and walk ahead toward an unknown goal. Directed and impelled by her surging soul, she forged ahead through the sheets of pouring rain and the blasts of roaring wind; yet to her mind came only an added sense of calm, and a vague thought of impending great events.

But the nomad girl was not alone in the storm-racked wood. Inspired with a like premonition of coming prodigies, the hermit also was astir, treading the familiar forest aisles and hearing in the scream of the tempest a half-formed prophecy that ere this night should pass, some wonder supernal should be wrought in him. The storm abated not, but swelled to great proportions. The trees swung their wild arms above the hermit's head, the while shrieking aloud their approval of destiny and its onward march of events. On walked the man, until it seemed to him that some inward greatness, some high ethereal vapour, was pressing for escape and well-nigh stifling him. Yet through it all was a warmth as though a furnace were being born, whose fire scorched with an ardour that he felt not as most of us feel heat or cold.

The two that wandered in the wood alone, for on such a night as this no forest creature dares breast the wrath of the gale, were now walking toward each other as swiftly and directly as though drawn together by an intangible but invincible cord of destiny. Knowing not whither their progress led, save as intuition hinted, each pressed onward with vague haste. Suddenly they met and paused, exalted by a fervent glow whose cause the darkness bid. Then all at once the glade was lit by a lightning flash whose fleeting effulgence laid bare the minutest details of the momentous scene. Face to face in mutual scrutiny stood the two, the godly hermit and the gypsy girl, who until that instant had never beheld each other's countenance. And now came to pass a marvel so great that the mind reels in the telling. Ere the flash had died away the man and the maid stretched forth their hands in an involuntary gesture of complete comprehension and recognition; and there, amid the wild tumult of the storm, came together once more the two souls that were all to each other, and that not even death had been able to sever. In reverent awe they embraced more closely than ever lovers embrace when they most grit their teeth and press each other to their bosoms with a passion which could never animate these two. Their love had always been the same. And as they stood there in sanctified silence, the heavens burst in twain. Down from the cloven empyrean shot a dazzling shaft of supernal radiance such as man had never seen before nor has seen since. A new, unearthly sort of day bathed for a second the forest and the neighbouring village; a day in whose instant of duration were heard celestial sounds like to none whereof men know. And when the skies had closed once more upon the holy light, behold—the inky clouds rolled gently apart from above the wood, and the pale moon, soft virgin queen of night, played with sweet argent archery upon two bodies stretched out side by side, with smiles upon their lips and faces, and with a lingering trace of the sureness of heaven in their open but unseeing eyes.

Great was the storm, and mighty the power that had shewn itself to all in the fury of the elements; yet was there revealed that night a power which, though manifest only to the two who were found so cold and silent, did in greatness surpass all the tempestuous forces so vividly displayed; even as the glory of Heaven surpasseth the splendour of earth. There is more power in the smallest thought of God or Good than there can ever be in the whole wide universe we see; even were all the various forces of that universe to be miraculously joined for a single purpose.

RESPITE

Through well-kept arbours fruitlessly I stray'd
In quest of respite from the causeless woes
That throng the weary spirit, and invade
The mind too seldom dreamless with repose.

Not neat-hedg'd path, nor garden's radiant grace,
Nor crystal fountain playing o'er the green,
Could cheer my heart, or from my soul efface
The tragedy of things that might have been.

The orchard boughs, bedeck'd with flow'rs of spring,
The verdant lawns, with skilful labour shorn,
To me no joy nor grateful thrill could bring;
In tears I came, and linger'd but to mourn.

One day, in idleness, my footsteps found
    The weed-chok'd slope that leads to sylvan deeps
Where leafy carpets clothe th' untrodden ground,
    And Nature, unadorn'd, her palace keeps.

'Twas there, in regions to mankind unknown,
    Where swamp and brake benignant spirits hide,
I stood at last, with Nature's God alone,
    And gain'd the respite that the world deny'd.

—H. P. LOVECRAFT

BY THE WATERS OF THE BROOK

Where waters slip like liquid lightning over polish'd stones,
Swift darting, glinting, flashing—shooting back the golden rays
Of dazzling sun; where one can hear the deep-voic'd undertones
Of diapason, and the overtones of crystal lays
Which sing through wooded canyon halls: there, free from toil and care,
In sweet abandon, loves my soul with Nature to commune;
For there abide the harmonies of peace, and all the rare
Enchantments and repose of life's sweet dream-imposing rune.

And by the waters of the crystal brook, which tumbling surge
Adown their stony bed, there comes to me the rhythmic swing
Of plashing sea like far-off chimes of silver bells; the urge
Of rolling tide and waves; the golden-russet glistening
Of ocean's wide expanse; the joyous shout of Wonder's call,
And all the charm of pent-up witcheries which so abound
In stream and sea, in fair cascades, and in the waterfall,
Which fashion symphonies supreme from riotings of sound.

'Tis there (O wondrous truth) as upward looks my eager ken
To search the rugged face of tow'ring crags, to scan the high
Encircling mountains, great and staunch—my soul feels glad that men
Nor cross my path, nor throw discordant thoughts into the sky

Of my content. My life is sweet, and peaceful are my days,
As hour by hour I sit within God's temple-close which He
Hath built for those who worship Him through Nature's songful praise,
And find themselves with Him in rapt accord and harmony.

'Tis there I strike from off my weary soul the binding thongs
Which so enthrall the freedom of life's joyous course; and there
In joy I quaff the chalice sweet of Nature's gladsome songs
Which pulse and throb like life upon the unpolluted air;
'Tis there I feel no more like bent and shackled slave, no more
Like one fast bound, and sold to do a task for shining pelf,
But like a free, upstanding soul which may in peace adore
The God supreme of all—the kindred to my highest self.

—EUGENE B. KUNTZ, D. D.

THE POOL

Above my head a leaf-lock'd sky,
A brown bowl set beneath my feet;
About my face pale ferns grow high,
And over all is silence sweet.

But Oh! sometimes in dreams I hear
A whisper, then a torrent's roar;
The shriek of wind, the belch of fear,
That I have known somewhere before!

—WINIFRED VIRGINIA JORDAN

IN THE EDITOR'S STUDY

The Proposed Authors' Union

It has been more than once remarked, that there is an intangible bond of kinship betwixt the highest and the humblest elements of the community. Whilst the bourgeois complacently busy themselves with their commonplace, respectable, and unimaginative careers of money-grabbing, the artist and the aristocrat join forces with the ploughman and the peasant in an involuntary mental wave of reaction against the monotony of materialism.

Never has this kinship been more plainly exhibited than in the present movement among a certain class of American professional authors to band themselves together in an honest workingman's union, and to affiliate with that peerless palladium of industrial independence—the well-known and far famed American Federation of Labour. That the professions of the average modern author and the day-labourer are remarkably alike in intellectual requirements, "The Conservative" has long been convinced. Both types show a certain rough vigour of technique which contrasts very strikingly with the polish of more formal times, and both seem equally pervaded with that spirit of progress and enlightenment which manifests itself in destructiveness. The modern author destroys the English language, whilst the modern strike-loving labourer destroys public and private property.

Nor can the ambitious author afford to despise the prodigious power to be gained by entrance into the ranks of organised labour. Since our obliging executive Mr. Wilson has established the precedent of national surrender at the least crook of Labour's gnarled finger, it may be justly assumed that the Writers' Brotherhood, as the most voluble and volatile of all the various bodies of workmen, will have complete power over all departments of the government; at least, until March 4, 1917. From this immeasurable height, our professional scribblers may brandish the quill of authority over a submissive Congress, and extort by due process of law every conceivable sort of advantage over the publishing fraternity, as well as over their less enterprising fellows—the non-union writers. It is barely possible that a strike of authors might be slightly less effective as a threat, than a strike of railway men; but so fond is our present idealistic executive of the beauties of rhetoric, that he would without doubt do much for the cause of fine words.

The place of literary radicals and imagist "poets" in this Utopian scheme demands grave consideration. Since the trade union movement requires at least an elementary amount of intelligence in its adherents, and is applied mainly to SKILLED labour; these deserving iconoclasts of the Amy Lowell school would seem to be left, Othello-like, without an occupation. But a moment's reflection serves to dissolve the difficulty. Here, indeed, is ideal material for that vague and awe-inspiring industrial "Mano Nera" known as the "I. W. W."! The benefits of such a coalition of "vers-libristes" and anarchists are patent to all. Since, save for its law and window breaking, the I. W. W. is in a condition of perpetual idleness, its leaders being generally out on strike, or out on bail; its imagistical recruits would naturally be constrained to follow the general example, inaugurating amongst themselves a sympathetic "walkout", and thereby delivering the public ear and the editorial waste basket from the annoyance of their effusions.

It is quite probable that the Brotherhood of Simplified Spellers would have to be created separately from both the American Federation of Labour and the I. W. W. Certain members of these learned societies, including expert hod-carriers and pick and shovel engineers, find difficulty enough with our language as now written, and could not possibly tolerate the presence of those reformers who are adding variability to its other faults.

The burning question of contemporary literature apparently concerns the eight-hour day for historians and the minimum wage for sonneteers. These things, and countless others which fret the artistic brain, could easily be solved by unionism. For instance; shall poets be paid by the hour or by the line? The one system discriminates unjustly against such careful workmen as Tom Gray, who consumed seven years on a job only 128 lines long, called "An Elegy Written In A Country Churchyard"; whilst the other system is too partial to speedy labourers like Sam T. Coleridge and Bob Southey, who, working together, built the poetic drama of "The Fall of Robespierre" between seven o'clock of an evening and the next noon. Also, pay by the line is unfair to writers of Alexandrines like Mike Drayton, while it unduly favours tetrameter bards like Sam Butler and Walt Scott, and leaves a bitter dispute to be settled amongst the balladmongers; who sometimes reckon their verses by long lines of fourteen syllables each, and at other times double the number of lines, the long heptameters being split up into alternate lines of eight and six syllables, respectively.

Amateur journalism, because of its free avenues of expression, would doubtless be suppressed as a hotbed of "scabs" by the Gomperses and Giovanittis of organised literature. Since it is the prevailing notion of trade unionism that no man has the right to labour without supporting a union and assuming the insignia of industrial blackmail, it may easily be deduced that literary unionism would utterly forbid all thought or expression by outsiders; and that it would, if necessary, resort to violence in cases of stubborn authorship by United members. Whether this violence would consist of stoning or of satire, is as yet uncertain.

A rather perplexing aspect of the case is afforded by the classic authors. These writers, having lived before the dawn of the New Slavery, are all necessarily non-union, wherefore a man who reads their work must logically be boycotted or placed upon the "unfair list" by the modern Knights of Grub-Street. The manner of establishing such a boycott would be interesting to determine; but the action will probably never be necessary, since but few up-to-date persons ever touch or peruse classic literature.

Looking ahead, as is the custom of all good radicals, the student may discern an age in which the whole domain of art; literary, pictorial, sculptural, architectural, and musical; will be placed upon a strictly union basis. Indeed, the modern Huns are already proving their efficient progressiveness by destroying the offensively beautiful non-union architecture of mediaeval religion in Belgium and northern France. "Down with the cathedrals, Comrade von Teufel" cries Bill Hohenzollern, head of the Berlin Butchers' Local No. 1914, "for they bear not the union label"!

Concerning trade unionism among authors as a whole, "The Conservative" will not venture here to render an opinion. Be it sufficient for him to say, that it would at least interest him to behold a new folly in a field whose potentialities of fatuity he had thought already exhausted.

Revolutionary Mythology

Events in our little sphere of amateurdom sometimes coincide remarkably with those of the world outside. The announcement in United circles of Mr. Henry Clapham McGavack's forthcoming essay on "Preliminaries of the American Revolution", wherein some hoary Yankee myths will be dissected, comes almost simultaneously with the storm of resentment awaked among professional American patriots by the lamentable faux pas of Prof. Wilson's pacifistical Secretary of War; who asserted in a campaign speech on October 16, that the Mexican banditti of today are comparable to the American revolutionists of Gen. Washington's army.

Secretary Baker has undoubtedly perpetrated another characteristically Wilsonian blunder in drawing a parallel between the pure-blooded Anglo-Saxon rebels of 1775, and the herd of half-breed swine, bent only on plunder, who are grunting, shooting, cavorting, and misbehaving generally below our southern border; but the loud denunciation comes rather from the truth he has let slip, than from the erroneous inferences he has drawn.

The American Revolution has created a more marvellous fund of genuine legendary lore than any other event in modern history. Not only to the proletariat, but to the bulk of our intelligent countrymen, the colonists who caused the withdrawal of America from the British Empire stand forth as heroes unsullied; as veritable Galahads, Bayards, and Sidneys. It is soberly believed by grown men, that the defiers of George III were a host of terrestrial Seraphim, the like of whom have never been known before or since. Willingly enough do we confess weaknesses on both sides of other intestine struggles through which our race has passed. In reflecting upon the Civil Wars which culminated in Cromwell's usurpation, we all acknowledge on the one hand that King Charles I was weak, that his promises were not inviolable, and that many of his adherents were luxurious and dissipated men; and on the other hand that the rebels were hasty, cruel, coarse, hypocritical, and animated by many absurdly false notions. Neither Charles nor Cromwell is to the descendants of his followers a supernal being "sans peur et sans reproche." But in mentioning the Continental army of 1775-1783, the average American assumes an unconscious accent of prayer, and damns any possible blasphemer with the true fervour of the fanatic. That the band of American colonists who seceded from the authority of Great Britain in 1775 contained at least several human beings, is well proven by careful students. That these beings possessed their full share of what we call "human nature", is likewise not unknown. Which compels "The Conservative" to smile a trifle at the legends of Revolutionary Gods and

Heroes preserved by each Yankee fireside, and transmitted both orally and verbally to each succeeding generation.

The American Revolution arose from a fatal misunderstanding between the Englishmen at home and those upon this continent. Neither side can claim the exclusive sanction of Heaven, nor must either side be blackened with the imputation of infamy. Saxon fought Saxon as men always fight men. The record of each army is as clean, or as soiled, as that of any other body of embattled human creatures who contend under the best traditions of civilised warfare. That a certain amount of looting, burning, and other irregularities existed on both sides, is no cause for surprise or indignation in the mind of the student or historian, for these things are inseparable from armed conflict of any sort, though training may modify them. Even the sainted Crusaders of old were less Christian toward the Saracens than we would like to imagine.

If the time has come when Revolutionary mythology may be placed in honoured banishment beside the similar lore of infant Rome; if men may at last be suffered openly to speak the truth about those brave Britons and Colonials of yesterday, it is to be hoped that justice may be done that most maligned class in all America—the loyalists, or "Tories". In the year 1775 this country was a legitimate part of the British domain, under the rightful authority of the King and his Parliament. The rebellious decision of a majority of the people can certainly form no ground for complaint against those Americans who felt that their duty lay with the existing government, and who upheld their Sovereign's rule with valour and distinction. That selfish interest dwelt beneath the acts of the "Tories" is often asserted, and may in some instances be true; but it is only the most crass ignorance or most malicious prejudice which can thus defame the multitude of patriotic American Royalists who willingly suffered or died in the service of the third George.

The Symphonic Ideal

Just a year ago "The Conservative" had occasion to refer to his contemporary, "The Symphony", whose discontinuance last July is a matter of such keen regret amongst United members. Though never formally affiliated with the Association, it was widely known in amateur journalism as an exponent of the acquisition of happiness through conscientious service to humanity. That so benignant a journal should lack the support necessary for continuance, is a circumstance reflecting unfavourably upon the mental temper of our age. We live in the midst of a new and outspoken cynicism; the result of declining orthodoxy on the part of the religious, and of aimless iconoclasm on the part of the philosophical. The happiness once acknowledged in our minor joys and moments of respite from the burden of life, is now laughed at and despised as a mere narcotic to the intelligence; and we are bidden to dismiss as unreal those simple and honest delights which alone make human existence endurable. If aught but the severe satisfaction of perfect intellectual, artistic, aesthetic, and moral beauty chance to please us, we are straightway damned as superficial, and censured for our childish triviality of taste.

There recently appeared before the public a rather unsophisticated volume entitled "Pollyanna", which preached a sweetly artificial doctrine of converting ills into blessings by the contemplation of possible calamities still more direful. After a period of enthusiastic laudation from the "jeune fille" type of admirer, poor "Pollyanna" became the target of every penny-a-line hack reviewer and little-wit in Grub-Street. They loftily demonstrated that the easing of melancholy by force of imagination is a vastly unscientific thing. Impossible, they vowed! Or, even if possible, it ought not to be; since 'tis a frightfully callow sort of mental regimen, quite unworthy of the mature mind! They all swore 'tis an affront to the eternal verities to be able to stop thinking of the world's evil and to gather a little joy from that idyllic goodness and virtue of which the world undoubtedly possesses, or seems to possess, a little. The "New York Tribune", in fact, deemed the inoffensive "Pollyanna" sufficiently culpable to merit a sneering editorial.

So runs the worldly-wise current of twentieth-century life! Your modern philosopher had rather be mature and miserable, than child-like and contented; and he deems you a monstrous imbecile if you can be happy at a time when he thinks you have not sufficient cause to be happy. Heaviness of spirit, he doth asseverate, is a sacred obligation of every thoughtful and responsible citizen. If you lack woes of your own, then go mourn at the wretched state of mankind in general!

"The Conservative" confesses to no little amusement at the wailing of these worshippers of morbid maturity. He even ventures to exhibit a leaning toward the side of immaturity; for is not maturity but the full-blown precursor of decay? It is dangerous to dabble in realities, and if more of us were able to retain the happy illusions of our infancy, those illusions would be so much nearer truth. Can any of our apostles of sophistication define what they mean by real happiness? Is it not more likely that all happiness is unreal; a golden fabric woven by fairies from the moonbeams of yesterday, and visible, like the Milky Way, only when more garish and conspicuous things are banished from the sight? A moment of retrospection, a snatch of song, a cadence of rhythm, a glance at the blue empyrean, the playing of the sun with the leaves of green trees, a chance act of benevolence—all these things sometimes bring what we uncultured barbarians are pleased to call happiness. Must we be utterly condemned if such happiness be found to have no cause save in physiological reactions or psychological stimuli? It is certainly grateful surcease from the pain of living, and what more could we desire? Is not fragrance fragrance, whether it come from the woodland violet or the stately cedar? If these simple pleasures be only drugs to help us forget reality, then let us accept the oblivion they offer. Nature designed them to soothe the roughnesses of our existence, and we should accept the gift with gratitude, rather than reject it with scorn. On the pleasures of the fancy rests all the mighty framework of art, poesy, and song. Stark, mature reality leads to the suicide's vault.

"The Conservative" has more than once been rather severely taken to task for his love of the idyllic happiness of the unreal. His pastoral verses have been scorned as archaic nonsense, whilst his whole literary style was condemned a year ago by a learned Jew, who with Semitic shrewdness declared that these pages, with their reverence for the storied past, savour of the "play world". But "The Conservative" is not unduly disturbed. He will linger on in his "play world", delighting in the pleasures of the imagination, calling up the shades of his beloved eighteenth century at will, and being as childish as he chooses, till second childhood itself overtake him. He may grow grey with years, but he will not accept dull "maturity", save when some pacifist, Anglophobe or simplified speller shall provoke him too far, and compel an occasional excursion into the bleak regions of unimaginative actuality! We are all much too serious, and too little disposed to promote the comfort of society. One refreshing zephyr of naturalness, whether in the primer-like and humour-lacking form of a "Pollyanna" or in the subtler shape of a "Symphony", is to our weary spirits worth an hundred laboured essays on the art of correct thinking or the science of being wisely miserable. Wherefore, though Reason may goad us on in our sterner search for Truth, let us not condemn the happiness which blooms by the roadside, nor cast aside unthinkingly the protecting cheerfulness of the Symphonic Ideal.

AMONG THE AMATEURS

Mr. John Russell of Florida, whose satirical and other verses have formed such a piquant feature of amateur letters, has recently accepted a position with the "Tampa Breeze". He will be in complete charge of the advertising department, besides having duties of an editorial nature. Mr. Russell will be pleased to receive literary contributions from the more experienced amateurs, which he will accept for publication in his paper.

"The Conservative" has not infrequently pondered in perplexity over the persistent use of the expletive "do", "does", or "did" by various amateur bards. Were these versifiers professed disciples of Dryden and his predecessors, there would be less cause for wonderment, but in view of their largely modern tendencies it appears highly peculiar that they should employ an archaic device censured and ridiculed ever since the reign of Queen Anne. No stigma of poetical puerility or lax scholarship is so patent as a line wherein we are informed that the poet "does sigh" because his Phillis or Chloe "did cast" him aside. Exceptions to this rule of abstinence may be made in certain cases of imitative archaism, but for the average amateur writer, total abstinence is the safer course.

The attitude toward our Association recently expressed by members of the Pedroni "United" is very regrettable. These worthy amateurs see fit threateningly to demand that we abandon our name in favour of their society, which they arbitrarily assume to be legally entitled to the designation "United". Whatever may be the advantages offered us by a more comprehensive title, we are certainly not to be frightened into a change by those who have at least no more right to the name than we.

In the Appleton, Wis., "Evening Crescent" for October 13 appears a highly interesting account of Maurice W. Moe's speech before the Northeastern Teachers' Convention, wherein our noted Private Critic treats of the uses of the phonograph in the teaching of English. Mr. Moe has opened up a wonderful field by his adaptation of the classics, beautifully rendered by the highest talent, to the daily routine of the class room. Incidentally, it will prove a surprise to many persons to learn that such classics as Milton's "Comus", passages from Shakespeare, and snatches from the later poets, have been made available to the public in the most artistic oral form through the refinement of mechanical science.

Though dread of triteness usually deters "The Conservative" from conventional comment on "exchanges", he cannot but remark the great and sustained merit of Mr. W. Paul Cook's new publication, "The Vagrant", whose September issue has just reached this office. Mr. Cook's editorials are of a closely personal character, and recall many incidents of interest to members of the preceding amateur journalistic generation. Though "The Vagrant" bears no official connexion with this Association, we may hope that it may reach most of our members; since it contains a phenomenally picturesque and searching sketch of a certain aspect of rural society from the pen of no less a philosopher than Pres. Paul J. Campbell.

The "Schuylerville (N.Y.) Standard" for October 12 contains an admirably interesting essay on the Mohawk Trail by our gifted and veneral poet and essayist, Mr. J. E. Hoag of Greenwich. More of Mr. Hoag's work may shortly be expected in "The United Amateur" in the form of a poem treating of several natural and historical aspects of his native state.

The United's 1916-1917 Year Book, to be issued by a committee of which "The Conservative" is chairman, will contain a rather unusual feature, in the form of a biographical dictionary or "Who's Who" of the more prominent members of the Association. The idea is due to the fertile brain of Pres. Campbell, and will, it is hoped, serve as a means of creating a closer tie amongst our gifted litterateurs. Members are hereby invited to send biographical notes to this office, for inclusion in the forthcoming annual.

THE UNKNOWN

A seething sky—
  A mottled moon—
Waves surging high—
  Storm's raving rune:

Wild clouds a-reel—
  Wild sounds a-shout—
Black vapours steal
  In ghastly rout.

Through rift is shot
  The moon's wan grace—
But God! That blot
  Upon its face!

—ELIZABETH BERKELEY

INSPIRATION

One fragrant morn, when Spring was young,

I roam'd the glen in eager quest,
Hoping with careful eye among
The grass to find the violet's nest;
But not a leaf or bud seem'd sprung
Up from the couch of wintry rest.
And yet, when all my greedy search was o'er,
By chance I spy'd the flow'r I miss'd before!

One night, within my chamber pent,
I strove my fancies to enchain
In breathing numbers, and to vent
Some portion of my bliss and pain;
But strife of soul my musings rent—
The sluggish pencil mov'd in vain:
Yet out upon the mead, the starlight brought
The long-wish'd song, unbidden and unsought!

—LEWIS THEOBALD, JUN.

The Conservative

Edited by H. P. Lovecraft in the Interests of the United Amateur Press Association. Published at 598 Angell St., Providence, R. I., U. S. A.

The Conservative, Vol. II, No. IV

Providence, R. I., January, 1917

Edited by H. P. Lovecraft

THE VAGRANT

A Wind walk'd in the West
    At edge of night,
While from a white star's crest
    It elbow'd light.

It to a garden sprang
    And gaily blew
Warm kisses, while it sang
    And filch'd the dew.

It tapp'd, with pretty blow,
    On nest-noos'd tree,
Then rapp'd, first swift, then slow
    And tenderly.

It leapt to black-brow'd hill;
    Tweak'd glow-worm's ear,
So damp and small and chill,
    With elfin leer!

It rac'd, on dancing feet,
    Into a dell
Where dreams creep in to meet
    And cast their spell;

And there, with merry cry
    And noisy shout,
It fleck'd them hasting by
    And chas'd them out!

Then on and on, with turn
    And lisping trill,
It came to golden fern
    Beside a rill.

It whisper'd low and long,
    On toes a-sway,
Then burst into a song
    And sped away.

And fast and far it went,
    For when the Dawn
Her soft-shod graylings sent—
    The Wind had gone!

—WINIFRED VIRGINIA JORDAN

THE UNBREAKABLE LINK

By Arthur W. Ashby

As we passed under the moss-covered lych-gate the ancient yew threw over us both its gloom and its serenity. They were welcome, for on the white road along which we came the blazing June sun bore down from above, and a stifling cloud of dust rose from below. Having passed the gateway we instinctively left the gravel path for the sake of feeling the spring of turf beneath our feet. Our ways parted; she was going to her father's grave, taking the first bunch of the season's white roses. I did not follow, for part of her life lies there, and I knew she would rather commune with it alone.

As I walked on, something impelled me toward the stone portal of the Church which, in the fierce light, stood placid and grey as it might in a winter fog. Time and weather have softened its lines, but only the vandal hands of men have greatly modified its appearance since the Normans laid their last stone. As I passed inside the air was chilly, it seemed almost freezing, and I felt my bones aching. In the middle of the centre aisle some new pews had recently been installed, so I went to try them; remembering the hours I had spent as a schoolboy in their predecessors of the high seat and the straight back. Sitting down, I noticed a ray of light playing hide and seek among the stanchions of the roof. It came from a Saxon window between the arches, outside which the Normans had extended the structure. And under that window was the great stone gargoyle that I so much dreaded as a boy. It is a head as of a horse, but with fierce eyes and teeth. Large, crude, and striking, it is typically Saxon.

My head dropped over the back of the pew. Strangely, weirdly, I heard the tramp of feet. Not loud, but distinctly regular, accompanied by the soft rustle and crunch of straw. A maiden with light, flowing hair came through the door, and by her side was the heavy, squat figure of a man clad in hodden-gray; behind them was a retinue of rickety followers. They took their seats on a flat bench before the altar steps. Shuffling peasants came in and scattered themselves about the building, and a man came to the altar. The pulpit corner had become a blank and the picture of the Lamb was obliterated. The man upon the steps began to speak in thick guttural tones, and the words were indistinct, but the audience obeyed them. They rose and sat, and rose again; presently there was a sound of a low, soft chant of voices unaccompanied by music, and then I saw the lady's page pick up her train as she stepped from the floor rushes on to a clay path outside. All was quiet.

Then I heard the sound of metal, also musical voices, more striking than those I had heard before. There were men chipping large blocks of white stone; these were also dressed in gray, their long flowing mantles girdled with stout grass ropes. Amongst them was a man dressed in colours, with golden spurs, and in the background a beautiful white arch, as yet uncompleted. Silence!........And then thought came again—I had seen the Knights of St. John, and the cunning monks and the white stone they imported from Normandy to adorn their chancel.

Years passed by; and when voices broke the silence once more, they were clear and familiar. All around was hurry of feet and clank of metal.

Horses neighed and champed outside, and through the general sound came whispers of "Essex" and "Rupert", "Parliament" and "Independent". I looked for the beautiful marble effigy left by the Knights of Jerusalem. It still remained intact. No! they were not Ironsides. They were ordinary Englishmen, but just a little excited. Their clamour lasted long, and when it subsided strange booms sounded in the distance. "Rupert" was in action.

The next scene was different. Three men—the parish overseers—sat by a large chest with a book before them. There was the chink of coin; men, boys, and women passed in and out. The last to go was a decrepit old grandmother, who would need to be carried the next time she came to church, probably in a pauper's coffin. The lid of the chest went down with a bang, and the door closed.

It soon opened again. A crowd of men rushed to the bellropes. The bells clamoured and clanged, and as the groaning men stretched down the ropes so that the tongues of the bells might speak again, there came in quick gasps, "Waterloo", "Wellington".

I saw and heard no more. Something gently brushed my lips. My eyes opened and they were met by two bright dancing lights. All illusions were dispelled by a sharp tremor that ran through my body. It was the Universal, the Unchangeable! The unbreakable link with the past! We walked out together, and the door gently closed behind me and my dream.

FUTURIST ART

The skill'd Apelles, by his Prince decreed
To paint with living line the panting steed,
Employ'd in vain each trick and study'd grace,
The likeness of the charger's foam to trace.
At length, in pique, his dripping brush he flung
Against the canvas horse before him hung—
When lo! by chance there spatter'd o'er each part
The painted lather that defy'd his art!
Thus the wild cubists of a later age
With freakish toil their fancies seek to cage,

Though their poor daubings all would nobler be
Should they splash paint as aimlessly as he!

—H. P. LOVECRAFT

IN THE EDITOR'S STUDY

The Vers Libre Epidemic

The alarming prevalence in contemporary periodicals of "poetry" without shape, wit, or artistic beauty, has caused no little alarm amongst the true friends of verse, and has given rise to the apprehension that the Aonian art has entered upon a definite phase of decadence. It is the belief of THE CONSERVATIVE, however, that the situation is more complex and less basically menacing than it appears from superficial indications.

It must be remembered that despite the kinship between human fancy and its mode of expression, there is a sharp distinction betwixt radicalism of thought and ideals, and mere radicalism of form; and that while the most notorious specimens of free verse represent complete chaos both of sense and of structure, the majority of that which gains admission to reputable magazines is decadent only in technique. The poetical fraternity have a new plaything, and all must needs have their hour of sport with it; but the better sort of bards possess too much inherent good taste and sanity to wander too far afield. They will soon be writing real verse by accident, in spite of themselves, for they cannot defeat the natural laws of rhythm in poetical expression. Even now, the work of these poets is replete with occasional reactions to normal rhyme and rational metre. Our fellow-amateur Mrs. Renshaw, a superlatively good poet despite radical theories, has recently composed a piece of apparent vers libre which is really a well-defined iambic composition with variation in the length of the lines. The innate poet has unwittingly triumphed over the radical theorist! We may, then, safely trust to time to bring the really gifted experimenters within the fold again.

The second or wholly erratic school of free poets is that represented by Amy Lowell at her worst; a motley horde of hysterical and half-witted rhapsodists whose basic principle is the recording of their momentary moods and psychopathic phenomena in whatever amorphous and meaningless phrases may come to their tongues or pens at the moment of inspirational (or epileptic) seizure. These pitiful creatures are naturally subdivided into various types and schools, each professing certain "artistic" principles based on the analogy of poetic thought to other aesthetic sources such as form, sound, motion, and colour; but they are fundamentally similar in their utter want of a sense of proportion and of proportionate values. Their complete rejection of the intellectual (an element which they cannot possess to any great extent) is their undoing. Each writes down the sounds or symbols of sounds which drift through his head without the slightest care or knowledge that they may be understood by any other head. The type of impression they receive and record is abnormal, and cannot be transmitted to persons of normal psychology; wherefore there is no true art or even the rudiments of artistic impulse in their effusions. These radicals are animated by mental or emotional processes other than poetic. They are not in any sense poets, and their work, being wholly alien to poetry, cannot be cited as an indication of poetical decadence. It is rather a type of intellectual and aesthetic decadence of which vers libre is only one manifestation. It is the decadence which produces "futurist" music and "cubist" painting and sculpture.

If concrete examples of the two sorts of unmetrical verse—the really poetical and the distinctly abnormal—be needed to illustrate their difference, the reader may compare Richard Aldington's "Inarticulate Grief" (THE POETRY REVIEW, August, 1916) with the following bit of sober nonsense, written by one of the so-called "Spectrists" without any idea of humour, but found by THE CONSERVATIVE in one of the whimsical paragraphs of a New York "colyum conductor"; where its complete ridiculousness and irrationality recommended it for citation. Mr. Aldington is a poet of genuine depth and feeling despite his awkward medium; the reader may judge of the following without aid of critic or commentator:

> Her soul was freckled
> Like the bald head
> Of a jaundiced Jewish banker.
> Her fair and featurous face Writhed like
> An Albino boa-constrictor.

She thought she resembled the Mona Lisa.
This demonstrates the futility of thinking.

And the futility of accepting the chronic free "poets" as serious factors in the literary situation today!

Amateur Standards

Amateur journalism has always been a battle-ground betwixt those who, cognizant of its better possibilities, wish to improve their literary skill; and those who, viewing it merely as a field of amusement to which they can obtain easy access, wish to indulge in mock-politics, pseudo-feuds, and cheap social frivolities. In 1886 this disparity of aims was sufficient to cause the better element to withdraw for a time, forming a short-lived "Literary Lyceum of America", but experience proved that the cause of unprofessional letters can best be furthered by combating its evils within the confines of the regularly organised press associations. Since 1914 the United has striven with varying success to occupy a materially higher plane in the world of culture and education; the campaign for betterment being led at different times by Mr. Moe and Mrs. Renshaw, and now by Pres. Paul J. Campbell. But there has arisen in opposition to the progressive policies of these leaders a reactionary movement of such blatant vulgarity and puerile crudeness, that THE CONSERVATIVE feels impelled to protest at the display of impotent malice and infantile bitterness shown by some of the treacherous anti-administration elements. Yellow journals have spread broadcast a silly series of attacks and aspersions on our best officials, setting by their glaringly plebeian atmosphere a dangerously bad example for the many youths whose cultural and literary improvement is the prime object of the Association. One of these peace-disturbers has wailed against the improvement of THE UNITED AMATEUR, declaring (despite the fact that it contained all but one of this year's laureate-winning pieces) that it has become a mere purveyor of "literary twaddle"; whilst another congenital "heckler" has recently launched a tirade of inexcusable commonness against President Campbell as a result of some disclosures in the news notes of the official organ. What President Campbell did was to expose some detestable trickery in the handling of proxy ballots last summer, and nothing save guilty resentment at this exposure could prompt this "heckler" to raise a veritable teapot tempest at Mr. Campbell's pleasantry regarding a former amateur; a pleasantry against which he rants with Pharisaical fervour. It is not the desire of THE CONSERVATIVE to enter the field of adolescent bickering, but he does deem it necessary and proper to warn the membership of the United against the sly malevolence, ambiguous statements, and apocryphal anecdotes whereby a fraction of malcontents is seeking to undermine confidence in the present administration; an administration whose leader has a longer and more brilliant record of amateur achievement than any other active member of the United Amateur Press Association.

WHEN NEW-YEAR COMES

When New-Year comes into your home
And smiles upon you with its cheer,
Turn then your back upon the gloam
Of all that in the past was drear.
Reach out your hand and grasp the new,
And let the old go as it will,
And drink Life's cup of sweeter brew—
Forget the draught that tasted ill!

Draw to your heart the tendrils fair
Of Friendship, such as never dies;
And give to others share for share
Of Love that charms and glorifies.
Tears may be yours, and anguish, too,
And hours of darkness and of pain,
But God will give, dear friend, to you,
The sunshine after sorrow's rain!

—EUGENE B. KUNTZ, D.D.

A REQUEST

THE CONSERVATIVE, as Chairman of the United's Year-Book Committee, will deem it a favour of great magnitude if every recipient of this paper will send him, as soon as possible, a set of autobiographical notes for use in the forthcoming annual. A complete biographical dictionary of amateurs is planned as a feature of that publication. The following specimen may serve as a guide to what is desired:

647c CAMPBELL, PAUL J., Farmer, Printer, Journalist. Born Georgetown, Ill., Nov. 8, 1884. Public School Education. Joined June, 1902, recommended by Ira E. Seymour. Published IDEAL POLITICIAN, SCOTTISH HIGHLANDER, PRAIRIE STATE JOURNAL, ILLINOIAN, SCOTCHMAN, and INVICTUS. Contributed 59 articles to the amateur press in 1906, his most active year. Elected Director in 1908, Treasurer in 1915, President in 1916. Interested in Literature, Religion, History, Philosophy, and Free Thought.

It is particularly desirable that each member convey some idea of his literary tastes. Those who have already sent biographical matter, either to THE CONSERVATIVE or to THE LOOKING GLASS, need not send further matter unless they wish to do so in order to include points previously omitted. The granting of this request by every reader will help to make the Year-Book the most interesting and valuable number yet issued by the United. THE CONSERVATIVE thanks the membership in advance.

THE CONSERVATIVE

Edited by H. P. Lovecraft under the Auspices of
the United Amateur Press Association. Published at
598 Angell St., Providence, R. I., U. S. A.

The Conservative, Vol. III, No. I

Providence, R. I., July, 1917

Edited by H. P. Lovecraft

IN VITA ELYSIUM

By Ira A. Cole

Mortal, why dream'st thou of the after-while,
And gods who wait thy death ere they may smile?
Why build thy heaven in some future time,
On other shores and in another clime?
Why mourn'st thou that the world is all awry,
And man alone must live that he may die?
Canst nothing see in all this beauteous land
So fair as that thou buildest with thy hand?
Canst see no heaven or no gracious God
In these fair hills or on this em'rald sod?
Canst feel no pulsing in this happy life
To tell thee that the world with love is rife?
Canst feel no rapture in the springtime's breath
So sweet as that thou dreamest after death;
Or see no beauty in the summer sky
To woo thee back to earth when thou shalt die?
Canst hear no music in October's rills
So soft as that thy fancy's heaven fills;
And canst thou never quite contented be
Save roaming worlds unknown to all save thee?
O Man! vain egotist! why search so long
For note to rival Nature's wondrous song?

Behold! thou mockest God, thou puny wight,
To find no favour in so grand a sight.
Dost think, thou sluggard, aught thy mind might build
Could rival this one world that God hath will'd;
Dost think thy craven intellect so vast
Could hold this earthly wonder still and last,
Ignoring yet that silent ether space
That night's bright multitudes in splendour grace;
Or those far realms beyond the faintest star
Where still God's wonders in their beauty are?
Go hide thyself alone, ungrateful wretch,
Midst those vast dunes where Afric's deserts stretch,
Or lose thyself in Arctic's icy waste,
If thou the mystery of life wouldst taste!
Go climb the mountain's height, or ride the sea,
Or learn life's vibrant song from forest tree;
Go hide thine arrogance 'neath tundras' tide,
And hear the notes the sedgy stringlets guide;
Or seek those inland seas of surging green
Where far the restless trades of fall careen.
Go! Go! vain man, to those unbounded fanes
Where God's one proven priest—fair Nature—reigns:
'Tis there, releas'd, (else blind and deaf thou art)
The chains that bind thy soul from thee will start—
Uplifted, glad, thy spirit then shall know
That life is light, and heaven's here below!

THE GENESIS OF THE REVOLUTIONARY WAR

By Henry Clapham McGavack

EDITOR'S NOTE: When Arthur James Balfour, Foreign Secretary and former Prime Minister of the British Empire, placed a wreath in tribute upon the sepulchre of George Washington, he paved the way toward an Anglo-Saxon unity of aims, ideals, and sympathies which will forever redound to the credit of this age. By his act, Great Britain expresses her fundamental faith in the institutions and principles of her American kindred, and removes the subtle barriers which have darkened both branches of the English race since the revolt of the Colonies one hundred and forty-one years ago. It is fitting that an American, speaking from sound knowledge and without prejudice, should meet the Mother Country half way in this mutual recognition of ideals, and seek to remove some of the mistaken Anglophobic notions which false history and biased text-books have implanted in the American mind. We should behold our valiant ally and ancestral nation as she is, not as we have learned to view her through the green spectacles of transmitted feuds and hereditary hatreds. The author of the following article, a Virginian by birth and blood, has made a lifelong study of diplomacy and Anglo-American history, and is unusually well qualified to deal with the problem of international relations. His frank historical statements, while perhaps startling to the lay reader, should be of immense value in doing away with the senseless idea that England is at heart an oppressor. Side by side, the Old England and the New must stand as of yore against alien tyranny. As joint inheritors of the blood which crushed the pride of Philip II and the Invincible Armada, we, the Anglo-Saxons of the world, again face armed despotism fearless and united.

H. P. L.

The erroneous impression of the Revolutionary War prevailing in America today is due to two causes; ignorance of Colonial history, and an absolute lack of knowledge regarding the political and commercial policy of 18th century England.

The Revolution was not, as is fondly imagined in these parts, the spontaneous outburst of a collected and united people against the misgovernment and tyranny of a diabolic power across the Atlantic; it was not fought with glorious patriotism, self-denial and valour by any great number of the colonists; it was not brought to a successful conclusion by any army or group of armies on American soil. It was, on the other hand, the outgrowth of sordidness and greed and pigheadedness and general incompetence all around; the major share of which attributes must be apportioned to the colonies.

The problem of colonial defence is the genesis of the Revolution. England chartered divers and sundry colonies from Massachusetts Bay to Virginia—and they were divers and sundry. Some were free commonwealths like Massachusetts, others fiefs of Lords Proprietors like Maryland, others Crown Colonies like Virginia. They had little in common except their allegiance to the King of Great Britain and Ireland. They were openly jealous of one another. They were always squabbling over boundaries, and endeavouring to knife each other commercially. In case of war England was in duty bound to protect them; her navy was the bulwark behind which they traded and bartered, quarrelled and bickered among themselves. In return they carried on all foreign trade with her or through her alone. This was the price of protection, and they paid it gladly, unquestioningly; for the economics of the eighteenth century were neither advanced nor scientific. For local defence they maintained, or pretended to maintain, militia; supported by taxes levied by authority of their own legislative assemblies.

The French and Indian War was fought, in America, for their security. Yet, such was their love of money and gain that they smuggled provisions to the French troops in Canada, and to the French ships in the West Indies, giving aid thus to the forces of the enemy when the English naval power had effectually barred to those forces help from France herself; so keeping alive a struggle which their own advantage demanded should be decided favourably at once. So far did greed take them, that the British army under Amherst lacked food because of their illegal and treasonable exportations to the enemy. Again, when called upon for their quota of men and supplies for the campaign, every colony held back; one fearing lest it do a little more a little sooner than the rest. The result was no men, no money, no transport, no defence save by the British Redcoat. Indians might burn and slay down to the very gates of Philadelphia itself, but the sacred principle that Pennsylvania could raise no more troops than New York might not be infringed upon.

In 1754 the British Government had called together the Albany Conference for the purpose of encouraging the Colonies to unite in matters of local defence. The conference came to naught because our revered ancestors could agree upon no plan of working together. So, in desperation, realising the terrible conditions along the frontiers due to Indian raids, the London Cabinet resolved to send British regulars to America for the purpose of checking inroads which the colonists seemed incapable of making any headway against.

The cost of this expedition, the English Government thought, could be very equitably and justly borne by the Americans themselves; for, in the first place, the people of the British Isles were undergoing exceedingly heavy taxation on account of previous wars, and in the second place, it did not appear that a prosperous community, such as America, would find an onerous burden in its own protection.

But the colonists thought very differently indeed—or rather, some of them did; upstarts and men on the make like Hancock and Adams, for instance. The result was the cry "No taxation without representation", and ultimately, the War of Independence.

Now the English were logically and legally right. In the first place, the colonies had demonstrated both their unwillingness and their inability to protect themselves. In the second place, England had made all preparations to render this protection herself. It certainly was only just that the Americans pay the material cost. So much for logic.

The legal aspect of the case is even stronger. The colonies, under the demagogic influence of men like Adams, declared that taxation was not repulsive to them; what they demanded was that they be represented at the source of taxation. They forgot, in the first instance, that they had been given an opportunity to form a union for defence at the Albany Conference and had neglected to avail themselves of it; and, in the second instance, they failed to recognise that the British Parliament, as inheritor of all the ancient prerogatives of the Crown, was through each and every charter granted, no matter in what form, to each and every colony the sovereign source of that colony's legal existence whose paramountcy had never been questioned nor denied. The fundamental basis of sovereignty is the power of taxation; hence to deny the right of the Parliament to levy taxes was to deny its sovereignty. Yet the colonies acknowledged the sovereign supremacy of the British Parliament, putting themselves thereby in an impossible position.

Moreover, the Parliament did not propose to levy internal taxes; customs duties formed the question at issue. Now, by all the precedents and all the charters and all the contemporary colonial policies, a mother country's control over the commerce of her satellites throughout the world was absolute and inviolable—and up till now the Americans had recognised the fact. Consequently, in attempting to levy duties at ports of ingress and egress on the Atlantic seaboard of the American Colonies, Great Britain was clearly within her rights; was only acting as any other colonial power of the time might have acted and did act; and was, moreover, levying these duties not for her own aggrandisement, but for the purpose of defending her colonies from their enemies.

Nevertheless the break came. It came because the colonies had possessed all of the benefits of separate existence without any of the responsibilities. The Empire had always protected them; they had never been called upon to defend the Empire except in a small, local way. When they were finally asked to share in imperial defence they balked. The commercial system of the age, entailing as it did colonial dependence upon the mother country, had made them myopic and selfish. Immersed in the petty details of provincial existence, they became blind to the vast expanse of the imperial life.

This commercial system, coupled with the pigheadedness of the eighteenth century political attitude and the stubborn colonial sordidness of spirit, sundered the Anglo-Saxon race.

SWEET FRAILTY

I should rather be
  A flow'r for a day
Than an age-old rock
  Grown harden'd and gray.

I'd rather be the tiniest flow'r
  That blinks in wonder at King Sun,
And shivers at rough North Wind's pow'r;
  That glows with hope, trusts Nature's heart,
And sweetly lives for **just one hour**,
  And then—is crush'd by careless feet!

Than be the mighty boulder grim
  That crowns some overhanging cliff
For ages long, pois'd on the brim,
  Defying storm and avalanche.
Untouch'd by dew or starlight dim,
  Then—falls to kill a caravan!

I should rather be
    A flow'r for a day
Than an age-old rock
    Grown harden'd and gray.

—MARY HENRIETTA LEHR.

IN THE EDITOR'S STUDY

A Remarkable Document

Friends of the Temperance cause, to whom the existence of the drink habit seems as inexplicable as it is lamentable and criminal, will take phenomenal interest in the article by Mr. Booth Tarkington entitled "Nipskillions", which appeared in THE AMERICAN MAGAZINE for January, and which was reprinted in THE NATIONAL ENQUIRER for April 12. This terse little essay, which takes its name from the slang word applied in certain circles to a man who has turned from drink to temperance through satiation, tells in remarkably vivid fashion of the precise sensations of the drinker, and of the damnably seductive false cheer of the cup which leads in so many cases to complete mental, moral and physical degradation. Denying the incurable addiction of the average drinker to his poison, the article throws an unusually grave responsibility upon the persistent tippler.

Mr. Tarkington, relating the true story of an artist friend who saved himself at the last moment from the clutches of alcoholism, makes a notable contribution to the temperance cause; not only through the authenticity of his account, but from the fact that he writes not as a moral or religious doctrinaire, but as a rational and discerning man of the world. He gives an infallible indication of the new temperance movement—a movement which has its foundation in common sense rather than abstract principle.

According to Mr. Tarkington, the prime incentive to drink is the desire for a greater degree of enjoyment and relaxation than is compatible with the normal mental and physical condition. In other words, human creatures long atavistically for the levity of an inferior state, and wish to throw off artificially the burden of dignity with which evolution from the simian ape has invested them. If this theory be universally true, then the drink problem is much more difficult of solution than as if it were merely an ingrained social custom. No one can deny that life in conventionally civilised communities is dull and monotonous to the point of loathsomeness; and if this basic ennui be so potent a factor in the desire for liquor, then we cannot expect to banish the evil till we have found some means of brightening the gloom which causes it. One of the greatest problems of the day, then, is a cure for the unutterable world-weariness which afflicts mankind; or if its complete cure be impossible, its alleviation. Not that the ordinary forces of temperance reform should be less active, but that we should be less Spartan and Puritan in our worship of duty at the expense of legitimate pleasure. It behooves the reformer to appear in a less forbidding guise, and to prefer grace to austerity in prosecuting his endeavours. Drink, we know, is abnormal; but if we are to banish this abnormality we must likewise banish the equal abnormality of excessive mental sabbatarianism. "Virtue itself offends," said an old writer, "when coupled with forbidding manners."

The United's Problem

In the April issue of THE WOODBEE, Mrs. Ida C. Haughton makes a much needed appeal to the members of our Association to preserve the amateur literary world from unmerited extinction. It may be that for some reason amateur journalism has lost its charm; and that our members, impressed with the difficulties of literary perfection, are turning to less exacting sources of diversion; but this THE CONSERVATIVE is loath to believe. Surely the benefits of amateurdom are as substantial as ever, and as worthy of enthusiastic support as they were in the proudest of the old Halcyon Days. A large number of amateurs will be unable to serve their country in active fashion during the coming period of trial, and how may they better spend the dark days of war than in the maintenance of an institution which cannot but alleviate in wholesome fashion the prevailing sombreness of the period? Let us write, and above all, PUBLISH. Publications alone can furnish the common bond of interest for our numerous and intellectually heterogeneous organisation.

The Conservative

Edited by H. P. Lovecraft under the Auspices of the United Amateur Press Association. Published at 598 Angell Street, Providence, R. I., U. S. A.

The Conservative, Vol. IV, No. 1

Providence, R. I., July, 1918

Edited by H. P. Lovecraft

LORD KITCHENER

By Wilfrid Kemble

He climb'd no lofty Pisgah, nor survey'd
    A land of milk and honey wide outspread,
    Where fervent warriors, stepping o'er the dead,
Would end their strife with victory long delay'd;
But he could view with pride one vast parade
    Of comrades arm'd, who, ne'er to warfare bred,
    Along each highway march'd with dauntless tread,
At Death's dark menace smiling undismay'd.

Not his in hallow'd ground to sleep outworn,
    His task erewhile to others' care resign'd.
        God took him almost from the soldier's tent
        With eye not dim and natural force unspent;
But o'er his unknown tomb none ever mourn
    Except the troubled sea and wailing wind.

THE SPIRIT OF SUMMER

By H. P. Lovecraft

Aerial Nymph, whose jocund sway
Can melt our vexing cares away,
Whose winsome train the valleys bless
With perfume, warmth, and loveliness;
From fulgent skies once more appear,
To spread thy annual gifts of cheer.
Let nimble Naiads cease their sport,
And gather wild-flow'rs for thy court,
While graceful Sylphs, admiring, lend
Their praises as thy feet descend.
How mild the zephyrs from afar
Fan with sweet breath thy gliding car;
How soft the Fauns of yonder grove,
Pleas'd with the sight, affirm their love!
Nature, rejoicing, hails thy reign,
And pleasure fills the grateful plain.
Now trip the agile hours in haste,
With new delights and comforts grac'd;
Though yesterday no bliss could give,
Today 'tis joyous just to live!
The bright'ning mind of genius glows
In warmer verse and livelier prose;
And o'er the dull terrestrial throng
Disports a breeze of Teian song.
The aureate sun, whose soothing rays
Pour languor through the noontide haze,
To each green bow'r a charm imparts,
And gilds them with enchanting arts.
Here may the pensive swain, at rest,
Behold, in robes of fancy drest,
The fays of air and sea and land,
Link'd in a sprightly saraband;
Old Pan, his brow with myrtles bound,
Young Satyrs, leaping o'er the ground,
Shy Oreads lur'd from distant hills

By melodies of reedy rills,
Ethereal Dryads from the wood,
And river-gods in festive mood,
All fir'd with Corybantian glee
To dance, Aerial Nymph, for thee!
Gay Goddess, may thy bounteous will
Diffuse more lasting treasures still;
Nor suffer these glad scenes alone
To form the province of thy throne;
'Tis thine in ev'ry heart to plant
Thy bliss, a true inhabitant,
That through far drearier days than thine,
The soul of summer still may shine!

THE DESPISED PASTORAL

By H. P. Lovecraft

Among the many and complex tendencies observable in modern poetry, or what answers for poetry in this age, is a decided but unjust scorn of the honest old pastoral, immortalised by Theocritus and Virgil, and revived in our own literature by Spenser.

Nor is this unfavourable attitude confined alone to the formal eclogue whose classical elements are so well described and exemplified by Mr. Pope. Whenever a versifier adorns his song with the pleasing and innocent imagery of this type of composition, or borrows its mild and sweet atmosphere, he is forthwith condemned as an irresponsible pedant and fossil by every little-wit critic in Grub-Street.

Modern bards, in their endeavour to display with seriousness and minute verisimilitude the inward operations of the human mind and emotions, have come to look down upon the simple description of ideal beauty, or the straightforward presentation of pleasing images for no other purpose than to delight the fancy. Such themes they deem trivial and artificial, and altogether unworthy of an art whose design they take to be the analysis and reproduction of Nature in all her moods and aspects.

But in this belief, the writer cannot but hold that our contemporaries are misjudging the true province and functions of poesy. It was no starched classicist, but the exceedingly unconventional Edgar Allan Poe, who roundly denounced the melancholy metaphysicians and maintained that true poetry has for its first object "pleasure, not truth," and "indefinite pleasure instead of definite pleasure." Mr. Poe, in another essay, defined poetry as "the rhythmical creation of beauty," intimating that its concern for the dull or ugly aspects of life is slight indeed. That the American bard and critic was fundamentally just in his deductions, seems well proved by a comparative survey of those poems of all ages which have lived, and those which have fallen into deserved obscurity.

The English pastoral, based upon the best models of antiquity, depicts engaging scenes of Arcadian simplicity, which not only transport the imagination through their intrinsic beauty, but recall to the scholarly mind the choicest remembrances of classical Greece and Rome. Though the combination of rural pursuits with polished sentiments and diction is patently artificial, the beauty is not a whit less; nor do the conventional names, phrases, and images detract in the least from the quaint agreeableness of the whole. The magic of this sort of verse is to any unprejudiced mind irresistible, and is capable of evoking a more deliciously placid and refreshing train of pictures in the imagination, than may be obtained from any more realistic species of composition. Every untainted fancy begets ideal visions of which the pastoral forms a legitimate and artistically necessary reflection.

It is not impossible that the intellectual upheaval attendant upon the present conflict will bring about a general simplification and rectification of taste, and an appreciation of the value of pure imaginary beauty in a world so full of actual misery, which may combine to restore the despised pastoral to its proper station.

ON SHORE

By Winifred Virginia Jordan

The trees are wailing,
And grim night—a grayling—

Swoops hawk-like down on
        The gale-gall'd day.

The sea, 'neath thunder
And wolf-winds' plunder,
On wreck-wound shore whacks
        The writhing spray.

And Oh, my soul's nearest,
My heart's own dearest,
Is out there tonight in
        A water-logg'd shell!

I can but be praying,
'Neath wind and sea's flaying,
And shut from my ears
        The Pollock's Rip bell!

CRITICISM OF AMATEUR JOURNALS

By Philip B. McDonald

Assistant Professor of Engineering English, University of Colorado

Someone has said that what the American people need is more and better critics. We are an optimistic, exuberant nation, interested more in quantity than in quality. Constructiveness appeals to us — getting ahead, progress, and quick results. Individuals who criticise are termed "knockers"; people who are conservative are called pessimists.

Yet our nation has got to a stage of development where quality is becoming as important as quantity. We are beginning to see the need for a more intensive training of the refinements, a cultivation of the "great imponderables." Americans are being brought to a stage of introspection and self-analysis; we are comparing ourselves with the Europeans with whom we are coming in contact.

Moderate criticism is valuable. It should, however, be liberal, kindly, and suggestive, rather than opinionated, rigid, and inflexible. Adverse criticism of one phase should be tempered with praise of another. We all like helpful criticism that points out our faults in a tactful manner, but we also like occasional praise—particularly if it seems spontaneous.

In writing, it is more important to be interesting than to be correct. Often as a writer becomes more correct, he ceases to be interesting. Almost anyone prefers to read an interesting journal, in spite of faults in grammar, to a dull paper that is correct. A touch of humanness that appeals to the readers, does more good than a wooden remark that is only rhetoric.

In matters of taste and opinion, there are as great differences as the world is wide. One man's hobby is another's pet aversion. *A* likes fat girls, *B* prefers them slender, *C* likes none at all, while *D* loves them all, and so it goes. This being a free country, it is well to be broadminded in matters of opinion. Democracy should not mean mediocrity at the expense of everyone agreeing with everyone else.

SELENAIO-PHANTASMA

Dedicated to the Author of "Nemesis."

By Alfred Galpin, Jr.

In Elysium-fann'd fields of my slumber,
In the wild-tinted beauties of night,
I have feasted on sights without number,
Recreated all Heav'n with my sight;
And I wake to the sunrise at dawning, fit close to the dusk's mad delight.

Shadow'd visions of beauties unpainted,
Shifting sights of a Heaven beyond,
Primal nature in pureness untainted,
Without Man and his slave-making wand,
Meet my sight in procession uncanny, unorder'd, and link'd without bond.

Mingling phantoms above Man's poor notion,
Phantasmas obscure and unknown,
Undulations and waves of wild motion

Into infinite variance grown,
I behold in my slumbers of madness, from far shores of mad Cynthia blown.

I have seen things of cryptical meaning,
Hinting life far above mortal view;
Superstitions of primitive gleaning
Blend with fancy to forms strange and new;
And my fetterless brain leaps the mountain of Science and dreams 'tis not true.

All the hopes of a life are entwined
With the greed of a fancy unchain'd,
While my thoughts, by the sleep undermined,
Wander wordless, uncheck'd, uncontain'd
O'er unearthly expanses of Spiritland, haunting where once they had reign'd.

When, in midst of this immundane dreaming
Come effulgent the first rays of light,
Bringing back my rapt soul with their beaming,
Lending splendour to all within sight;
And I wake to the sunrise at dawning, fit close to the dusk's mad delight.

TIME AND SPACE

By H. P. Lovecraft

Of the various conceptions brought before the human mind by the advance of Science, what can be compared in strangeness and magnitude with that of eternity and infinity, as presented by modern astronomy? Nothing more deeply disturbs our settled egotism and self-importance than the realisation of man's utter insignificance which comes with knowledge of his position in time and space.

Life, or at least life upon the earth and the other planets of the solar system, extends but a little distance, relatively speaking, into the past; for the nebular hypothesis of Laplace can trace the ancestry of the sun and planets to a gaseous, incandescent mass which could under no circumstances support the vital principle. And this condition, removed from us by innumerable years, is obviously but a matter of yesterday as eternity is reckoned. Nor is the future prospect of much greater extent. In a few billion years, a mere second in eternity, the sun and planets must lose the heat bequeathed to them by the parent nebula, and roll black, frozen, and untenanted through space. Therefore the very existence of life and thought is but a matter of a moment in unbounded time; the merest incident in the history of the universe. An hour ago we did not exist; in another hour we shall have ceased to be.

Turning to the consideration of infinite space, we are no less paralysed with "thoughts beyond the reaches of our souls." In our own solar system we discover the apparently boundless earth to be a comparatively small planet, and in the immediate universe we find the entire solar system but an inconsequential molecule. What, then, shall we think when we learn that all that universe is but one of an infinite number of similar star-clusters, only the nearest of which are to be seen from our part of space? And besides all this, we must ever recall that space has no boundary; that the illimitable reaches of vacancy extend endlessly out beyond our sight or comprehension, perhaps beyond the apparently infinite region of the luminiferous ether and beyond control of the laws of motion and gravitation. What mind can venture to depict those remote realms where form, dimensions, matter, and energy may all be subject to undreamt-of modifications and grotesque manifestations? All that we know, see, dream, or imagine, is less than a grain of dust in infinity. It is virtually nothing, or at best no more than a mathematical point.

But whilst all these considerations may well serve to diminish the presumption of the petty philosopher, they should not be permitted to discourage humanity in its devotion to the ideals it has always pursued. Life and mankind have their place in the natural plan, however infinitesimal that place may be; and the laws of Nature are too obvious and well-defined to warrant a feeling of futility and unrest. The essential reality and rationality of our aspirations and moral code should, notwithstanding all the revelations of Science, be apparent even to the most thorough materialist.

UPON THE BRINK

By Eugene B. Kuntz, D. D.

I've often stood upon the brink where Death
Holds out his wither'd hand to lead one hence
To realms invisible; and there the breath
Of strangest mystery from worlds immense,
Pass'd gently o'er my soul like odours sweet
From blossoms of immortal grace. I've stood
And long'd to go—and yet held back my feet
From paths which end in Life's eternal good.

So oft I've wearied of the task which holds
Me fetter'd to my earthly lot, and sigh'd
For freedom and for rest from clinging folds
Of Time's habiliment; and yet when wide
Dun shadows crept my way, me to embrace
In that long sleep, and bear me to Death's shore,
I've turn'd to Earth again my tear-stain'd face,
Content to linger for a moment more.

'Tis not because I fear to die, my heart
Grows eager to remain; but Oh, there seems
So much one needs to do; so great a part
One dare not leave undone; so many dreams
That should be brought to sweet fruition's goal;
So many Whys and Wherefores yet to test;
So many parts to join, so that the whole
May lastly answer Life's most eager quest.

MERLINUS REDIVIVUS

By H. P. Lovecraft

In humanity's age-long struggle for emancipation from the ignoble chains of superstition, no retarding influence has been more potent than that of national distress. The inevitable result of a great war or social crisis, is to cloud the atmosphere for rational perception; to inflame the imagination beyond the realm of calm analysis, and to give unbounded license to untrustworthy impressions, superficial doctrines, antiquated fallacies, distorted coincidences, psychopathic delusions, and irresponsible thoughts to which wishes alone are the fathers.

Throughout the war-torn world there is now being born a more dangerous and degrading era of superstition than history records for many centuries past. Excited by a wild desire to communicate with the vast numbers of the honoured dead; rebellious against the thought that these splendid souls are totally lost to the earth; the public have turned with the irrationality of deep grief to the hoary frauds and delusions of cruder ages, and have lent willing ears to the charlatans and eccentrics whose claims of spiritualistic insight are normally dismissed with a smile.

Amongst the uneducated, an atavistical relapse of this sort was but natural. We do not marvel at the legends of the Marne where the shades of our old English bowmen are said to have come to the assistance of the army and saved the day; or of Mons, where angels are reputed to have battled on the side of right against the Hun. These, and the usual mediumistic nonsense and amulet-wearing of the ignorant, were to be expected. But we do marvel at the extent to which the scientific perspective of supposedly wiser classes has become distorted.

Spiritualism, whose adherents now number many former men of science who should know better, is a frank surrender of judgment to vague subjective impressions. None knows better than the sober psychologist how vivid some apparently occult manifestations may be to certain types of persons; yet the sober thinker can see further than the spiritualist, and can analyse the phenomena, tracing them to a material cause in the consciousness of the subject.

The prime obstacle to truth in this struggle is the will. Overpowered by a desire to believe in the supernatural, men are everywhere ignoring patent scientific principles and encroaching upon borderlands where evidence is highly coloured with illusion. Against common sense is arrayed a flimsy mass of dream-stuff which under ordinary conditions would be laughed out of court.

Were material communication really possible, or the dead able to make themselves known to the living, it is safe to state that the world would be a very different place. Secrecy would be non-existent, and death would be no mystery. In fact, the very rarity and frivolity of alleged spiritual messages are enough to condemn them as frauds or hallucinations.

However general may be the relapse of the world into mediaeval credulity, it is to be hoped that Anglo-Saxon sense and conservatism may exempt our particular realm from so pitiable an intellectual debacle.

THE PRODIGAL

By Ernest Lionel McKeag, R. N. R.

On an African desert, remote and far-reaching,
In a region of heat where the sun ever burns,
The half-buried bones of a trav'ler lie bleaching—
He has gone to that bourn whence no mortal returns.

Midst a fair English garden where robins are mating,
In a cottage with roses abloom by the door,
A weary-eyed mother is waiting, ay, waiting,
For the prodigal son she will gaze on no more.

IN THE EDITOR'S STUDY

Anglo-Saxondom

When the historian of the future shall look back upon the stupendous events of this age, it is likely that he will find, aside from the general defence of civilisation, no event of greater magnitude and significance than the new understanding which is daily being cemented between the two political divisions of Anglo-Saxondom.

The war has stripped many shams and delusions from the social and political life of the world; and paramount amongst these is the pernicious fallacy, fostered by and for the unthinking immigrant rabble, that America's path must lie apart from that of the Mother Empire.

The strongest tie in the domain of mankind, and the only potent source of social unity, is that mystic essence compounded of race, language, and culture; a heritage descended from the remote past. This tie no human force can break, whatever political revolution may by such an agency be effected. It may be temporarily submerged by the base prejudices of passion and the detestable contamination caused by alien blood, but rise it must when overwhelming stress calls out man's deeper emotions, and sweeps aside the superficialities of arbitrary modes of thought.

Today we know that, as in the beginning, England and America are spiritually one; one undivided rampart of liberty and enlightenment ordained by the Fates to defend for humanity the priceless legacy of classical civilisation.

Amateur Criticism

The somewhat remarkable attack of an amateur editor upon the United's critical bureau, made just a year ago, has apparently inaugurated a long period of debate regarding this phase of our literary activity. Exponents of mildness and severity, vagueness and frankness, personality and generality, archaism and modernism, each have had their say; without arriving at any very perfect community of ideas or consensus of opinion.

The Conservative in this issue publishes a brief contribution to the fray, from the pen of Prof. Philip B. McDonald, Chairman of the Department of Private Criticism. Prof. McDonald is a modernist and liberalist; and while his remarks are undeniably the fruit of much erudition, mature reflection, and sincere conviction, it is hard to let them pass unchallenged. As former Public Critic, The Conservative feels impelled to defend the policy whereby he was always a strict upholder of classical standards and impeccable technique.

Prof. McDonald affirms, 'that it is more important to be interesting than to be correct,' and in enunciating this dictum he is indeed speaking truly. All things, however, have their limits; and there are certain standards of technique below which no author may fall without impairing his literary strength, and distracting the attention of his readers by the grossness and numerousness of his faults. Style should be imperceptible;

the crystal medium through which the theme is viewed. Laxity of technique is the least excusable of literary deficiencies; since it depends not on a want of natural parts, but on pure haste and indolence. We may pardon a *dull* writer, since his Boeotian offences arise from the incurable mediocrity of his genius; but can we thus excuse the *careless* scribbler whose worst blunders could be corrected by an extra hour of attention or research? The contemporary tendency to condone carelessness for the sake of brilliancy is as illogical as it is pernicious. No man ever wrote the duller for being correct, whilst many have transformed commonplaceness to pleasing urbanity by means of a graceful mode of expression.

Among amateur journalists, technique is the most neglected branch of literary art. We have scores of brilliant writers whose productions lose a considerable percentage of their possible force through lack of polish. Concretely, it may be pointed out that of our well-known poets only Messrs. Kleiner, Lowrey, and Loveman have an absolutely comprehensive and unfailing mastery of their medium, whilst the writers of elegant and musical prose are scarcely greater in number. It is in no spirit of cavilling or assumed superiority that The Conservative and other official critics have consistently laboured on the side of correctness. Any other course would have seemed, in their eyes, a flagrant dereliction of duty.

Regarding the element of individual taste and personal preferences in official criticism, it would be foolish to insist that the reviewer suppress all honest convictions of his own; foolish because such suppression is an impossibility. It is, however, to be expected that such an one will differentiate between personal and general dicta, nor fail to state all sides of any matter involving more than one point of view. This course The Conservative sought to follow during his tenure of the critical chairmanship, with the matter of *vers libre* as a single possible exception. That abominable species of artistic Bolshevism, condemned with equal vigour by every person who has ever been connected with the United's critical bureau, has no more right to a defence than political Bolshevism or any other sort of anarchy. Fortunately but few specimens have been inflicted upon our Association.

Within the last few weeks one of amateurdom's most prominent critics, a man who has served for more than a decade on either the public or private board, expressed in a personal letter the belief that all amateur criticism is futile; that if honest it offends too deeply to instruct, and that if "sugar-coated" it has no power to inculcate ideas. The Conservative does not entirely coincide with this view, but experience and observation have done much to remove from his mind the opposite opinion.

The United, 1917-1918

The Conservative views with profound gratification the official year just completed by the United Amateur Press Association, proud to have borne the honour of the presidency through this period of cultural excellence and intensive development. Too much cannot be said in grateful praise of the perfect harmony and complete fidelity of the official board, and of the tireless effort and brilliant work of the critical bureaux. *The United Amateur* has surpassed all standards hitherto known to amateur journalism, writing the names of Miss McGeoch and Mr. Cook imperishably into the pages of our history. The lack of numerous publications has been more than atoned for by the quality of those which have appeared. *The Vagrant* is a magazine worthy to be compared with anything the amateur world has produced since the beginning, and the smaller publications have been close rivals in quality, however much exceeded in bulk.

For the new year the prospect is encouraging. The war will naturally curtail the production of papers to a greater or less extent, but that our present high ideals will be sustained and amplified, there is no reason to doubt. Free from friction with contemporaries, whose correct and liberal attitude is most heartening to observe, the United moves prosperously in its chosen sphere.

The Amateur Press Club

Attention is directed to the new international organisation of amateur journalists founded in the Mother Country by Messrs. Benjamin Winskill and Joseph Parks, and denominated "The Amateur Press Club." This society, which now possesses nearly an hundred members both in England and the States, is designed for the diffusion of higher literary standards amongst amateurs, and commands the services of such earnestly progressive writers and critics as Sub-Lieut. Ernest Lionel McKeag and Miss Vere M. Murphy. THE CONSERVATIVE not long ago joined the Amateur Press Club, and believes it would be to the advantage of amateurdom if his readers were to do likewise; for the drawing together of amateur interests on both sides of the sea is something much to be desired in this period of decreased general activity. Detailed information may be obtained from the Secretary, Joseph Parks, Esq., 38, Garnet St., Saltburn-by-the-Sea, Yorkshire, England.

Ward Phillips Replies

THE CONSERVATIVE acknowledges a communication from Ward Phillips, Esq., whose recent ulalumish poem entitled "Astrophobos" was so unfavourably contrasted with Mr. Kleiner's "Ruth" by a reviewer in the May *United Amateur.* Mr. Phillips would make it plain, that if he so desired he could work with perfect ease in a simpler, tenderer, and more popular medium; and as an answer to his critics he has graciously favoured this office with the following effusion, in the metre and manner of his distinguished contemporary:

Grace

With Unstinted Apologies to the Author of "Ruth."

By Ward Phillips

In the dim light of the unrustled grove,
    Amidst the silence of approaching night,
I saw thee standing, as through boughs above
    Filter'd the pencils of the dying light.

Grace! I had thought thou wert by far too proud,
    Too harden'd to the world and all its pain,

To pause so wistfully, with fair head bow'd,
Forgetting all thy coldness and disdain.

But in that instant all my doubts and fears
Were swept away as on the evening breeze,
When I beheld thee, not indeed in tears,
But rack'd and shaken with a mighty *sneeze!*

Les Mouches Fantastiques

Extreme literary radicalism is always a rather amusing thing, involving as it does a grotesque display of egotism and affectation. Added to this comic quality, however, there is a distinct pathos which arises from reflection on the amount of real suffering which the radical must, if serious, endure through his alienation from the majority.

Both of these aspects lately impressed The Conservative with much force, as he glanced over a new and most extraordinary amateur publication entitled *Les Mouches Fantastiques,* published by Miss Elsie Alice Gidlow and Mr. Roswell George Mills of Montreal. Miss Gidlow and Mr. Mills are sincere and solemn super-aesthetes, fired with the worthy ambition of elevating dense and callous mankind to their own exalted spiritual plane, and as such present vast possibilities to the humourist; but it is also possible to view their efforts in another light, and to lament the imperfect artistic vision which imparts to their utterances so *outre* an atmosphere.

The Gidlow-Mills creed, so far as may be discovered from their writings, is that Life is a compulsory quest of beauty and emotional excitement; these goals being so important that man must discard everything else in pursuing them. Particularly, we fancy, must he discard his sense of humour and proportion. The sceptical bulk of humanity, who cannot or do not enter upon this feverish quest, are (as Miss Gidlow tactfully tells us) "unnecessary."

And of what do these great objects of Life, as revealed in the pages of *Les Mouches,* consist? The reader may, up to date, unearth nothing save a concentrated series of more or less primitive and wholly unintellectual sense-impressions; instinct, form, colour, odour, and the like, grouped in all the artistic chaos characteristic of the late Oscar Wilde of none too fragrant memory. Much of this matter is, as might be expected, in execrable taste. Now is this Life? Is human aspiration indeed to be circumscribed by the walls of some garishly bejewelled temple of the Dionaean Eros; its air oppressive with the exotic fumes of strange incense, and its altar lit with weirdly coloured radiance from mystical braziers? Must we forever shut ourselves in such an artificial shrine, away from the pure light of sun and stars, and the natural currents of normal existence?

It seems to THE CONSERVATIVE that Miss Gidlow and Mr. Mills, instead of being divinely endowed seers in sole possession of all Life's truths, are a pair of rather youthful persons suffering from a sadly distorted philosophical perspective. Instead of seeing Life in its entirety, they see but one tiny phase, which they mistake for the whole. What worlds of beauty—pure Uranian beauty—are utterly denied them on account of their bondage to the lower regions of the senses! It is almost pitiful to hear superficial allusions to "Truth" from the lips of those whose eyes are sealed to the Intellectual Absolute; who knows not the upper altitudes of pure thought, in which empirical forms and material aspects are as nothing.

The editors of *Les Mouches* complain very bitterly of the inartistic quality of amateur journalism; a complaint half just and half otherwise. The very nature of our institution necessitates a modicum of crudity, but if Miss Gidlow and Mr. Mills were more analytical, they could see beauty in much which appears ugly to their rather astigmatic vision.

THE CONSERVATIVE, in order to forestall conjecture, desires to state that 'Consul Hasting,' signed to the following parody, is not a pseudonym for himself. The *nom de plume* cloaks one of our most brilliant new members, a young man of great attainments and infinite promise."

TWO LOVES

(After, and with apologies to, Miss Elsie Alice Gidlow in the June *Vagrant.)*

By Consul Hasting

I have two loves, who haunt me unceasingly.

Which shall I choose?

One is ugly to men's sight, and arouses repulsion in them;
Not so to me; for I know the true heart within.
Yes, he is ugly and repulsive to the many—
His robust mien and his plebeian companions dishonour him.
But they are as he:
For his heart is as pure gold, the gold
Scorned in sham by the would-be poetic, but ever true and useful.

He is constant, and I could love him forever;
Yea, with dishonour stamped on his brow by the mob, I yet do love him.
For his heart is as the heart of a thrifty and comely woman sought by all of thought.

He hath a hard skin, and is difficult of acquaintance;
But to him who searcheth beneath, he is a rich mine of delicious treasure.

In my sensuous dreams I behold him, and long for him;
When all the world is heartless and I am aweary of it,
Then do I long for him.

The other I would shun; for he is traitorously fair and beauteous:
But he draws me to him inevitably, as the raft through many streams to the ocean.

His soul burneth as the hot torrents that prompt love—
Ever youthful and daring in heart, but changing ere ultimately carefree;
Inspiring hesitant fear at a distance, but enticing and ever victorious.

He is not constant,
Except as he forceth me to everlasting constancy;
For he is exacting.
He draws me to him and I drink of his luscious beauty—
But O the aftermath! The satient afterwhile!

He would destroy me;

He has become a part of my soul, and meaneth my ruin;
And yet I should die without him.

His beauty sparkles, and is given fastidious care.
His speech flows swiftly and fluently, and is the language of all who are subject to his sway.
Yea, him I long for passionately, and the other is only a comfort.

I have two loves who woo me unceasingly;
One is bologna and the other Scotch Whiskey:
Which shall I take?

THE CONSERVATIVE

Edited by H. P. Lovecraft, under the Auspices of the United Amateur Press Association. Published at 598, Angell St., Providence, R. I., U.S.A.

The Conservative, Vol. V, No. I

Providence, R. I., July, 1919

Edited By H. P. Lovecraft

SONG

By Samuel Loveman

In the spring of the year, in the silver rain,
When petal by petal the blossoms fall,
The robins begin to mate again,
But the heart forgets not all.

For within the budding flow'rs and leaves,
A spirit of Joy awakens and stays;
But the soul of Grief remembers and grieves,
All her lonely and alien days.

TOUCHING ON EUPHUISM

By James F. Morton, Jr

The average fairly well-read person, if asked for a definition of Euphuism, would undoubtedly affirm that it was an affected and artificial style of speaking and writing, current in the Elizabethan period, which originated in the vogue of a book named Euphues, by John Lyly, and might add that Shakespeare's Love's Labour Lost was written largely to ridicule this contemporary vice of speech, much as Moliere, in the following century, dealt by his Precieuses Ridicules a death blow to a somewhat similar extravagance of language and manner.

As to reading Euphues and thus seeking enlightenment on the subject at its source, practically nobody dreams of so hazardous a procedure. The modern reader, in fact, is wont to neglect the literary masters of the past. He will join in the general acclaim with which their names are pronounced; but reading their books is quite another matter. Are not the bookstores crammed with the latest works of contemporaries? Let the dead past bury its dead, while we proceed to feed our minds on the effusions of living writers. It is much, if we condescend now and then to pick up a volume of Dickens or Thackeray, or one of the three or four novels of Scott which are conceded to be "interesting" to a generation stuffed with the near-literary fiction of Marie Corelli, Florence Barclay, Robert Chambers, Harold Bell Wright and other wretched specimens of cheap ephemeralism. We pronounce Hugo's masterpiece, the greatest novel of all time, "too long," Balzac "too slow," Duman "too old-fashioned." To confess to the occasional reading of Jane Austen, or of Richardson, Fielding, Smollett, Sterne or Defoe, is to be dubbed an incorrigible highbrow, whose idiosyncrasies may be charitably tolerated by mere men and women. And while it is universally granted that the Elizabethan age surpassed all others in the production of great works of English literature, how many readers of these lines have so much as dipped into the works of any writer of that age, except Shakespeare? Aye, and how many know even their Shakespeare through and through, and recognise as a personally loved companion the mighty master, who is the eternal glory of the English race? A few of Bacon's essays, a handful of lyrics found in some anthology, a little of Chaucer and Spenser and something of Milton's poetry (rarely by any chance his great Areopagitica or any other of his prose works); these represent nearly everything in English literature prior to the eighteenth century, so far as known by actual reading to the vast majority of "well-educated" readers of our day.

This is not as it should be. If ever there is to be an improvement in literary taste, it must be signalised by a reversion from the flashy and bodiless books of the "best seller" class to the real literature which lives for all time. "Whenever a new book comes out, I read an old one," said Lamb in deprecation of the tendency to neglect the deathless for the ephemeral. This, however, is going to the other extreme. While human nature remains intrinsically the same from age to age, its manifestations vary; and each epoch brings with it new problems. We need to study the men and women of our own day in their present setting, and to grapple with the issues of our own period. Nor is literary talent wanting to the present generation. In the single department of English fiction, such writers as Hewlett, Wells, Locke, Smith and Mrs. Voynich are by no means deserving of neglect; while the still greater names of Hardy, Meredith and James shed undying lustre on the latter portion of the nineteenth and the earlier years of the twentieth centuries. Equally important are latter day contributions in poetry, history, science, criticism and many other branches. Our worthy contemporaries deserve something better than neglect at our hands; but we are incapable of rendering to them their true meed of appreciation, unless we have prepared ourselves by familiarity with their predecessors to trace the historical and psychological connection between the past and the present. Nor are the older writings "dull" to any alert mind. The fascination of the Morte d'Arthur is perennial, as is the delight to be taken in those glorious relics of our ancestors embedded in Percy's Reliques of Ancient Poetry. "Marlowe's mighty line" has not lost its power to thrill; nor has the charm of The Faery Queen faded away.

Returning to euphuism, the digression from which is more apparent than real, the current view is that reflected in most books dealing with English literature, although in many cases the writers who pronounce it show evidence of having based their verdict on the testimony of others, instead of searching for themselves to learn "whether these things were so." Thus, the Standard Dictionary defines euphuism as "an affectation of elegance in writing; especially, a high-flown, periphrastic style; originally, the style of John Lyly in his Euphues, marked by antitheses, alliteration, pedantic affectation, obscurity, subtle similes, and fantastic conceits."

The Everyman Encyclopaedia speaks of Euphues as "a very tedious story," which is remarkable for its prose style, which is chiefly characterised by a continuous straining after antithesis and epigram.

The Concise Oxford Dictionary defines Euphuism as "artificial or affected style of writing (prop.) in imitation of Lyly's Euphues; high-flown style."

John Berkenhout, M. D., in his Biographies Literari, violently attacks Lyly's work as "a most contemptible piece of affectation and nonsense." Equally condemnatory are the expressions of Gifford, the first editor of the Quarterly Review, few of whose judgments have stood the test of posterity; John Payne Collier, Henry Hallam and innumerable others. More kindly are the words of Professor Marsh, Stopford Brooke and Charles Kingsley, the last-named of whom shows unequivocal signs of having proceeded to the unusual extreme of himself having read the book about which he was writing.

As to Lyly's motives, the majority of critics seem to suppose that it was his deliberate intention to corrupt the English language, by furnishing a new and highly objectionable model of style. Others express themselves variously. Thus the Everyman Encyclopedia declares: "His idea was not to improve, but to amuse." Auguste Filon, in his Histoire de la Littérature Anglaise, says: "The book—it is the author who says so—had no other ambition than to deserve a place on the knees of ladies, by the side of their favourite dog, in order that they might play with the animal when they should be tired of the pretty fancies of the writer."

A contrary view is thus expressed by Stopford Brooke, in his Primer of English Literature: "The story is long, and is more a loose framework into which Lyly could fit his thoughts on love, friendship, education and religion than a true story." In like manner, John W. Cousin, in his Short Biographical Dictionary of English Literature, credits Lyly as being "largely inspired by Ascham's Toxophilus, and aiming at "the reform of education and manners. Charles Kingsley more emphatically declares that if parents "could train a son after the pattern of his Ephoebus, to the great saving of their own money and his virtue, all fathers, even in these money-making days, would rise up and call them blessed." The chief purveyor of misconceptions concerning Lyly and his work is undoubtedly Sir Walter Scott, who in The Monastery has given us a self-named euphuist in the Person of Sir Piercie Shaffon. This fantastic knight has schooled himself to make use in the presence of ladies and persons whom he considers his equals or superiors of a high-flown jargon such as no mortal ever heard before or since. How far his personality and style are removed from his supposed model, may be judged by a single comparison.

Here is a specimen of Sir Piercie's manner of addressing a lady:

"But who can talk of discords, when the soul of harmony descends upon us in the presence of surpassing beauty? For even as foxes, wolves and other animals void of sense and reason do fly from the presence of the resplendent sun of heaven when he arises in his glory, so do strife, wrath and all ireful passions retreat and as it were scud away from the face which now beams upon us, with power to compose our angry passions, illuminate our errors and difficulties, soothe our wounded minds, and lull to rest our disorderly apprehensions; for as the heat and warmth of the eye of the day is to the material and physical world, so is the eye which I now bow down before to that of the intellectual microcosm." No wonder that Mary Avenel could find no other answer than "For heaven's sake what is the meaning of this?"

Now consider the words of Euphues on a somewhat similar occasion:

"As there is no one thing which can be reckoned either concerning love or loyalty wherein women do not exceed men, yet in fervency above all others, they so far exceed, that men are liker to marvel at them than to imitate them, and readier to laugh at their virtues than emulate them. For as they be hard to be won without trial of great faith, so are they hard to be lost without great cause of fickleness. It is long before cold water seethe; yet being once hot, it is long before it be cooled: it is long before salt come to his saltness; but being once seasoned, it never loseth its savour. I for mine own part am brought into a paradise by the only contemplation of women's virtues; and were I persuaded that all the devils in hell were women, I would never live devoutly to inherit heaven; or that they were all saints in heaven, I would live more strictly for fear of hell. What would Adam have done in his paradise before his fall without a woman, or how could he have risen again after his fall without a woman?"

This quotation by no means unfairly represents the general tone of Lyly's work. Here is no far-fetched hyperbole of expression, but the clear setting forth of a proposition, and its reinforcement of analogies. The peculiarity of Euphues is not to be found in turgid phrases, like those of Sir Piercie, but in the innumerable similes brought forth to emphasise each point. Take the following, as a fair example:

"Beware of delays. What less than the grain of mustard-seed; in time almost what thing is greater than the stalk thereof? The slender twig groweth to a stately tree; and that which with the hand might safely have been pulled up, will hardly with the axe be hewn down. The least spark if it be not quenched will burst into a flame; the least moth in time eateth the thickest cloth; and I have read that in a short space, there was a town in Spain undermined with coneys, in Thessalia with moles, with frogs in France, in Africa with flies. .... Think this with thyself, that the sweet songs of Calypso were subtle snares to entice Ulysses; that the crab then catcheth the oyster when the sun shineth; that Hiena, when she speaketh like a man, deviseth most mischief; that women, when they be most pleasant, pretend most treachery."

This long harping on one string is what wearies the modern reader, in attempting to enjoy Euphues. Yet I do not hesitate to assert that the occasional pain is well rewarded. Of obscurity there is little or none, save that few will be familiar with all the historical and mythological references to be found therein, or with the immense number of mediaeval beliefs introduced with regard to imagined properties of plants and animals. The story is slight; but the picture of the times is of distinct interest. The first part, entitled Euphues, The Anatomy of Wit, deals with the experiences of a young Athenian, contemporary with the author, who learns by sharp lessons that cleverness and brilliance of intellect are insufficient means whereby to achieve the higher aims of life. Disappointed in love and friendship, he turns first to intellectual labour and then to the consolation of religion, becoming pious even to the verge of fanaticism. A dialogue with an Atheist, whom Euphues beats from his position rather by threat of divine wrath than by such arguments as would be considered requisite in these days, and an elaborate and (for its time) wholly admirable treatise on the education of youth, occupy about a third of the entire work. Its sequel, Euphues and His England, deals with a journey to England, and contains some ingenious conversation, love-making of a highly edifying sort, moral tales and the inevitable eulogies of the flattery-loving Elizabeth and her court.

Of the influence of Lyly on Shakespeare there can be no question. A simple comparison of style shows that no preceding writer except Marlowe is so clearly to be traced throughout the earlier works of the supreme dramatist. Even Love's Labour Lost, commonly supposed to be a satire on euphuistic phraseology, shows more of Lyly in the seriously treated characters than in those held up to ridicule. Pedantry and highly elaborated language are indeed unsparingly satirised; but there is no trace of the manner of Euphues in Holofernes, Sir Nathaniel or even Don Armado; while it is abundant in Biron and his companions and in the ladies of the French court. Two Gentlemen of Verona abounds in expressions typical of Lyly's influence; and few even of the later plays are without traces of it.

In two instances at least, Shakespeare has not failed to draw directly from Euphues for subject matter, to be worked over by his incomparable genius. Note the advice of old Eubulus to Euphues:

"Be merry, but with modesty; be sober but not too sullen; be valiant, but not too venturous. Let thy attire be comely, but not costly; thy diet wholesome, but not excessive; use pastime as the word importeth to pass the time in honest recreation. Mistrust no man without cause; neither be thou credulous without proof; be not light to follow every man's opinion, nor obstinate to stand in thine own conceit."

Out of this passage, with the addition of suggestions from certain other precepts to be found in Lyly's work, Shakespeare elaborated the famous counsel of Polonius to Laertes, with which every school child is familiar.

The other example is that of the famous passage in Act 1, Scene 2, of King Henry V, in which the Archbishop of Canterbury describes the commonwealth of the bees. This is modelled on a passage in Euphues and His England, wherein Fidus, an old nobleman retired to country life, discourses to Euphues and Philautus concerning his observations of the social organisations in which the bee serves as a model to human society.

That the name euphuism was applied to a grossly affected style of conversation, which came into vogue the latter portion of Elizabeth's reign, and grew yet worse during the subsequent degenerate period of the worthless Stuarts, is not to be denied. For this corruption, however, Lyly is in no way responsible. There is no trace of any effort on his part to thrust his own style of writing upon others, still less the later perversion which has little of Euphues besides the stolen name. As a matter of fact, his style differs less from that of his contemporaries and immediate predecessors than does that of Thomas Carlyle from the English style current in his day and in ours. Not only are its extravagances far less than represented; but, such as they are, they merely represent his individuality, departing no further from the normal than do the very different manners of Ben Jonson and Christopher Marlowe. His message was a sincere attempt to improve the manners and the morals of his time; and the language employed was that which best fitted his individuality as a means of his wholly laudable end. In this day, when so many idols are being shattered, it is surely not amiss to correct one of the great injustices of literary history, and to remove from John Lyly a reproach which has so long been wrongfully cast upon him.

CONSTANCY

By Andrew Francis Lockhart

The blood-red sun sinks deep,
    Deep in the bowl of space;
And snow-white clouds like sheep
    Stray o'er the evening's face.

A lone star glimmers pale,
    Above the mountain's crest,
And like a fading sail
    The moon dims in the west.

A stillness reaching far;
    Night....and the Loneliness!
And yet in one lone star
    Lie Hope and God's caress!

THE FIELD OF NIGHT

By Willis Tete Crossman

(W. Paul Cook)

It is dark, dark. It seems to be always night, black, black, unrelieved night. Not a sky decked with stars, but a black, fathomless pit above me. Not a sign of a light in so far as my eyes can see or any of my other senses perceive. It is night, always night. Night in so far as my eyes can tell me, and night to my poor tired mentality. My brain is tired, tired. It has worked too hard, poor thing. It was tired out, tired out, and must rest. My eyes, too, were tired, tired. They once never closed for how long I do not know. Now they never open.

Occasionally, though, my brain registers once again the impressions taken by it during its last days. But there is nothing new, always swift, vanishing photographic prints, one at a time, like the single pictures in a cinema reel. Never a connected impression. And never aided by my eyes, my poor, tired, tired eyes. It is difficult to build up a story from thousands of haphazard photographic negatives—a picture puzzle is simple in comparison. Then when the pictures are arranged in sequence, it is strange, so strange, to seem to stand off and watch a completed story—one's own story—flashed before one.

Where am I? I do not know. I only know I am tired, tired. My poor body is tired. My eyes are tired. My weary brain is still, so still, yet striving to register impressions. Can I catch and put together and convey to you this story—the story which I now view as a spectator, yet knowing the actor was indeed I?

After all, it is indeed a sordid story, hardly worth the trouble of recording. This man was wealthy, perhaps not enormously wealthy, but possessed of means enough to purchase all the necessities and many of the comforts of life. He had not shown his miserliness, nor his meanness of soul, nor his wonderful intellect, when he caught and married this girl. But he soon revealed himself. She was a virtual prisoner in this once magnificent but now rotten and rambling old mansion on the outskirts of the town far from her home.

With clothes in which she dared not show herself to strangers, with an insufficient quantity of the poorest food, a slave to the whims of a man of ungovernable passions and splendid but perverted intellect, she had been but a few feet out of the decaying edifice since he brought here there, a bride.

How long ago that was, she did not know. Sometimes she thought it but yesterday. At other times it seemed aeons and aeons ago. Her arms were black where he had seized her with his hands. Her limbs were blue where he had kicked her. She walked with a bowed back, where he had thrown her against a corner of the kitchen chimney.

And now he was sick, sick unto death it seemed. He lay in the only room in the house protected from the elements. Here were his books. Here was a small printing outfit on which some of those books had been produced. Other volumes were old folios of black-letter, and rolls of vellum and parchment and papyrus. He had once compelled her to read one of these books and sat watching her mirthfully as she shuddered at the forbidden things revealed therein. But after quieting with some medicament of his own compounding the extreme hysteria into which the reading had thrown her, he forbade her to touch any of the books again. Many of them were in strange languages, and he once mentioned that one of them, he alone of living men could read.

And now he was ill, here on this cot among these forbidden books. And she, she must watch over him and wait on him, giving him this or that in such and such a fashion, mixing according to his directions, grinding this herb to compound with that, while his burning eyes never left her. Once when she left him for a moment apparently asleep, she was recalled by an unearthly shriek commanding her to return. She must not close her eyes. She must not lie down. She must remain ever alert, hour after hour, ready to obey his slightest wish. This man, sick unto death, had resolved by his black knowledge and his powerful will to remain alive. Remain alive he did, until finally he was more alive than the ghost attending him. Once she fell asleep on her feet while standing over him, and was awakened by falling upon his body. He cursed her in known and unknown languages, commanded her to take a certain draught of a medicine prepared for him, and when it had given her an artificial strength and wakefulness, he gave her minute instructions for the next three hours. He was going to sleep or into a coma, he said. Three drops of this was to be forced between his teeth every quarter hour. A spoonful of that was to be given every half hour. He could swallow them without difficulty, he said. At the end of one hour he was to have a hypodermic injection of the greenish liquid, exactly there, where he made an ink mark. Exactly at the stroke of the third hour she was to inject the syringe full of the colourless liquid. These instructions were vital. The colourless liquor, especially, was not to be touched except as ordered. The result would be fatal if administered otherwise.

He sank into a senseless shape. She faithfully gave the first draught. But she was so sleepy. Perhaps she could snatch ten minutes' rest. Quite useless. Though her brain was numb for lack of sleep, she could not sleep. That devil draught he had made her take was designed only to prolong her agony and keep him, the Evil One himself, alive and in the flesh.

She picked up the hypodermic syringe with the colourless liquid. She leaned over him. He was in so deep a coma that his breathing was scarcely discernible. She bared the place on his body marked for the final injection. The needle was about to be inserted when the arms of the man came up; one hand grasped her throat, the other forced the syringe away from his body. His eyes were open — burning, hell-fire eyes with a malignant triumph and yet an unearthly horror in their depths. Not a word was spoken. With the strength of the insane she forced his hand from her throat, and kneeling with her whole weight on his body forced the needle in and pressed the piston home.

With a convulsive and superhuman effort the man threw her off and gained his feet. She scrambled to the door on all fours, then rose to her feet and ran, ran out of the house, through the rank shrubbery of the front lawn and into the roadway, the man pursuing her with giant strides. She continued her career down the road toward the village; when the man came to the roadway he sank forward on his face, such being his inertia that he ploughed several feet of the roadbed with his face ere he came to rest.

Two men driving from the village, one of them the doctor, stopped their team as they saw running and swaying toward them a nearly naked woman. They left their buggy and seized her as she came to them. She offered no resistance, but collapsed in their arms. Conceiving it a faint, they attempted to revive her, but to no purpose. The doctor said she was sleeping, perfect sleep, but sleep from which for days she could not be awakened. At last her eyes opened, but she saw nothing. She spoke, but she said nothing.

The doctor was puzzled. Driving out to the old house he discovered nothing of the man. The body must have been removed by someone who for some reason did not declare himself. The doctor thoroughly explored the house; finally arriving at the room of books. Here he spent some hours, coming out shaking as with an ague, with white face and burning eyes. One small volume of modern print he put in his pocket. Then he carried, all alone, can after can of naphtha and more violent refinants of petroleum into that room. A train was laid to the outside of the house. The doctor cast a match into that train and took to his heels. In an incredibly short space of time the whole countryside was lighted by flames from the old mansion. The doctor did not leave the spot until late the next day, after he had thoroughly ransacked the embers above which had lain the room of books. No, nothing remained.

The woman was placed in an asylum, and the doctor locked the little book in the very innermost compartment of his safe, washing his hands after he had touched it.

It is dark, dark. Dark to my eyes, dark to my brain, dark to my senses. I am tired, tired. I would sleep. The pictures have ceased. Perhaps I can sleep. Ah, I sleep!

THE JOY OF BOOKS

By Arthur Goodenough

When suns are dim and skies are grey,
And clouds obscure and blur the day,
When flow'rs are few and fields are brown,
And lifeless leaves in gusts whirl down;
When radiant Summer's gorgeous dress
Gives place to rags and nakedness,
And wreck and refuse choke the brooks,
I love to lose myself in books!

And too, when Nature lies asleep,
And over earth the snow falls deep,
And all the bliss and bloom of old
Is slain and silenc'd by the cold;
When hope is low and ev'rywhere
The winds the restless grief declare,
And all the future loveless looks,
I love to sink myself in books!

And when these inner moods of mine
The tempest and the cold combine,
And envy, hatred, and deceit
Have brought about my worst defeat;
When all my hopes in ruins lie,
And Fortune makes me no reply,
And men forbid me with their looks—
Naught soothes me like the charm of books!

IMAGISM

By Maurice Winter Moe

The essence of imagism, aside from the deliberate casting away of all restraint as to form and taste, is an intense concentration on the percept of every sensation. The imagist concentrates his attention on any object or phenomenon he happens to select for description and then, turning his mind in upon itself, strives to capture the exact image of every sensation at the very instant it registers on his brain. After it has been assimilated and classified as a concept, it no longer interests him.

Now I must confess that this is not the easiest thing in the world to do, for the economy of our mental life has through long years taught us to combine into concept groups the multitudes of perceptions that are constantly impinging on the consciousness. Life is too short to deal with each of these percepts lightly. If we did, we should have no time for the larger units of thought that constitute real intellection; we should be living on a plane just one degree removed from that of the unthinking animal. But it can be done. There is a trick about it, and the novelty of the effort, childish as it is, at first proves rather fascinating, just as it proves exhilarating for grown-ups occasionally to cut loose in the antics of boyhood days and play leap-frog and prisoner's base. One "poem" I discovered recently describes the imagist as a child sitting in a sunny corner and letting the brightly-coloured pebbles of life trickle through his fingers. And that's it exactly: he is playing with his sensations, watching them sparkle and glance in the sun, but not using them for any real purpose in the business of existence.

This—even if we forgive the imagist his anarchy of form, which I do not—lays bare the fundamental weakness of the whole cult: there is absolutely no attempt at interpretation. Amy Lowell herself takes pride in admitting this. We take the exact picture and present it to the reader without comment, she says; it is for him to put his own interpretation upon it. But images are in quality—not in content—all alike; stark, bare, and lacking any touch of personality. It is the interpreting touch of the artist that gives to a word-picture the subtle touch of his personality. In the volume of imagistic poems entitled "Others," almost any one of the poems might have been turned out by any one of the "Others," so lacking are these formless attempts in style and personality. That such otherwise sane critics as William Stanley Braithwaite and such otherwise sane publications as the New Republic bow down at the new fane, is utterly beyond me.

If this be poetry, then anyone, even I, can be a poet. To prove this I wrote one of these things myself. I never thought I should be guilty of such a thing, but I did it in the interests of good literature. One morning as I was "coming to the surface," my first thought was that it would be a good experiment to scrutinise my waking sensations one by one. So I took about five minutes to wake up, noted carefully every sight and sound that trickled in upon me, then rose and hastened to record the whole hodge-podge. "Seven O'Clock" is the result. Maybe it isn't real imagism, but if it isn't, the distinction is beyond a poor ordinary reader like me. If this is the new poetry, Lord help literature!

SEVEN O'CLOCK

By Maurice Winter Moe

I heave one hugely weighted eyelid—
The other refuses to budge.
Through the pillow come big, vague ticks
Of my Ingersoll.
At the edge of the curtain
Shows a narrow slice of greenish yellow.
I turn my head slowly toward the door—
A tall slit of yellowish blue.
Spokes of black shadow
Swing leisurely across the ceiling
With the door-slit as an axis:
The wire-workers hurrying by.
Crisp, brittle sounds on the icy sidewalk
Plusk-plusk-plusk-plusk ......
Swelling, chaotic, diminishing words,
One nasal female louder than the rest:
"Well he seen me; why didn't—"
Others:
"No—I said—If she—all around—"
Plusk-plusk-plusk-plusk ......
Between groups
Silence wedges in:
But into the silence
Pours a low cataract of sound,
Microscopic,

Insistent;
The far-off roar of the dam decreeing forever
That perfect silence
Shall not be in Appleton.
More plusk-plusking
Breaking into a run
As a distant whistle,
Shrilling and needle-like,
Stabs into the silence.
A nearby bassoon now takes up the tune,
And the chorus is swelled
By three or four more.
Shouldering in between blasts
Come the four double-bells:
Clang-clangg! Clang-clangg! Clang-clanggg!
Then a lower note; mellow, deliberate:
Bong-bong-bong-bong-bong-bong-bongg ! !
Time to get up!

APRIL SHADOWS

By Winifred Virginia Jordan

I shall hide from April shadows;
    I shall lightly tread the grass;
I shall leave no sign behind me
    To betray where I must pass!

For my Love waits in the Junetime,
    Beautiful and sweet to see;
Only sunshine shall enfold her,
    Only joy her portion be!

BEREFT

By Agnes Richmond Arnold

He rideth up; he rideth up;
The red, red sun o'er a glassy sea;
And there be ships as will gang a-wrack,
And lads as will never come sailing back
To their true, true loves in their ain countree.

They tell it oft at break of day—
The wise old tars who have sail'd the main—
"When the blood-red sun climbs the heavens' dome,
The storm will gather and fret to foam
The merciless sea ere he sets again."

They say it now and will say it aye—
The wise, wise ones who have watch'd in vain—
"The heart that awaits a lover's return,
O'er the waves that swell and the seas that churn,
Is the heart that bears its burden of pain."

He rideth low; he rideth low;
The lurid sun o'er a choppy sea;
And the black, black night comes a-swooping down
Where true-loves wait in the spray-swept town
For those afar from their ain countree.

MOTHER SEA

By Ernest Lionel McKeag

Hold me gently on thy bosom,
Like a child I cling to thee;
With thy gentle waves caress me—
I am tired, Mother Sea.

Long have I withstood thy calling,
Long my ship has kept me free;
Now my ship lies in thy stronghold—
I must follow, Mother Sea.

One last look at Earth and Heaven,
Quite content—I make no plea.
Close my eyes with gentle fingers—
I am ready, Mother Sea.

Now I feel thee swift enfold me;
Feel thine arms close over me;
Sink I to thy crystal caverns—
I am thine, O Mother Sea!

AT PROVIDENCE IN 1918

By Rheinhart Kleiner

I left my own Manhattan, seeking pleasure,
And having journeyed hence
A hundred miles, I found it in full measure
In teeming Providence!

I sought her hidden ways and quaint old places
That nestled ev'rywhere,
And found that Time had left benignant traces
On alley, street, and square!

I thought of one for whom these ways had beauty
And splendour all their own:
My friend, whose path of pleasure and of duty
These scenes had only known.

And over all the cloud of war hung drearly;
The summons to the strife

Was soon to come; and one whom I held dearly
Was near the close of life!

But with unclouded brow and heart uplifted,
All unaware, among
These scenes and sights, by golden summer gifted,
I mov'd—for I was young.

WHO WILL FARE WITH ME?

By Winifred Virginia Jordan

Oh, who will fare afar with me?
Oh, who will fare with me?
We'll tread the green and happy land,
We'll sail the salt blue sea!
And east and west and north and south
We'll take the trail away,
And always with Tomorrow hold
The joys of Yesterday!

We'll take the Trail of Dreamers out
Across the leagues of dew;
We'll pass where grand green willows lean
In bonnets silv'ry blue.
We'll play with young white violets
In velvet pinafores,
Just taken, sweetly scented, from
A May-elf's woodland drawers.

We'll take the Trail of Dreamers, that
Is gay with bloom begun;
And as we're faring onward we
Will sail a sea of sun;
We'll find our way to shaded wood
Where pools lie, still and deep,

And tease from them the secrets that
We know they cannot keep.

We'll take the Trail of Dreamers to
The minstrel folk of dream;
We'll beg their charm that we may hear
The fairy singing stream;
We'll hear the jolly river wind
Sing songs it learn'd at sea,
A-rollicking with fantasies
As sweet as sweet can be.

We'll take the Trail of Dreamers on
An hour that's all our own,
When hope's glad thrilling kisses are
Upon the skyways blown;
And love will fare on with us, and
Will shield from stress and strife,
And grant the gift of happiness
To bless us into life!

Oh, who will fare afar with me?
Oh, who will fare with me?
We'll tread the green and happy land,
We'll sail the salt blue sea!
And east and west and north and south
Well take the trail away,
And always will Tomorrow hold
The joys of Yesterday!

DISAPPOINTMENT

By Wilfrid Kemble

Their lustrous eyes still glow in wood and mead,
The flow'rs that drew my infant steps astray

From home, while yet, with purpose bent on play,
To grander sights above I gave no heed.
But when at length I felt a larger need,
As grew the heat and burden of the day,
I sought relief in visions far away,
Whose glories would the spangled earth's exceed.
Alas! I hear the battle's deadly roar,
And mark the glare of burning shrine and street,
Whose smoke ascends to Heaven's fast-clos'd door;
And sick at heart with surfeit of deceit,
I fain would be a little child once more,
Content with daisies flow'ring at my feet.

IN THE EDITOR'S STUDY

The League

Endless is the credulity of the human mind. Having just passed through a period of indescribable devastation caused by the rapacity and treachery of an unwisely trusted nation which caught civilisation unarmed and unawares, the world purposes once more to adopt a policy of sweet trustfulness, and to place its faith again in those imposing 'scraps of paper' known as treaties and covenants; this time setting up as its bulwark against barbaric inroads a prettily and abstractly conceived 'parliament of man and federation of the world' popularly and semi-officially labelled as "The League of Nations." It is to be a very nice and attractive League, we are told; brimful of safeguards against ordinary war, even though somewhat deficient in safeguards against Bolshevism. War, in fact, is to be formally and distinctly prohibited, or at least discouraged; which is of course an absolute guarantee of an immediate millennium of universal peace! Ultimately, as the grave proponents of the scheme condescend to inform us, all nations are to be included in this Utopian circle of friendship and confidence; thus giving us the valued collaboration of our highly honourable German, Turkish, and Bulgarian brothers in the momentous task of governing the future earthwide Elysium. Verily, it is a pleasing vision.

But visions generally become dangerous when mistaken for practical possibilities, and the present case is not likely to prove an exception. Since a war-weary and mentally fatigued world is really listening soberly to the vague theorising of league-advocates, it behooves us to awake to full consciousness and examine this roseate rhetoric in the white light of reason, history, and science. To sign any hastily drawn and clumsily patched league covenant without such an examination would be contrary to the traditions of a free and enlightened people.

Is it indeed true that man has suddenly discovered an infallible panacea for all political ills? Is it indeed certain that a general entanglement of diverse and in many case opposed countries offers a solution of all national difficulties? Have we indeed exchanged the natural laws of mankind and this earth for those of fairyland? To all these queries The Conservative is inclined to venture a negative reply.

Warfare, whose minimising is the avowed object of the proposed league, is something which can never be abolished altogether. As the natural expression of such inherent human instincts as hate, greed, and combativeness, it must always be reckoned with in some degree. Men will submit to argument only up to a certain point, beyond which they invariably resort to force, however great the odds against them. Would the league reduce warfare? On the contrary, it would probably have a precisely opposite effect. By multiplying international contacts, it would multiply international animosities; and upon each outbreak of trouble the indirectly involved powers would be less likely to act constitutionally as suppressors, than to divide according to sympathy and previous alignment, and to participate as combatants. Oaths and treaties are worth no more than the honour of those who make them. Set up one league, and it will soon be undermined by a score of clandestine inner leagues.

What we need as an international safeguard is not a cumbrous and futile federation of miscellaneous nations good and bad, with the independence of each one virtually destroyed; but a simple and practical alliance betwixt those powers such as the United States, Great Britain, France, and Italy, which inherit in common the highest ideals, and which possess almost no conflicting interests. Those who hold up our Federal Union as an example of a "League" in working order would do well to mark the fact that the component states are all of one general type, and not in any way comparable to the widely diverse nations of the globe. Such an alliance, properly armed, would constitute an almost resistless and stable force in world-politics; affording the best defence possible for our civilisation, and providing the best possible guarantee against needless wars.

Let us cease to think in unrealities, or to mouth such benevolent but empty catchwords as "disarmanent" and "universal brotherhood." We are living not in Paradise but on Earth ;and will fare best if we marshal the harmonious forces of civilisation in a sensible way for an attainable object, rather than rashly yoke together opposed and dissimilar cultures in the vain hope of realising a fantastic and impossible ideal.

BOLSHEVISM

The most alarming tendency observable in this age is a growing disregard for the established forces of law and order. Whether or not stimulated by the noxious example of the almost sub-human Russian rabble, the less intelligent element throughout the world seems animated by a singular viciousness, and exhibits symptoms like those of a herd on the verge of stampeding. Whilst long-winded politicians preach universal peace, long-haired anarchists are preaching a social upheaval which means nothing more or less than a reversion to savagery or mediaeval barbarism. Even in this traditionally orderly nation the number of Bolsheviki, both open and veiled, is considerable enough to require remedial measures. The repeated and unreasonable strikes of important workers, seemingly with the object of indiscriminate extortion rather than rational wage increase, constitute a menace which should be checked.

To a certain extent, our government will probably meet these conditions with legislation affecting seditious speech and treasonable acts; but if a permanent cure is to be accomplished, something deeper and more educational will be needed. It will require propaganda to combat propaganda. The present agitation undoubtedly arises from the false belief in the possibility of a radically altered social order. The workers who strike, and the shouters who incite to crime, are obviously possessed of the notion that the property of the wealthy could practicably be shared with them; that even if they were to seize the things they covet, they could continue the enjoyment of civilised existence and of protection against violence.

We need a new Menenius Agrippa to proclaim and demonstrate widely the total fallacy of such an illusion. Our present social order, whilst capable of some degree of liberalisation, is the product of the natural development of human relations. It is not ideal, nor could anything on earth be ideal—but it is inevitable. Just as long as some men are more intelligent than others, so long will there be inequality of wealth. The type of persons who indulge in strikes and socialism seem never to realise how much they depend on the brains of their hated "economic masters." They do not reflect that if they were to seize the factories and governments as they desire, they would be totally powerless to run them. The lawless I. W. W. sometimes boasts of its prospective ability to overthrow orderly government and substitute a sanguinary reign of the so-called "proletariat." Perhaps such a catastrophe will come, just as the Russian catastrophe came; but how little will the blind anarchists gain therefrom! With the intelligent element removed, the rabble will use up the resources of civilisation without being able to produce more; cities and public works will fall into decay, and a new barbarism arise, out of which will spring in time the natural chieftains who will constitute the "masters" of another era of capitalism. Far better that the impressionable and inflammable masses be taught these things before they embark upon a futile revolution which will ruin all civilisation, themselves included, without helping anyone.

FOR OFFICIAL EDITOR—ANNE TILLERY RENSHAW

Associational politics, happily dormant since the sordid period of 1916, has once more raised its sinister head to challenge the achievements of those who have laboured in behalf of the United's evolution; and distasteful though the subject may be to the true friend of amateur literature, prompt discussion is necessary if the work of recent terms is not to be undone. Out of its native darkness after a welcome absence of three years comes the turbulent Cleveland element (apologies to Mr. Samuel Loveman—shining exception!) with its attending train of blatant vulgarity and innuendo, bent on seating in the Official Editor's chair a candidate of such conspicuous unfitness for power that his defeat becomes a public duty on the part of those who cherish the progress and paramountcy of the United.

Direct comment on The Cleveland Sun and what it represents is obviously impossible in these columns, because of the boorishly sneering attitude which that contemporary has chosen to adopt toward The Conservative and his efforts in amateurdom. Comment, under these circumstances, could not but reflect a certain amount of personal disgust and purely subjective opposition. But no such inhibitions of good taste restrain the pen which would point out reasons why one William J. Dowdell of Bearcat notoriety must not be allowed to acquire the enormous—almost supreme—influence as a molder of policy which goes with the Official Editorship of the United Amateur Press Association.

Mr. Dowdell, ever since he became old enough to entertain opinions of his own, has consistently favoured the cruder and less desirable side of amateur journalism. His bitter and puerile hostility to those improvements of 1915-16 which placed the United upon its present cultural basis, and his very singular oversights as Secretary in mailing proxy ballots, are too well known to require citation; while his more recent complete devotion to the National speaks for itself. The absurd anti-Campbell outbursts appearing in the Bearcat three years ago worked greatly to the detriment of the United, and gave the National ground for one of its illiberal attacks upon us. As a publisher—and it is as a publisher par excellence that he makes his appeal for votes—no one can fail to see that Mr. Dowdell's claims far exceed his accomplishments. He is, indeed, a veritable Prince of Broken Promises. Members of the United who contributed cash for the co-operative paper he was to issue in 1916, are still awaiting the arrival of that paper; meanwhile wondering why their literary matter was pirated by Mr. Dowdell's personal Bearcat, and why their money has not been refunded!

Mr. Dowdell glibly pledges himself to a continuance of the McGeoch editorial policy if elected. Do his past and present performances warrant such a prediction? Since actions speak louder than words, it appears to The Conservative that the election of Mr. Dowdell would result in an abrupt drop in the official organ from classical to plebeian standards. Mr. Dowdell is clever, and could go far in literature if he chose; but up to now he has shown no inclination to succeed except on a very low cultural plane—the plane of commercial "yellow" newspaper journalism. His artistic birth has not yet taken place. It is probably no exaggeration to say that the Bearcat and Sun, as now conducted, are fair specimens of the grade of official organ which Mr. Dowdell would give us—when he might condescend to give us any. Need more be said? Forewarned is forearmed!

The vote of every well-wisher of the United Amateur Press Association should be cast for Mrs. ANNE TILLERY RENSHAW as Official Editor. Mrs. Renshaw, now an Instructor in Pennsylvania State College, and a reciter and poetess of repute, needs no introduction to amateurs. Her work as a recruiter has been the greatest constructive force in the United during recent years, and of available candidates she alone is able to maintain the McGeoch editorial standards. Under her guidance the official organ can continue to act as a nucleus for the intellectual activities of the Association, without it, the organ must inevitably lose prestige, and the best elements of our membership become dormant or disappear entirely from amateurdom. Few realise how much of next year's programme hinges absolutely upon Mrs. Renshaw's election.

It would be interesting to analyse the motives of those "dark forces" which have set up a candidate in opposition to Mrs. Renshaw. Significant indeed is their close connexion with the rival society—Mr. Dowdell is now a National member only, and has not been in the United for a period of more than two years. These Clevelandites come to us from the National with plans which if successful will tend to submerge our Association and restore to the senior organisation its long-coveted ancient supremacy. Shall we not rally to the defence of the United with votes for Mrs. Renshaw as Official Editor?

AMATEURDOM

Judging from the quality of most of the United papers which have lately reached The Conservative's desk, amateur journalism has now attained a cultural level not before touched since the later eighties and early nineties. At what other period in recent years has the space of six months afforded such a display of wit and intellect as is included in the journals appearing since the dawn of 1919? To mention The United Amateur would be redundant. Under the McGeoch regime that organ is wholly beyond praise; a model which our competitors both envy and emulate. But the uniformity with which individual publications maintain high standards, is as remarkable as it is encouraging. In steady succession have arrived The Recruiter, Pine Cones, The Hellenian, Corona, and The Piper; the last named of which comes just in time for admiring recognition in these columns.

Pine Cones and Corona represent a departure from conventional typography which establishes an excellent precedent. Too much importance has been attached to the printing-press in modern amateurdom, and it is gratifying to observe that editors are beginning to realise the more basic object of literature—the diffusion of thought irrespective of medium. It is noteworthy that these non-printed journals occupy the highest rank, intellectually, amongst the season's products. If this worthy example is followed as it should be, our circle will be enriched by the utterances of many learned and cultural members hitherto inarticulate through inability to issue printed papers.

The untimely death of Mrs. Helene Hoffman Cole is a source of lamentation throughout amateurdom. In the loss of so gifted and diligent a worker, the cause suffers immeasurably. United members perused with melancholy interest the May official organ, which contained numerous tributes to Mrs. Cole, and which forms a literary monument to her honoured memory. Of corresponding value will be the forthcoming *Hellenian,* commenced by Mrs. Cole but shortly before her demise, and completed by Mr. Cole as an affectionate memorial.

That amateurs of intelligence are not indifferent to man's chief solace and source of inspiration, is well demonstrated by the almost simultaneous appearance of two poems in praise of books; one by Mr. Kleiner in The Piper, the other by Mr. Goodenough in these columns. Both pieces represent genius of a high order, and both will awaken an universal response from those readers who have weighed carefully the relative value of life's various blessings.

Mr. John Milton Samples' regularly issued monthly, The Silver Clarion, is an amateur journal whose progress and development should be watched with interest. At present censured by certain critics for its atmosphere of sanctity and unsophistication, it has lately enlarged its editorial staff and embarked upon a course of steady artistic development. Its policy, however, will not be altered; and it will remain as a sturdy exponent of honest Anglo-Saxon virtue in an age tainted with degeneracy and continental ideals.

The Conservative

Edited by H. P. Lovecraft under the Auspices of the United Amateur Press Association. Published at 598, Angell St., Providence, R. I., U. S. A.

The Conservative, Twelfth Number

March, 1923

Edited by H. P. Lovecraft

THOMAS HOLLEY CHIVERS

(Buried at Decatur, Georgia)

Beneath these pines and lucent skies,
Forgotten, save by those that know,
The loneliest Immortal lies—
A poet and the friend of Poe.

Somewhere on Heaven's chancel floor,
Where wandering stars and orbits meet
So high, it dared no longer soar,
His song rose marvellously sweet.

He sang of Heaven ere twilight fell,
Of cherubim and seraphim,
And in the radiance visible,
Their loneliness crept over him.

Something half-alien and remote,
A sense of gold on lips athrong,
And from that perilous lyric throat,
The wonder of celestial song.

And he who utter'd in his mood
The music of the stars and sun,

Lies here as any mortal would,
A serf to long oblivion.

—SAMUEL LOVEMAN,
Georgia, 1918

AN AMATEUR HUMORIST

By Frank Belknap Long, Jr.

Notwithstanding a dearth of genuine humour in recent Amateur periodicals an opulent wit breathes, and has its being within the "magic circle." And this jocularity is in nowise forced, or deliberate. It springs as naturally from the well of being as a fluctuant imp from a fabulous Arabian bottle. Amateurs have coldly courted the smile, have ceaselessly strained after brilliancy. And Laughter has pensively folded her wings, and with tear-stained visage and melancholy mien has hid herself away in some dim cavern, inaccessible, remote. But the new voice is oracular—its message is replete with the cryptic wisdom of an ancient clown. It resembles the insensate quips of some King's jester with green cap and golden bells lost amid the melancholy of funereal bearers. And this brilliant joker (what a figure of Romance he is, in sooth) devotes his uncanny insight, his almost spiritual penetration to—the Poets of Amateurdom. And in a recent issue of THE ORACLE we behold him in all of the glory of his prismatic raiment. He dances in wild glee before the adamant and ivory throne of a King, and displays to the sad eyes of the tolerant but unhappy monarch the exceedingly colourful back of a baboon. Occasionally he stretches forth his long, yellow snout and bites the King viciously upon the ear with sharp, black teeth. And then he retreats in panic, awed, but still defiant, his finger to his nose. The King smiles a wan, indulgent smile, and perhaps in his heart he pities the jester. He is an eminently kind-hearted King. But the jester is happy. He has succeeded in creating a sensation; admiring eyes have been turned for one brief moment in his direction, and it should be said at once that the jester lives for that sort of thing. He is well pleased, and all concede him wit. But as the gifted playboy lacks even the rudiments of a creative imagination he does not know that he wearies the King—and he lingers on and says many absurd and childish things. One characteristic of a jester is his utter lack of all sense of beauty. The divinest strain from the most enchanted lyre drives him to a gnashing of teeth and an insane stamping of feet. His appreciation of the arts is limited. He is in a small measure interested in "thought" and he is very careful to warn us that Matthew Arnold and Milton were also profoundly thoughtful individuals. And yet it is certain that all of the nuances and subtleties of thought escape him. And as for beauty and feeling, which are of far greater import, he does not even concede their right to exist. He is hopelessly black in this respect; he has no colour in his soul; he has never gazed upon a spiritual prism. But his multi-hued raiment is so bright and dazzling that one can forgive him. He is such a jolly fellow. He mentions vision, and passion, and like a small boy who juggles with large phrases, he has not the slightest realisation of the occult significance back of the symbols. But he dotes upon the frozen didacticism of Arnold. He does not say so, of course. He is divinely witty. Oh, divinely witty. But how poor old Arnold must shock him at times. He must shriek with horror at the mere thought of Dover Beach, and one can imagine him astutely grimacing at certain other passages:

"Vainly does each as he glides, fable and dream, of the lands which the River of Time had left ere he woke on its breast, or shall reach when his eyes have been closed."

The jester is interested in no age but his own. To dream of other happier, lovelier lands on the marge of the River of Time is not to be thought of; it destroys that humility, and balance, and gray resignation so much esteemed by the whole tribe of Lacimaginatus.

But I seem to recall a poet named Samuel Loveman who sings in a voice of "surpassing beauty" of ultimate, dim thules, and of distant alien mainlands, of far incredible sea beaches, and of dim pools of ebony in centuried forests on whose banks grow monstrous red nenuphars; of miraged cities lying "within the dim West," cities of alabaster, and of bronze, and of porphyry, with tall emerald towers from the narrow windows of which ruby lights glow and send thin streams of liquid radiance out across the blue and yellow waters; and of midnight seas; and of cold, Northern suns; of griffin-guarded gateways of ivory and gold; of buccaneers from the Spanish Main; of buried treasure, and Isles lost in the misty Hebrides—but above all else he hymns the praises of that beauty which is lost to the world forever—the great, white, silent beauty of immeasurable antiquity—a beauty whose fleeting garments and fire-ensandalled feet pass with the rapidity of silver lightning in an ancient dawn. There pale white ladies wander endlessly beneath skies of opal fire, their blue eyes wide with wonder, their yellow hair wind-blown, and their cheeks suffused with ecstasy. For Samuel Loveman has "felt the eternal woes of the soul that aspires, and knows," and there can be no closing of the book for him. He has awaked from the common dream, and in big eyes the white splendour lingers still, and in his ears there still rings the "music of the spheres." He has passed through lands where nightingales sing eternally, and where the foliage is wrought of the purest gold; and he has glimpsed the beauty of the silver night; the morning beauty of stars, and wind, and rain; and he knows the beauty of the enormous void, and the beauty of the Tomb. And he has seen other stranger, sweeter things—his eyes are still open upon that Supernal Loveliness that dwells in Heaven upon a sapphire throne, and communes with the seraphs who chant in ecstasy a golden antiphon. But the jester laughs with mirthless mockery, and sends up his impotent protest to the pale stars. He has never heard the wind moan about the purple promontories of Mytilene; he has never looked upon the face of Sappho, her eyes congealed with the wind and silver spray; never has he beheld the dream-enchanted Isles lying white and still in a sea of the deepest blue, where "grew the Arts of War, and Peace!"—never has he beheld Delos rise, and Phoebus spring. What to him are the "Islands of the Blest" and the pity of beauty vanishing before the day?

There is a faculty divine called imagination—the jester does not know it. There is vision, and passion, and pity, in the world—the jester does not know it! There is tolerance, and understanding, and sympathy in the world—this excellent joker stamps his feet, and grimaces. He has annoyed the Monarch on his adamant throne, and no one will deny him wit.

But he is so utterly naive! He reads "A Triumph in Eternity," and all of its unearthly beauty and splendour of vision is lost upon him. Loveman has wrought with moonlight, and iris, and pearl, but to the jester these lovely attributes are merely "fireworks"—a framework upon which to hang the poem (or was it the other way about)? He then proceeds to dissect this exquisite lyric with a pair of rusty tweezers, and flatters himself that the experiment is a strictly scientific one. But after he has pulled it all to pieces he discovers to his horror that each individual fragment glows with a spectral beauty of its own. There is but one thing left for him to do; he must consign the poem to everlasting perdition. So he confers upon it the following splenetic benediction: "In anyone but an amateur poet with an amateur perception of things held sacred in a Christian country the whole piece would be considered blasphemous!" There was a time when a statement of that sort would have called the gods down from the sky; unfortunately the gods today are occupied with more important matters. But here is a gem: "It may fairly be asserted that the time when readers are interested in the antics of pagan gods is gone forever." When Swinburne read anything of that sort he emitted a low scream, and vanished. I shall emulate him. OOOOoo!

IN THE EDITOR'S STUDY

Rursus Adsumus

Again the dispensations of fortune permit THE CONSERVATIVE to appear before the public in wonted guise; mellowed perhaps by the passing of time, yet in essence as unchanged as his title would indicate. In the world around, the spectator beholds a multitude of mutations; as younger minds arise to impugn the values and discard the manners of former days. With such bold adventurers THE CONSERVATIVE will contend less bitterly than of yore, for with age he hath grown mindful of the spirit of originality; yet for himself he will crave the reciprocal indulgence of his juniors, and assert on their own ground of individuality the right to cling to his accustom'd periwig and small-clothes. Whilst they, in hectic style, dissect the smallest particles of thought and invade the remotest recesses of consciousness; it may perhaps be permitted to an old gentleman to view the world as a natural whole without the microscope of modernity, and to express himself in a fashion which, if stilted, is scarce more so than the fashions of youth with their misused words and pertly artificial affectations.

Rudis Indigestaque Moles

The Conservative, observing the complacent indifference of most amateurs toward the present state of literature and general aesthetics, hath frequently wondered how acute be their realisation of just what is taking place. The average amateur paper, when it can spare the space from subjects so titanic as politics, conventions and personalities, is unique in its allegiance to the accepted art and literature of the past; and in its happy oblivion regarding the menaces offered by the present and future. To read such a paper one would gather that Tennyson and Longfellow are still taken seriously as poets, and that the sentiments and sentimentalities of our fathers are still capable of awakening the Muse and forming the basis of future works of art. A protest against this species of myopia was some time ago uttered by one of our ultra-radicals; but lost force because of its origin and form. Perhaps it would not be improper for a CONSERVATIVE, whose sympathy with extreme manifestations is little enough, to call renewed attention to the situation.

Do our members realise that the progress of science within the last half-century has introduced conceptions of man, the world, and the universe which make hollow and ridiculous an appreciable proportion of all the great literature of the past? Art, to be great, must be founded on human emotions of much strength; such as come from warm instincts and firm beliefs. Science having so greatly altered our view of the universe and the beliefs attendant upon that view, we are now confronted by an important shifting of values in every branch of art where belief is concerned. The old heroics, pieties and sentimentalities are dead amongst the sophisticated; and even some of our appreciations of natural beauty are threatened. Just how expansive is this threat, we do not know; and The Conservative hopes fervently that the final devastated area will be comparatively narrow; but in any case startling developments are inevitable.

A glance at the serious magazine discussion of Mr. T. S. Eliot's disjointed and incoherent "poem" called "The Waste Land," in the November DIAL, should be enough to convince the most unimpressionable of the true state of affairs. We here behold a practically meaningless collection of phrases, learned allusions, quotations, slang, and scraps in general; offered to the public (whether or not as a hoax) as something justified by our modern mind with its recent comprehension of its own chaotic triviality and disorganisation. And we behold that public, or a considerable part of it, receiving this hilarious melange as something vital and typical; as "a poem of profound significance", to quote its sponsors.

To reduce the situation to its baldest terms, man has suddenly discovered that all his high sentiments, values, and aspirations are mere illusions caused by physiological processes within himself, and of no significance whatsoever in an infinite and purposeless cosmos. He has discovered that most of his acts spring from hidden causes remote from the ones hitherto honoured by tradition, and that his so-called "soul" is merely (as one critic puts it) a rag-bag of unrelated odds and ends. And having made these discoveries, he does not know what to do about it; but compromises on a literature of analysis, chaos, and ironic contrast.

What will come of it? This we cannot say; but certainly, great alterations are due amongst the informed. European culture has reached the Alexandrian stage of effeteness, and we probably cannot hope for anything better than diverging streams of barren intellectualism and of an amorphous, passionate art founded on primal instincts rather than delicate emotions. The emotions will be minutely analysed and laughed at; the instincts will be glorified and wallowed in. The hope of art, paradoxically enough, lies in the ability of future generations not to be too well informed; to be able, at least, to create certain artificial limitations of consciousness and enjoy a gently whimsical repetition and variation of the traditional images and themes, whose decorative beauty and quaintness can never be wholly negligible to the sensitive taste. It is, for example, hardly possible that moonlight on a marble temple, or twilight in an old garden in spring, can ever be other than beautiful in our eyes. Bourgeois and plebeian literature, of course, will undoubtedly go on without change; for the thoughts of the great majority are rarely affected by the subtleties of progress. The Edgar A. Guests are secure in their unassuming niches. But it is only by the higher strata that we can judge a literature in its historic perspective, so that the permanent residuum of folk or ballad aesthetics does not figure in the problem. Never before, it is interesting to note, have the popular and the sophisticated types of literature been so widely divergent as at present.

Meanwhile it is singular that so few echoes of the prevailing turbulence should have reached our amateur press. Shall we remain comfortably cloistered with our Milton and Wordsworth, never again to know the amusing buzzing of such quaint irritants as LES MOUCHES FANTASTIQUES? THE CONSERVATIVE confesses himself curious to know what other amateur authors and editors think of "The Waste Land" and its bizarre analogues!

The Conservative

Edited and Published by H. P. Lovecraft, 598 Angell St., Providence, R. I., under the Auspices of Amateur Journalism and the National and United Amateur Press Associations.

The Conservative, Thirteenth Number

July, 1923

EDITED BY H. P. LOVECRAFT

TO SATAN

By Samuel Loveman

"Tu tires ton pardon de l'eternal martyre
Inflige sans relache aux coeurs ambitieux."

—BAUDELAIRE

To H. P. L.

WHEN, mid the hyacinth deep that girds the sky,
You saw, O Brother, ere your eyes grew dim,
In wrath and loneliness the sight of Him,
Amid His bow'd and litten hierarchy:
Heard songs that fell from lips half-strange with years,
Outcast and ruin'd, beautiful in flame,
You—with the lost among the damned few,
The fallen rebel crew—
Hearing the flattery that fawned His name,
Turn'd back to hell a face that shone with tears.

Did you not at the sunken portals wait,
And where the golden estuaries fell,
Gazing at heav'n before the glow of hell,
Stretch forth your hand to where the tyrant sate?

With the first cry that shook th' enslaved world,
Swift, silver, clarion, Lo! I make you free,
Free as the winds and as the waters are,
Sons of the morning-star!
O souls of mine, I give you liberty—
No withering hate into the darkness hurl'd!

Not from those spaces charm'd to dusk and rose,
Nor in the scarves with light and music pent,
Came the soft wail of disillusionment,
But lower than the lowliest in their woes,
The trodden and the dispossess'd of fate;
These, brooding in a quiet flash of tears,
By stars that to the massive night are graven,
Recall'd their austere haven—
The sorrow and the bitterness of years,
Conceiv'd in ruin and embalm'd in hate!

And now shall men no longer fear and dread!
For heav'n is shatter'd, faded is the host,
That without pity judg'd the tortur'd lost,
And radiantly parcell'd forth the dead.
See! where your molten throne uprears in night
The legions gleam, the drowsy vultures wing;
That which first met your plaintive, human eyes,
Ev'n that, is paradise......
At last, my Brother, the awakening!
Ere Dawn appears, a perfect chrysolite.

FELIS

A Prose Poem

By Frank Belknap Long, Jun.

OH, how delightful it is to stroke the sinuous hair of felicitous cats. Long, long ago I discovered that these happy creatures know more than Adam our father because they have never been tempted by the evil one, have never eaten of the forbidden fruit and have never fallen. I know that in their great, tearless, seductive eyes there lurk sinister secrets, pre-incarnate hieroglyphics which only the gods can fathom, secrets and signs which portend nothing but evil for man. And they are immortal; you cannot kill them. When the tiny sphere which certain weary seers have agreed to call the earth, for lack of a better name, shall have permitted itself to become cold through sheer ennui there shall yet remain the cats. They are immortal and shall live always, even as the old stone gods, even as the voluptuous Venus, even as the albine and implacable Oelphic Apollo. Long have I studied them, and I have become, in a degree, their slave. They have begun to exercise an unholy fascination over me and have even stolen into my dreams, into the secret chambers of my fancy. I shall always see them now, whenever I dream, large, and sinewy and soft with prismatic eyes, scintillating eyes, vacillating eyes, eyes green and blue, and pale, washed-out yellow, like the mournful orbs of the melancholy Kakue bird of Paraguay who possesses the immortal soul of a negress. And in my dreams they climb over my arms and legs and purr and whine disconsolately. And when I reach out, fascinated, and smooth their long fur I experience a joy at once profound and awful—*because their fur is soft and burns my fingers.* There is something *outré* about their fur. I have seen great waste places entirely inhabited by cats. I have seen cats of all colors, of all shades, of all hues, and of every shape and size. I have seen skeleton cats and cats with elephantiasis and deformed and misshapen and dwarfed cats. I have seen cats that could talk and cats that could laugh and, yes, I have actually seen a cat who could dance. But whenever I dream of cats I see the spiced mummy of some august Pharaoh, or a skeleton rider carrying a scythe riding furiously around an ever widening circle or a radiant corpse swinging gracefully under a cloudless blue sky. When I walk the streets of our great cities I am haunted by cats. I see them everywhere, behind the smooth glass of costly limousines, on street corners, in the languid eyes of women, by deserted waterfronts, in the smoke of a man's pipe, on top of tall buildings, down dark and unfrequented alleys, and in the pale yellow light of the city's gas lamps. Some day I shall drown in a sea of cats. I shall go down, smothered by their embraces, feeling their warm breath upon my face, gazing into their large eyes, hearing in my ears their soft purring. I shall sink lazily clown through oceans of fur, between myriads of claws, clutching innumerable tails and I shall surrender my wretched soul to the selfish and insatiable god of felines.

THE CROCK O' GOLD

By Lilian Middleton

When the round moon's shining and the timid dew' a-glisten,
And the corn-crake calls the night-long from the far-off wold,
You can hear the fairies singing if you'll only stop to listen,
And the lepracauns a-dancing round their treasur'd Crock o' Gold!

'Tis a land of strange enchantment,—and oh! its songs and stories!
And the blue sky wraps the mountains softly, fold to fold,
But I left that world of magic, with its age-old, misty glories,
To travel to the Rainbow's End, to find the Crock o' Gold!

Oh! I know the gillygowans on the mountain-side are glowing,
And the blackbird in the hawthorne whistles clear and bold,—
And I'm sick to death with longing, for 'tis now that I am knowing
That my island was the Rainbow's End, and there the Crock o' Gold!

INTUITION IN THE PHILOSOPHY OF BERGSON

By A. T. Madison

THE idea of intuition, while not the most novel of M. Henri Bergson's singular contributions to contemporary philosophy, appears to be fundamental to his entire system; and is indeed the key to understanding the methods by which this strange personality arrives at his notions. We find scattered throughout his writings several attempts to analyse it, more frequent references to its value as a new philosophical *method,* and a continual practice, quite consistent with his preaching, from which he derives many essentials of his philosophy.

This insistence upon mystical method is perhaps Bergson's most vital connexion with contemporary thought, and therefore one of the chief causes of his now fading popularity. This is palpably an age in which mysticism, if not dominant, is at least an element to be reckoned with. Moreover, it makes acceptance of Bergson's system easier to the normal person, because it seems to lend an extra-intellectual plausibility to many of his vagaries.

While reference to it is so frequent in his works, particularly in his *magnum opus,* I have been unable to find a reasonable analysis of the method anywhere. In chapter two of "Creative Evolution," after stating that instinctive and intelligent life are two complementary directions of the central life stream, he says: "These are things that intelligence alone is able to seek, but which, by itself, it will never find. These things instinct alone could find; but it will never seek them." There seems to be a difficulty here, which Bergson recognises even more explicitly a trifle later: "But a glance at the evolution of living beings shows us that intuition could not go very far. On the side of intuition, consciousness found itself so restricted by its envelope that intuition had to shrink into instinct."

The difficulty here is heightened by the difficulty of finding any experiential background for this analysis—it is another offspring of Bergson's "intuition." I have shown that his analysis of the functions of instinct and intellect, overlooking its other faults, seems unable to give us any clearer comprehension of intuition; but some of his other statements are superficially more satisfactory. In one place he says that intuition is "instinct that has become disinterested, self-conscious, capable of reflecting upon its object and of enlarging it indefinitely." The word "reflection" would seem to posit a certain co-operation of intellect in the process, and elsewhere Bergson recognises this. His view seems to be perfectly honest, and fairly consistent. He is in possession of a certain rather undefinable method of thinking, closely connected with the traditional sense of the word "intuition." He makes laudable efforts to explain this process, and manages to convey to us, in an indirect way, much of its essence.

Assuming, therefore, that Bergson is unable to give a scientific justification of his method, still is it not superior to that of the intellect? Bergson apparently thinks so. His whole analysis of the function of the intellect is a marvellously clever demonstration of his claim that intellect can not handle life, but is only at home in restricted spaces, with inert matter. But does his own method negate intellect? He is unable to define it, however nebulously, without including its expressed enemy. He admits outright more than once, that his "instinct" is by itself as helpless as intellect—indeed more so, for how can instinctive knowledge become conscious knowledge except through intellect? He does not say; therefore we may assume that instinct plays the initiatory role, but that it can only become knowledge when it reaches the higher thought centres.

There is, however, a vital contradiction to intellectualism, in that the intellect is not accepted as the ultimate source of knowledge, or judge between contradictory sources, and is discredited as far as possible from any participation in the knowing process. This is Bergson's mysticism; what does it mean?

The basic assumption in his plea for a new method, is that this "letting oneself go," this mystical *introspection,* can produce uniform results if philosophers apply themselves to it with proper zeal. There is something ludicrous about the vision that comes to my mind when Bergson pleads for a "new method" in philosophy. What a waste of perfectly good mathematical ability! Why not import spirit mediums into the profession, and be assured of fuller, if perhaps less accurate data? But that is beside the point, which is to find out what Bergson's intuition is and whether it will do all he thinks it will.

In the case of Bergson himself, there is apparently a large element of imagination, particularly of a *visual* sort, in his mentality. His figures of speech are distinctly pictorial; he has a habit of mistaking a particularly clear figure for a logical explanation. His picture of the vital impetus, of the evolution of life, is especially strong in imaginative quality. One is lead to suspect, then, that his own "intuition," from which he apparently derives the general notion of the process in others, has a great deal of the poetic imagination in it.

Now, the difficulty about imagination, however well it be grounded in reliable "instinctive knowledge," is that it differs so markedly in the individual. It is an attribute of genius, perhaps the most inseparable of them all, but geniuses are notorious for following their own bent, and for being different from all who have come before. In Plato it gave the supra-sensible world, in Spinoza the "all", in Leibnitz the monad. And worst of all, it is impossible to argue with the authoritative visions of genius. The whole panorama is a vast postulate, no part of which will its parent allow to be argued from the rest. While intellect is a common meeting ground, in which all ideas must subscribe to the laws of logic and common experience; on the other hand, intuition is so indefinite that no two individuals can possibly have the same understanding of it, and it authorises the individual experience in sharp distinction from the common.

Reality, reached in this clandestine and subjective manner, becomes determined by the emotional association of the individual. And at this point Bergson seems to stop. He is effective from some points of view, in attacking intellect; but his own vision is not of the sort which spreads, like that of Swedenborg or Bruno, or Plotinus. Intuition, as far as I can see it, becomes contradictory to real philosophy when it is emphasised in preference to reason. It necessarily gives the individual his data for speculation, and is a necessary attribute of great philosophy. But to seek the intuition rather than the why and wherefore, is an emotional process, which modern psychology is gradually showing to be merely one form of self-delusion. In persons of strongly imaginative temperament it means much; in art, literature, and the more refined contacts of life, this vague fellow-feeling is much more necessary than conscious syllogism. But it is not philosophy, and to ask philosophers to adopt it as a method is ridiculous.

The real effect of Bergson's plea is to make disciples of a certain cosmic temperament akin to his own, and to give them the groundwork of an inner mystical life. But it does not stimulate research into reality. If you care to agree with Bergson you will probably have little independent contribution to make. If you don't, more than likely you will reach a reality entirely distinct from the reality of Creative Evolution; or your introspection may lack the credibility of Bergson's, and you may be forced to abandon the method entirely.

The whole appeal, then, as I see it, is for people to sympathise with the opinions of this queer, this unique thinker. His philosophy is almost entirely without social connections, in essence or in presentation. Other philosophers feel themselves one of many, or at least recognise themselves as philosophers. Bergson seems to think of himself as an eye apart. He speaks disapprovingly of "metaphysics," "philosophers," "scientists," "the intellect," and even of his old occupation, mathematics. His intuition is personal, it places originality higher than consistency, and it seeks personal participation. For this reason it always seems to me that Bergson is persuading rather than convincing. He wants to wheedle one to his side, and he will use the most plausible argument at hand.

On the other hand, adopting a broader and sympathetic attitude, one may see much of value in the emphasis, at least, in Bergson's method. Like James, Nietzsche, and other typical modernists, he wants to inject *life* into philosophy. But Nietzsche puts life above truth; James makes life the criterion of truth, while Bergson has fundamentally nothing more to contribute than the mystics of the past. He wants, it might be put, to make philosophy interesting—he is in a certain sense a romanticist, even an impressionist. But I rather fear he is working in the wrong material. Philosophy is an ancient and sedate institution; break through it, like one of Bergson's rockets, and when the sparks have died down the eternal Logical Mind must analyse the light and bring it into focus with proved or accepted facts of past philosophers. His own most important additions to the stream of thought have been those in which he was most consistent, either within himself, or with experience. Apart from these isolated arguments; his temporalism, his conceptions of life and intellect, and so on, he is important only because of his spirit—his intuition. He had a gorgeous cosmic vision and he used every resource of argument, language, and feeling to make that vision common to mankind.

THE STORM

By John Ravenor Bullen

Beware! Beware! that sullen cloud,
        The Tempest's ebon form.
Though deathly still....its darkness dense
Is herald of a wrath intense....
        The calm before the storm.

Hark to the distant moaning sound,
        The soul with dread it fills;
The trees are trembling with affright,
As the wind shrieks out of the dismal night,
        And echoes through the hills.

Behold the raging tempest's might,
        The heav'ns are streak'd with fire.
The lightning paints its lurid scars,
The thunder bursts its prison bars,
        So fierce the storm king's ire.

Lash'd by the gale, the once calm sea
        Now writhes in tortur'd pain,
The foam-capp'd billows roar with rage,
And fierce in fight with the shore engage,
        But rear their crests in vain.

Stay! but stay! the scene is chang'd,
        All, now, is quiet and calm;
The driven clouds have ceas'd their tears,
The Earth hath cast away her fears,
        Peace reigns where once alarm.

ENNUI

By Anatol Kleinst

When the earth blossomed and was green again, I denied the god of desolation and went among the trees. I breathed incense, and I knew that the gods of the forest were breathing their offerings to the implacable blue sky. I breathed of it as would the sky, had it any soul, and knowing that the sky had none, I was a god. For a moment joy was in me.

But the spirit of desolation was angry, and smote me. I did not see him; the grass, the flowers, sun and wind still moulded their evanescent palaces of warm perfume; but the will of my god is mighty, and he supplants these things. Then desire glistened in my brain, like a grey moon when the stars are out; I desired joy and lo! it had slipped away, and left not even sorrow in its place. And my desire grew strong, and I felt the strength of it through all my spirit; and I envisioned my dead sister Pain and would have sung to her in a high and melancholy voice. I would have sung to her of the cruel moist lips of love, and of the agony that creates hope, of immeasurable fair gardens that mock the frenzy of fine words, of the ruin that comes to dreams in the morning: I would have chanted to the lonely bones of the desert the purity and exaltation that was once Pain. But the words were harsh, and the savour of their sickly passion suddenly cast me into despair. "Ai; Ai! Thou that dreamed of mountains and would be a God! Thou that spurned men and rebuilt fallen castles, and sang at night, in the desert, the anthem of your immemorial pride! Thy voice is pallid, it is not the voice of man, it is not the hymn of thy sister Pain; and as you speak you dishonour the crystalline vapours that are words, for your soul is empty, and its voice is hollow." And I beat my breast, and quaffed unspeakable wines, and called to my garden the dancers of Eudemia, who danced before me with no garment, and were not ashamed, for they loved me. And I cried at them to go away, and pored over the beautiful mad parchments of old poets, and knew the thing that drove them mad. But in all this the voice of despair laughed always as men do not ever laugh, while it sucked the blood of my heart and sent it poisoned through strange channels in my breast.

Then I regained my voice, and it rose to the grey mansion of my God, saying, "Behold, you have taken away joy and beauty, give me now suffering, that I may feel one of men, and let me weep with the beggar at the cross-roads!" But my God spoke only in his old accents of despair……

Then I grew angry, and denied again my God. And the mocking sharp voice of despair rose higher and became pale song. And this is what it sang, to the tepid sands of my little desert, as the sky was silent.

FAUSE MURDOCH

By James F. Morton, Jun.

FAUSE MURDOCH stude in gude greenwode,
Aneath a tall elm-tree;
He's set his horn intil his mouth,
An' blawn laud blasts fu' three.

He' blawn sae laud as he can blaw,
Wi' mickle micht an' main;
An' sune he saw his merry men a'
Cum ridin' o'er the plain.

"Licht doon, licht doon, my merry men a',
Ye's need na steed today;
There roams a stag amang these trees,
Which we maun find an' slay."

Wi' that out spak the bauld MacPhail;
His sister's son was he;
"Sae mony men to slay ae stag,
I trow this needna be."

"Thou brags too sune, thou bauld MacPhail!
The stag that we maun slay
Wears antlers keen an' hoofs of steel,
An' dreads na mortal fray."

"I dinna fear his antlers keen,
Na mair his hoofs of steel;
An' gin I meet him in the chase,
My knife he's quickly feel."

"Now hauld thy word, thou bauld MacPhail!
I pray thee hauld thy word!
That stag we seek's the proud Gordon,
Wha ne'er shunn'd foeman's sword.

"Fu' mony a deep an' deadly aith
I've sworn, his bluid to spill;
An' I maun win his ladye's luve,
Or bend her to my will."

A' this beheard a little footpage,
Fast hid ahind a tree;
An' he's awa' to seek his laird,
Sae fast as he can hie.

"Why rinn'st thou sae, my little footpage?"
"O flee for luve of Heaven!
Fause Murdoch comes to seek thy life,
Bot' an' his followers seven!"

"Thou leest, thou leest, thou little footpage!
Sae loud's I hear thee lee!
Young Murdoch is my ain cousin;
Wad ne'er wark ill to me."

"Yet haste, yet haste, my ain dear laird!
Ise rede thee haste awa';
He's sworn to win thy fair ladye,
An' spill thy bluid today."

"Rin fast, rin fast, thou little footpage!
Gae seek my brithers twain;
An' bid them cum to succour me,
Before that I be slain."

The little footpage sped sae fast,
Nae swallow sae micht fly;
Bot ere he fand those bauld brithren,
The Gordon's faes were nigh.

An' foremaist cam' the bauld MacPhail,
Wha aye socht bluid an' strife;
An' he is gane to the proud Gordon,
To reave him of his life.

He's aimit a blaw at the Gordon's head,
Wad gar an ox doon fa';
The Gordon steppit swift aside,
An' gat na hurt at a'.

He's raised his arm, a' wode wi' rage,
To deal a deadly smart;
Bot the Gordon, wi' a stroke sae keen,
Has pierc'd him to the heart.

He's turned himsel', an' set his back
Until a braid aik-tree;
"Fause traitors, ere ye win my life,
There's some of you sall dee!"

They've drawn their swords, wi' murd'rous spite,
An' ran at him amain;
Bot ere they had their wicked will,
Three traitors mair lay slain.

Bot aye wae warth the fause Murdoch!
And an ill death mout he dee!
He's creppit behind wi' a coward's stroke,
An' cut the Gordon's knee.

"Wae warth, wae warth thee, fause Murdoch!
For I may ficht na mair.
Bot hadst thou fac'd me like a man,
Thou'st rued thy treason sair!"

An' they hae slain the proud Gordon,
An' left him in his bluid,
An' gane to seek that fair ladye,
Wi' a' the speed they could.

The ladye stude on catle wa',
Beheld baith dale an' down;
She saw fause Murdoch an' his men
Cum ridin' to the town.

"What news, what news, gude young Murdoch?"
"Ill news, thou fair ladye;
Thy laird lyes wounded in the wode,
An' cries for sicht of thee."

"Gae not, gae not, my fair ladye!"
"Fye, fye, thou serving-dame!
Young Murdoch is my laird's ain cousin;
An' sall he wark me shame?"

They've mounted themseles on their steeds sae tall,
An' her on a fair palfraye;
An' they're awa' to gude greenwode,
Whereas her dear laird lay.

An' when she saw his pale, cauld corse,
She's flung her to the ground,
An' wept sae laud, that hills an' trees
Wi' echoes rang around.

"O wha has dune this bluidy deed?"
"Be still, thou ladye fair;
Gif yon dead man has lo'ed thee much,
I'll lo'e thee ten times mair."

"Now woo me not, thou young Murdoch!
I swear by God abuve,
Sin' my ain laird's sae basely slain,
Ise hae na ither luve."

"By fair or foul," quo' fause Murdoch,
"Thoust sune belang to me!
I've slain thy laird to win thy luve,
An' winna let thee free."

He's taen her by her waist sae sma',
An' seized her lillye hand;
She shriek'd, an' struggled a' in vain
The traitor to withstand.

Richt then beheard her laird's twa brithers,
Wha cam' to seek him there;
They heard that bluidy traitor's threats,
The ladye's wild despair.

An' they hae drawn their trusty brands,
An' sped wi' micht an' main;
An' sune fause Murdoch an' his men
A' on the ground lay slain.

"Weep not, weep not, thou fair ladye,
An' gie thy sorrow o'er;
See where the traitor an' his men
Lye yonder in their gore."

"I canna joy, though the fause traitor
Lyes stiffening in his bluid;
I still maun weep for my ain dear laird,
To me he was e'er sae gude."

I WILL LEAD THEE

By Betty Earle

Announcement in March number of *Modern Age*:

"Some of the most delightful, most spontaneous songs come from children. Recognising this, we announce that hereafter this page will be devoted to the original poetry of contributors between the ages of nine and fourteen."

Letter sent to editor of *Modern Age* from Burmah:

"I realise how inadequate are these translations. In vain have I tried to reproduce the melody, the sweetness, the divine simplicity of these songs.

Only an aged poet of tremendous faith could come as he does in his boat upon the river, turn his great blind eyes to the stars, and plucking his lute here and there, sing these songs of creation.

He loves his solitude. But since his generous spirit has permitted me to accompany him to these lonely places, I try to withdraw myself from his consciousness, so that he can sing or sit silent with his large thoughts upon him, as if he were altogether alone."

Poem sent to the editor of *Modern Age* by David Paul, aged nine, Lillith, Missouri:

The Quiet plays behind the stars,
    The holy notes break forth in nestled glories.
Clouds shape and stain themselves with unnamed colors,
    shifting before the wonderment of worlds.

With the silvering strains upon them, the little stars lie still.
And there is no exhausting, no tiring, no faint farewell of lute
In the untroubled music behind the stars.

Letter sent to David Paul, Lillith, Missouri, by the editor of *Modern Age:*

"If you read the announcement in the March number of *Modern Age,* you will discover that all poems submitted must be original and must be written by the contributor, whose age must not exceed fourteen years. This fact, of course, bars from publication the poem you submitted."

Letter sent to editor of *Modern Age* from Burmah:

"Like the translations the picture fails to do him justice. You can see only a white-haired, white bearded face, the hair parted softly in the middle, the eyes introspective, dark and sad. But I see a face of strength and awful humility, a race of vision and steadfast purpose. I believe—I cannot help but believe—his singing is divine.

The seventh song is the first I have heard him sing on shore. He had walked without faltering along the reeds by the river. He seems to have an inner vision that makes guiding unnecessary. It was sunset, and the lotus was red. *'The sunlight will walk down the river-path to meet me—'* I reached hurriedly for pencil and pad."

Poem mailed to editor of *Modern Age* by David Paul, aged nine, Lillith, Missouri:

"A light will spread from sea to sea and whisper my spirit to rest;
The lotus flowers will spill their blood at my feet;
Pale they will glow and radiant-white, throwing their gladness toward me,
The sunlight will walk down the river-path to meet me,
And the flowers will come crowding to my hands."

Letter to David Paul, Lillith, Missouri, by the editor of *Modern Age:*

"I must confess I do not know where you are getting these unpublished poems. But you are, perhaps, too young to know that when you copy almost word for word the songs of another, you are committing what is called plagiarism in a publisher's office and theft in a commercial world."

Letter sent to editor of *Modern Age* from Burmah:

"With what sorrow must I send you this last song, written before he died, September the ninth.

The evening had come quietly upon us. He sat with silent fingers resting upon his lute. He spoke almost without moving. I felt that he was not speaking for the Father in saying,

'I will lead thee by the hand—,'

but that he was speaking for himself, as if he were the leader, and another, a weaker, were being led.

Still light of evening fell upon his face. So quiet he was, a wall crept up between us, a sort of holiness shutting him away from me; so that I turned my eyes to the water, knowing it was wrong to see.

When I looked at last, I knew he would never sing again."

Poem mailed to the editor of *Modern Age* by the mother of David Paul, Lillith, Missouri:

"The shadows shall grow large upon my coming.
My lamp shall descend upon thee, where men shall seek and never find.

I will lead thee by the hand into the pure, unhanging twilight.
There shall be soft stars to listen, but never, never a breath."

Letter copied and mailed to David Paul by the editor of *Modern Age:*

"I felt that he was not speaking for the Father in saying
'I will lead thee by the hand—',
but that he was speaking for himself, as if he were the
leader, and another, a weaker, were being led.
Still light of evening fell upon his face....
When I looked at last, I knew he would never sing again."

Message scrawled upon back of envelope that had been addressed to David Paul; now returned unopened to the editor of *Modern Age:*

"David Paul: Died, September 9th."

SONG XVIII CENT.

By Lilian Middleton

Because you are so calm,
M' dear!
Because you are so calm,
Unto your sweet Madonna-face
I fain would sing a psalm!
But 'faith, before such saintly grace
I shrink, a witless, hopeless case,
Because you are so calm!—

The harpischord you play,
M' dear!
The harpischord you play,
A-straying go your fingers ten,
Your gaze is far-away!
Ah! would I had an artist's pen
To paint that lovely picture when
The harpischord you play!

In church I sit in awe,
M' dear!
In church I sit in awe,
My restless limbs a-twitching make
And I would laugh haw-haw!
'Tis thus your saintly glances shake
My wits, as when a-twitch, a-quake
In church I sit in awe!

I seek to rouse your mirth,
M' dear!
I seek to rouse your mirth,
Repeat the scandal of the town,
The latest death, or birth!
So ho! you neither smile nor frown,
But mildly look me up and down,
When I would rouse your mirth!

Altho' I love your poise,
M' dear!
Altho' I love your poise,
You deem I have but slender wit,
My jocund face annoys,
I'll tarry here no more with it
Where St. Cecelai-like you sit
Altho' I love your poise!

IN THE EDITOR'S STUDY

A DESPERATE NEED of amateurdom today is an enlightened critical standard which shall save us from devotion to false, conventional, and superficial values, and blindness to all that is sincere, vital, penetrating, or genuinely ecstatic in art. The relative rarity of young blood has begun to give us a perilously Philistine bias, so that the path of the uncompromising artist in our midst is much thornier than it should be. These are times when a flash of subtle emotion or a colourful appeal to obscure and fantastic recesses of the imagination is likely to evoke a superior titter if the words sound in the least extravagant or unfamiliar to a mind bred on Dickens or the *Saturday Evening Post.* Good homely common sense, no doubt, but sadly disastrous to amateur literature.

It is time, The Conservative believes, definitely to challenge the sterile and exhausted Victorian ideal which blighted Anglo-Saxon culture for three quarters of a century and produced a milky "poetry" of shopworn sentimentalities and puffy platitudes; a dull-grey prose fiction of misplaced didacticism and insipid artificiality; an appallingly hideous system of formal manners, costume, and decoration; and worst of all, an artistically blasphemous architecture whose uninspired nondescriptness transcends tolerance, comprehension, and profanity alike.

These reflections are elicited by the urbane warfare of Philistine and Grecian so opportunely precipitated by Mr. Michael White's critique of Mr. Samuel Loveman's poetry. Mr. White, taking his stand with the hard-headed and condemning an artist who employs such strange materials as ecstacy or imagination, has naturally aroused the opposition of certain ardent fantaisistes like Mr. Frank Belknap Long, Jun., whose impressionistic reply appeared in these columns. And now we find Mr. Long the recipient of some priceless comic-supplement sarcasm from the admirers of Mr. White, a typical Boston group to whom New England's Puritan heritage has denied that touch of ethereal madness which makes for the creation and appreciation of universal, fundamental art.

Just what do these mild hostilities signify? Should we after all denounce our Eminent Victorians merely because of their support of the critic who classifies Macaulay, Carlisle, (sic) Emerson, and Shaw as "great poets", attributes unique limitations to the word *chorus,* and sits stolid in the beams of imaginative art? Is this protest of humorous, sensible clearness against symbolic, colourful intensity indeed a mark of Victorian obtuseness instead of a sane defense of tradition in the face of chaotic innovation? Certainly the position of Mr. White's circle is flawless if we are to accept art as an affair of the external intellect and commonplace, unanalysed emotions alone. THE CONSERVATIVE dissents only because he believes with most of the contemporary world that the actual foundations of art differ widely from those which the prim nineteenth century took for granted.

What is art but a matter of impressions, of pictures, emotions, and symmetrical sensations? It must have poignancy and beauty, but nothing else counts. It may or may not have coherence. If concerned with large externals of simple fancies, or produced in a simple age, it is likely to be of a clear and continuous pattern; but if concerned with individual reactions to life in a complex and analytical age, as most modern art is, it tends to break up into detached transcripts of hidden sensation and offer a loosely joined fabric which demands from the spectator a discriminating duplication of the artist's mood, The Philistine clamour for a literature of plain statement and superficial theme loses force when we assign to literature—especially poetry—its proper place in aesthetics, and compare it to such modes of expression as music and architecture, which do not speak in the language of primers.

THE CONSERVATIVE is no convert to Dadaism. Nothing, on the contrary, seems more certain to him than that the bulk of radical prose and verse represents merely the extravagant extreme of a tendency whose truly artistic application is vastly more limited. Traces of this tendency, whereby pictorial methods are used, and words and images employed without conventional connexions to excite sensations, may be found throughout literature; especially in Keats, William Blake, and the French symbolists. This broader conception of art does not outrage any eternal tradition, but honours all creations of the past or present which can show genuine ecstatic fire and a glamour not tawdrily founded on utterly commonplace emotions.

Thus the shrill laughter of the thin-blooded literalist at the ecstatic artist is founded mainly on one-sidedness and conventionality of background; the scoffer being nearly always a follower of an obsolete tradition, steeped in the orthodox English literature of the middle nineteenth century rather than immersed in the universal stream which knows neither time nor country. Such a sage, like the proverbial *homo unius libri,* may prove a formidable and witty antagonist; but his parochial limitations obviously unfit him for anything like an authoritative pronouncement on laws touching the entire human spirit. *"Les esprits médiocres,"* says La Rochefoucauld, *"condamnent d'ordinaire tout ce qui passe leur portée."* Before intelligently approaching a work of art a critic must absorb at least the rudiments of the background from which it was developed—which takes us back to the problem of dealing with the Victorian scolding and giggling which bid fair to discourage sincere aesthetic endeavor in amateur journalism.

The Conservative would unassumingly urge a slight course of literary research upon those critics who are hurling the English 19th century in our faces with so much gusto, finality, and drollery. Without wishing to emulate their own fetching pageantry of mighty names across the learned page, he would bid them consider such titans as Walter Pater, Lafcadio Hearn, Arthur Symons, Arthur Machen, Wilde, Gautier, Flaubert, Baudelaire, Verlaine, Rimbaud, Mallarme, Laforgue, D'Annunzio, or Croce—titans about whom much may be learnt even through reviews. Once really aware of the existence of this wider field, and of the extent to which it has influenced contemporary ideas of art, our conscientious Philistines could not but enlarge their horizons of tolerance. How much they might actually understand or sympathise, is a temperamental matter alien to the problem.

MR. CHARLES A. A. PARKER, with characteristically sprightly wit, remarks on the loyalty shown toward royalty in distress. At least, this is what we believe he means, although the colloquial operation of Grimm's philological law has somewhat enriddled the text. He is to be congratulated upon his able exemplification of his paragraph, as shown by a nobly satiric scorn of all foes of the snowy Archangel Michael.

MR. H. A. JOSLENS *Gipsy* is an unique and by no means unwelcome addition to amateur journalism, supplying the place of the long-departed *Les Mouches Fantastiques.* In his valiant attempt to break away from mediocrity and imitative stupidity, the editor shows a healthy artistic instinct. It must now be his care to avoid the excess of sheer revolt for revolt's sake, and the vulgarity sometimes resulting from an anti-Puritanism itself Puritanical in seriousness. Beauty, lightness, delicacy, and just a touch of irony—these are the marks of a true art independent of social or ethical barnacles, and founded on a just conception of life's essential triviality and futility.

THE APPEARANCE of a book by an amateur is always an occasion for legitimate rejoicing in our circle; and when the author can count no less than 92 years to his credit, we may be pardoned something like positive jubilation. Such is the case this month, which brings to view the complete Poetical Works or Jonathan E. Hoag, carefully edited and fittingly bound. Since Mr. Hoag is still writing with undiminished fecundity, we may expect another volume from him as he becomes a centenarian.

FEW LITERARY recommendations are more apt than that of Mr. Edward H. Cole in the *Hub Club Quill,* whereby we are advised to read the periodical essays of the eighteenth century. In many respects this glittering, cynical, rational period is closer to our own disillusioned time than any other; for it represents a dominant intellectualism and critical and analytical spirit exactly paralleling this era of Anatole France, Cabell, and the columnar sophisticates. Just as the post-Renaissance world as a whole is nearer classical antiquity than the Middle Ages, so is our 20th century much nearer the 18th than the intervening 19th century. It has long been the opinion of The Conservative that the 18th century marked a glorious apex of many kinds of taste; notably that in prose style and in all ordinary forms of architecture, furniture, and decoration. The correctness of this view seems rather pleasingly confirmed by the return to Colonial patterns now practised by American homebuilders and city-planners, and we may hope for further confirmation in the literary field.

UNUSUAL INTEREST attaches to the prospective volume of the late Mrs. Jennie E. T. Dowe's collected Irish verse, to be issued next autumn by Mr. Charles A. A. Parker for sale at a dollar and twenty-five cents per copy. It is possible that this may be the forerunner of many similar volumes of the work of amateur poets; an event of the greatest possible benefit to amateurdom, and one which would enshrine Mr. Parker as a Prince of Pioneers.

A NEWS NOTE of more than passing amateur interest is furnished by Mr. Alfred Galpin Jun.'s receipt of a Graduate Service Scholarship in the University of Chicago, for the year 1923-24. Our erstwhile infant prodigy will not only study, but teach 80 hours per quarter; thus early arriving at an academic distinction always predicted by those who unqualifiedly consider him the greatest intellectual ever connected with amateur journalism.

THE SUBTLY MIRTHFUL commentator E. M., in *L'Alouette,* curiously mistakes a Swinburnian *scream* for a *groan;* and expresses doubt as to the identity of the "Amateur Humorist" described in Frank Belknap Long's recent critical phantasy. Speaking of doubt, The Conservative presumes it is Mr. White's scholarly article which E. M. means, in alluding to something whose value equals "ooOOOO" minus the rims.

AMONG the interesting problems raised by the current Philistine-Grecian controversy in amateurdom, is one which both concerns and contains humor—the problem of when and when not to laugh in dissecting an unusual literary production seriously offered by an author whose general achievements set him definitely above the throng of the inept and the extravagant. To many, and especially to the older critics, the answer would appear farcically simple; and would involve an amused insistence on the right of a Cheshire cat to exercise his hereditary prerogative on all occasions, thus establishing the inference that possible ludicrousness in writing, if *unintentional,* is always *unconscious,* and therefore a fatal artistic defect.

This ordinary attitude is at first sight of such weight that the merest questioner exposes himself to a share of its possessors' cachinnations. Examples of really hilarious gravity are so prevalent that their recollection overshadows all the nuances of the ultimate problem. But a dispassionate view, free from the glare of the obvious, reveals one important modifying consideration in the fact that comicality always depends wholly on the system of thought and values held by the perceiver; that, in short, ridiculousness is *relative,* and conditioned by the truth, inflexibility, or paramountcy of certain common ideas which are absolute to the multitude yet merely virtual to the closer inquirer. Intelligence and education, as they open new fields of risibility, close old ones; so that the laughing-stock of one stage of culture is often the gospel of the next, and vice versa.

Remembering these things as we turn to literary criticism, we perceive the difficulty of laying down permanent laws of laughter in an age when all standards are plastic. Much of the serious and accepted literature of the past, especially where human motives and cosmic purposes are involved, is broadly comical to the mind informed in contemporary science and philosophy; and much in modern writing, where the conceptions touch on the subjective and imaginary instead of the real world, is screamingly funny to the mind accustomed to nothing but literal reality and inherited beliefs.

Thus it would seem wise to look before you laugh. A subtle writer's imagery often takes a turn which has its conceivably comic side, yet which is not only admissible but sometimes powerfully original when viewed as part of a fabric as exotic, individual, subjective, and essentially decorative as the pictured phantasmata of Sime or Beardsley. Such an artist is not unconscious of the humorous interpretation which prosaic literalism may give his occasional bizarrerie—often he laughs himself—but he retains his quaintly carven Buddhas and Sivas just as zealously, knowing that they fit his far, strange realm of alien moonlight and incense-perfumed dream, however odd or ludicrous they may appear in the workaday sunshine of Main Street.

Far be it from The Conservative to decry humor in amateur journalism. High Pegana knows how badly we need the genuine article! But are there not times when its judicious discipline augments our power of creation and appreciation in certain fields? Who will say that Lord Dunsany's delicate Arabesque touch has not suffered as his wit has become less and less detached from it, or that Arthur Machen is not the stronger for the childlike naivete of his outlook on the dream-world? And is it not possible that some of the Philistine hyperticklishness at unaccustomed whimsies springs from a lack of that deeper and more pervasive humor which sees in all human life and effort an ironic comedy? Verily, laughter is an art for the discriminating!

The Conservative

Edited and Published by H. P. Lovecraft, 598 Angell St.,
Providence, R.I., under the auspices of Amateur Journalism.

From the Press of C. A. A. Parker, 30 Waite St., Malden, Mass.

Other titles published by Arktos:

Beyond Human Rights
by Alain de Benoist

Carl Schmitt Today
by Alain de Benoist

Manifesto for a European Renaissance
by Alain de Benoist & Charles Champetier

The Problem of Democracy
by Alain de Benoist

Germany's Third Empire
by Arthur Moeller van den Bruck

The Arctic Home in the Vedas
by Bal Gangadhar Tilak

Revolution from Above
by Kerry Bolton

The Fourth Political Theory
by Alexander Dugin

Hare Krishna in the Modern World
by Graham Dwyer & Richard J. Cole

Fascism Viewed from the Right
by Julius Evola

Metaphysics of War
by Julius Evola

Notes on the Third Reich
by Julius Evola

The Path of Cinnabar
by Julius Evola

Archeofuturism
by Guillaume Faye

Convergence of Catastrophes
by Guillaume Faye

Why We Fight
by Guillaume Faye

The WASP Question
by Andrew Fraser

War and Democracy
by Paul Gottfried

The Saga of the Aryan Race
by Porus Homi Havewala

Homo Maximus
by Lars Holger Holm

The Owls of Afrasiab
by Lars Holger Holm

De Naturae Natura
by Alexander Jacob

Fighting for the Essence
by Pierre Krebs

Can Life Prevail?
by Pentti Linkola

Guillaume Faye and the Battle of Europe
by Michael O'Meara

New Culture, New Right
by Michael O'Meara

The Ten Commandments of Propaganda
by Brian Anse Patrick

Morning Crafts
by Tito Perdue

A Handbook of Traditional Living
by Raido

The Agni and the Ecstasy
by Steven J. Rosen

The Jedi in the Lotus
by Steven J. Rosen

It Cannot Be Stormed
by Ernst von Salomon

The Outlaws
by Ernst von Salomon

Tradition & Revolution
by Troy Southgate

Against Democracy and Equality
by Tomislav Sunic

Nietzsche's Coming God
by Abir Taha

Generation Identity
by Markus Willinger

The Initiate: Journal of Traditional Studies
by David J. Wingfield (ed.)

CPSIA information can be obtained
at www.ICGtesting.com
Printed in the USA
BVHW032037030222
627702BV00003B/107

9 781907 166303